"Mason." Harper stood, but kept her desk between them, a pencil in her hands.

Her hair was shorter than he remembered. Her eyes as blue, with the tinge of violet around the edges that he'd never forgotten. She didn't look any happier to see him now than the last time he'd looked at her. The morning after...

"Harper." Hands at his sides, he stood there in a moment of uncharacteristic hesitation. Not sure what to do, how to take control of his interview. Hugging was definitely out.

Mentioning the past...ditto.

"You look good." She wasn't quite smiling, but there was no chill in her gaze, either.

"So do you." He hoped to God the wealth of feeling in that statement didn't reveal itself to her.

They'd known each other since Bruce had brought her home from work more than six years before, a new recruit, to have dinner with the family one night—but he'd never taken much time to actually talk to her.

After his initial rea............il.
he'd been hit by a
deliberately shiec
was his brother's

Dear Reader,

This is a story that has been toying with me for pretty much my whole life. It's a story about family. About what makes family. It's a story that throws down all the chips and waits to see what family really means. It's the story of two brothers who both love the same woman. And the woman who, in different ways, loves them both.

I've never been in love with brothers. Or personally known anyone who was. But I have always been a huge believer in family. In a body of love that's yours no matter what you do. A body that might turn you in if you commit a heinous crime, but do it with tears on cheeks. A body that will then sit beside you in court and visit you in prison every single week. A body that, no matter what—no matter what—will love you.

I believe in my responsibility as a family member. My heart is open and the love is there...always. No matter what. Life has forced me to see the proof of this, to live by it, and I now know the statement to be completely true. So...*Falling for the Brother* was ready to be written. And read.

All the best,

Tara

TaraTaylorQuinn.com

USA TODAY Bestselling Author

TARA TAYLOR QUINN

Falling for the Brother

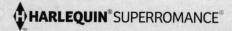

For Scott Gumser, my "little" brother, my family, a huge part of a small pool of unconditional love. We've been on both sides of many fences and always, always, our arms are open, and our backs are protected. That means more to me than you'll probably ever know…

ISBN-13: 978-1-335-44914-6

Falling for the Brother

Copyright © 2018 by Tara Taylor Quinn

Printed in U.S.A.

www.Harlequin.com

Having written over eighty novels, **Tara Taylor Quinn** is a *USA TODAY* bestselling author with more than seven million copies sold. She is known for delivering intense, emotional fiction. Tara is a past president of Romance Writers of America. She has won a Readers' Choice Award and is a seven-time finalist for an RWA RITA® Award. She has also appeared on TV across the country, including *CBS Sunday Morning*. She supports the National Domestic Violence Hotline. If you or someone you know might be a victim of domestic violence in the United States, please contact 1-800-799-7233.

Books by Tara Taylor Quinn

HARLEQUIN SUPERROMANCE

Where Secrets are Safe

Wife by Design
Once a Family
Husband by Choice
Child by Chance
Mother by Fate
The Good Father
Love by Association
His First Choice
The Promise He Made Her
Her Secret Life
The Fireman's Son
For Joy's Sake

A Family for Christmas

Shelter Valley Stories

Sophie's Secret
Full Contact

HARLEQUIN HEARTWARMING

Family Secrets

For Love or Money
Her Soldier's Baby
The Cowboy's Twins

MIRA BOOKS

The Friendship Pact
In Plain Sight

Other titles by this author available in ebook format.

Cast of Characters

Lila McDaniels—Managing director of The Lemonade Stand (TLS). She has an apartment at the Stand.

Wife by Design (Book 1)
Lynn Duncan—Resident nurse at TLS. She has a three-year-old daughter, Kara.
Grant Bishop—Landscape developer hired by TLS.
Maddie Estes—Permanent TLS resident. Childcare provider.
Darin Bishop—Resident at TLS. Works for his brother, Grant. Has a mental disability.

Once a Family (Book 2)
Sedona (Campbell) Malone—Lawyer who volunteers at TLS.
Tanner Malone—Vintner. Brother to **Tatum** and **Talia Malone**.
Tatum Malone—Fifteen-year-old resident at TLS.

Husband by Choice (Book 3)
Meredith (Meri) Bennet—Speech therapist. Mother to two-year-old son, Caleb.
Max Bennet—Pediatrician.
Chantel Harris—Police officer. Friend to Max and his deceased first wife.

Child by Chance (Book 4)
Talia Malone—TLS volunteer. Public-school scrapbook therapist. Student of fashion design.

Sherman Paulson—Political campaign manager. Widower. Single father of adopted ten-year-old son, Kent.

Mother by Fate (Book 5)
Sara Havens—Full-time TLS counselor.
Michael Edwin—Bounty hunter. Widower. Single father to six-year-old daughter, Mari.

The Good Father (Book 6)
Ella Ackerman—Charge nurse at Santa Raquel Children's Hospital. Member of the high-risk team. Divorced.
Brett Ackerman—TLS Founder. National accreditation business owner. Divorced.

Love by Association (Book 7)
Chantel Harris—Santa Raquel detective. Member of the high-risk team.
Colin Fairbanks—Lawyer. Member of Santa Raquel's most elite society. Principal of high-end law firm. Brother to **Julie Fairbanks**.

His First Choice (Book 8)
Lacey Hamilton—Social worker. Member of the high-risk team. Child star. Identical twin to daytime-soap-opera star **Kacey Hamilton**.
Jeremiah (Jem) Bridges—Private contractor with his own business. Divorced. Has custody of four-year-old son, Levi.

The Promise He Made Her (Book 9)
Bloom Larson—Psychiatrist in Santa Raquel. Domestic violence therapist. Divorced.

Samuel Larson—Santa Raquel high-ranking detective. Widower.

Her Secret Life (Book 10)
Kacey Hamilton—Daytime-soap-opera star. Identical twin to **Lacey Hamilton**. Volunteer at TLS.
Michael Valentine—Cybersecurity expert. TLS volunteer. Shooting victim.

The Fireman's Son (Book 11)
Faye Walker—Paramedic. Divorced. Sole custody of eight-year-old son, Elliott, who is in counseling at TLS.
Reese Bristow—Santa Raquel fire chief.

For Joy's Sake (Book 12)
Julie Fairbanks—Philanthropist and children's author. Sister to **Colin Fairbanks**.
Hunter Rafferty—Owns Elite Professional event-planning business, specializing in charity fund-raisers. TLS is one of his clients.

Falling for the Brother (Book 13)
Harper Davidson—Former city police officer, head of security at The Lemonade Stand. Divorced. Has sole custody of four-year-old daughter, Brianna.
Bruce Thomas—Decorated undercover detective. Harper's ex-husband. Father to Brianna.
Mason Thomas—Private crime scene investigator, national government security clearance. Estranged uncle of Brianna.

CHAPTER ONE

MIRIAM THOMAS. INSTANTLY ALERT, Harper Davidson stared at the report on the computer screen in front of her. Miriam Thomas. It wasn't a common name. But not a stretch to think there'd be more than one woman bearing it.

As newly promoted head of security at The Lemonade Stand, a unique 5.1-acre resort-like women's shelter on the California coast, Harper made it her first task every morning, after dropping Brianna at the day care on-site, to take a look at the resident status report. Kind of like a doctor looking at patient charts. In the month she'd been doing so, the task had consisted of nothing more than a simple wellness check. The fifteen new residents who'd arrived in those four weeks had all joined them during waking hours and she'd been notified immediately.

Miriam Thomas had been brought in at 2:00 a.m. with a broken arm and multiple contusions on her chin, as though someone had held her head still with great force.

Harper skimmed the basic details in the overview, suspended from any kind of reaction, as she searched out identifying information that generally wasn't her primary concern. How old was the newest resident and where was she from?

Seventy-five. Albina, California.

Hands shaking now, Harper moved her mouse. Clicked. And clicked again, typing codes and passwords that would get her into a database containing the complete file. She was alone in her small office off the main building at the Stand, coffee not even made, and could hear the silence like the roar of the ocean just wooded acres away.

Miriam? At The Lemonade Stand? What had happened?

Her screen changed and she was in. She typed Miriam's newly acquired resident number.

Who'd brought her here? She had to get further in to find out details. Why hadn't Bruce let her know?

The Stand would've had no reason to call Harper unless Miriam had asked them to. Which wasn't likely. Harper's background check had mentioned her ex-husband by name, but not his family, and it wasn't like anyone would have memorized that information anyway. She'd never taken the Thomas name. And even if she had, it wasn't all that uncommon.

She'd never taken the name because she never should have married Bruce.

But…

The page opened and Harper pulled back. In her three and a half years on staff at The Lemonade Stand she'd seen a lot of disturbing injuries and broken women. They were an everyday fact. Not that she ever grew desensitized. But she'd learned early on to draw boundaries around her personal emotions—just as she had as a cop when she'd been first responder at a deadly car crash. Or a murder.

Gazing into the meek stare coming from Miriam's photo, she lost those boundaries. Miriam, meek? And the bruises on that soft chin… Her face bore little resemblance to the face Harper was used to—one more prone to smiling with confidence that all would be well. Miriam had been the ultimate law-enforcement family member. The wife of a detective. The mother of a detective. The grandmother of a cop. She'd taken it all in stride, certain that her men would survive and make it home in time for dinner.

Or whenever they were expected.

They always had, too.

Her husband had died at home, from kidney disease. Her son, Bruce and Mason's father, had passed away at home, too, from a heart attack due to being a hundred pounds overweight—not that Harper had been there. She'd only heard about it from Bruce when they'd met in his driveway to pass Brianna back and forth for his bimonthly visitation overnighters.

Taking a minute to catch her breath, on what had started out as a normal Tuesday morning in July, Harper got a bottle of water out of the small fridge beside her desk and sipped from it. Then she swept nervous fingers through her short blond hair and reached for the mouse. Scrolled slowly past that photo.

Miriam had been brought to them from the urgent care in Albina; the report didn't say who'd brought her in and she assumed someone from the urgent care had called The Lemonade Stand. One of Harper's employees—probably Sandra, who was the most senior officer on duty the previous night—would have driven over to pick her up. Harper would have a report on that, too.

Scrolling further, she stopped. Stared.

Miriam's abuser was... Bruce Thomas?

She blinked. Read it again. Picked up the phone and hit the first speed dial.

"Lila Mantle." The newly married managing director of The Lemonade Stand—a woman who'd given Harper more courage than she knew—answered on the first ring, her tone as calm and level as always.

Lila might smile more readily these days and

go home to her family every night, but the fifty-three-year-old was still as dedicated, reliable and firm as she'd been all the years Harper had known her. And, based on what she'd heard, just as she'd been since the opening of the Stand more than a decade ago.

"Our new resident…"

"Miriam Thomas, yes. She's in Bungalow 7."

Harper could see that. In a bedroom by herself.

"She's HSR?" She'd get to the Bruce mistake in a second. High Security Risk meant that someone from Harper's staff had to be watching her at all times.

"Yes."

Another sip of water went down with difficulty. The guard assignment wasn't a problem. She'd do it herself, for any of their residents, anytime the need was there.

What the hell had Miriam gotten herself into since her son had died? Bruce's father, Oscar, had moved in with his mother after Bruce left home. Made sense, since both of them lived alone in houses way too big for either one of them.

Miriam needed someone to take care of. And Oscar, an Albina police captain, had worked ungodly hours protecting the public and had wanted someone to take care of him at home.

"Why is she HSR?" Harper asked the question before she was ready for the answer.

"Her abuser's a decorated member of the Albina PD."

Harper shook her head. "Who?" she asked. One of Bruce's friends? That might explain the name mix-up.

"Her grandson. Bruce Thomas. He works as an undercover officer and apparently has the skills to convince anyone of anything he wants them to believe. And he has cop friends all over the state. If he doesn't already know where she is, we can assume he will soon enough. He isn't being formally accused, and the police aren't officially involved as of yet. No one wants to ruin a decorated public servant's reputation unless there's solid proof that he's done wrong."

She couldn't believe any of this.

"Bruce wouldn't hurt his grandmother."

Lila's silence seemed to echo through the line, and Harper realized she'd spoken aloud.

"You know Bruce was my husband," Harper said.

"Of course."

"He wouldn't do this, Lila. I swear to you. He adored his grandmother." But someone had hurt Miriam. She couldn't quite grasp it. And...

"Has anyone called Mason? He's Bruce's older brother. He's a special crime scene investigator based in LA, but travels all over the country. He'll vouch for Bruce."

For most of their lives, Bruce had idolized Mason.

From what she knew, the rift between them hadn't healed, but they talked occasionally. And if the chips were truly down, they'd defend each other to the death. The Thomas family was just that way.

"Mason Thomas is the man who delivered Miriam to us." Lila's tone didn't change. The calm didn't waver.

Sitting forward, Harper put her water bottle on the desk with such force, water sloshed over the top and puddled. She grabbed a tissue, sopped up her mess. "Mason was here?"

She hadn't seen him since the week before she'd married Bruce.

And tried not to think of him. Ever.

So her assumption about how Miriam had arrived at the Stand was wrong. Had the urgent care in Albina called him?

But…wait a minute. "Miriam told you Bruce did this to her…" She went back to the picture of a battered Miriam. Staring at it. As though that would make all of this seem possible. Make some kind of sense. "And you're telling me now that Mason corroborated her story?"

"Not quite. Miriam Thomas claims she fell

off a stepladder in her kitchen and sees no point in being here. Mason Thomas is the one who's claiming the abuse. He insists that she stay inside the grounds at all times until further notice."

Confused, alarmed, just plain beside herself, Harper pursed her lips and studied the screen. Scrolling down. Then up. Then down again.

"But...what about the police? You said they aren't officially involved, but is there a report waiting to be filed?" As a private facility, the Stand could keep Miriam if she chose to stay. But only if she wanted to be there. They weren't a prison.

Or...she could sign a form asking them to prevent her from leaving, for her own safety. Until she'd had some counseling. So many times victims who'd undergone years of mental or emotional manipulation would feel they had to run back to their abusers. They couldn't trust their own minds.

It happened. More often than Harper would ever have believed.

If Miriam had signed the form, Harper and her team would prevent her from leaving, but only for the designated period of time. Or until she signed a retraction in the presence of witnesses, including a Stand counselor.

"Miriam has refused to talk to the police or

press charges. She's not budging from her step-ladder story."

Frowning, Harper began to focus. "So why is she here?"

"She made an agreement with Mason. If she agreed to stay here, and to sign a VNL, he'd do an investigation himself without making it formal or involving the police." VNL. The voluntary no release form.

"And Miriam signed it?"

"Yes." That report would be waiting in her in-box, too. She'd just gotten to work and clicked on resident status... "For how long?"

"Two weeks."

Mason had been there. At the Stand. And would be around for the next two weeks? Or, at least, somewhere between Santa Raquel, where the Stand was, and two hours north in Albina, where Bruce lived—if he was, indeed, investigating.

There were going to be ramifications. She knew it and could feel them building. She and Mason in contact... Bruce being accused... She had to get all the facts she could before she started to feel things that had nothing to do with Miriam. Or her job.

"Bruce didn't abuse his grandmother," she said with certainty.

Why the hell would Mason do this to him?

And then it occurred to her. The brothers must be working together. They knew who'd hurt their grandmother—someone she was protecting—and Bruce, with his undercover skills, and Mason, with his investigative talents, were going to put the guy at ease. They'd let him think he'd gotten away with it, then set him up somehow, in order to find the proof that would trap him and put him away without Miriam's needing to testify against him. Which, clearly, she was terrified to do. You didn't get those bruises on your chin by falling from a stepladder.

It was a long shot, considering the fact that the brothers hadn't had much to do with each other—as far as she was aware—in five years, but Bruce would put all differences aside to protect Miriam from danger. And Mason would come running if Bruce needed him.

"Bruce's brother is absolutely certain he did it." Lila's tone had a different quality to it now. Not defense. Or even authority. More like… compassion?

"Did you talk to him yourself?"

"Yes." Then that meant…

"You were called in?"

"Yes."

Prior to her marriage, Lila might have been at the Stand in the middle of the night, since she used to stay at her apartment there as often as she went home to the condo she'd owned. Calling her in had been more common then, too; she'd had no family, no one else who needed her. But that had all changed since she'd finally allowed herself to love again.

She'd taken her son back into her life, trusting herself to love him and his family well. And married the man who'd been the only one able to break through the barriers she'd put around herself.

But now, to call Lila out of bed in the middle of the night… Someone had been pretty damned concerned.

Maybe Mason hadn't known he could trust Lila with the truth—that he and Bruce were working together?

"So Bruce is still working and living his life as usual?"

"That is my understanding."

"And Miriam's injuries…they're non-life-threatening…" She read over them again. Severe facial contusions in the chin area and a broken arm.

"Correct."

"Maybe she did just fall." The chin bruises, if she'd landed with her chin in something—say, the gold egg carton she was so fond of.

"According to Mason this isn't the first time."

Wow. She simply couldn't grasp the reality. Couldn't imagine how it must make the brothers feel, knowing someone was hurting their grandmother.

Brianna.

She became aware of the first ramification stirred up by this mess.

"How many times before?" Until a month ago, four-year-old Brianna had spent every other Friday night and half of Saturday with Bruce. And, since Oscar's death two years before, since Bruce had moved in with his grandmother to help her out, Brianna had been with Miriam, too.

"The doctor suspects, based on previous bone cracks he could see on the X-ray, at least three."

"To the same arm?"

"Yes."

It made no sense to her at all.

"And the cracks had time to heal." Which meant that whatever had been happening had been going on for a while.

"Yes." Lila didn't often point out the facts, didn't explicitly share what she knew. Her way was to give her conversational partners the time and space—usually with a bit of guidance—to find the truth on their own. To figure it out for themselves, rather than be told. She was a huge proponent of helping people think their own thoughts, draw their own conclusions.

Because so many victims of abuse—as everyone now knew Lila had been—were denied that right to the extent of believing themselves incapable of trusting their own thoughts.

"Brianna stayed in that house every other Friday night."

"I know the two of you used to go to Albina on your weekends off. I suspected she might've been visiting her father."

"And my parents," Harper said, her screen steady on the picture of an injured Miriam. "They have a small vegetable farm and I'd stay with them. Brianna would spend Friday night at Bruce's. From Saturday afternoon until we came home on Sunday, we'd be with my folks."

"What's happened with her visitation since you accepted the new position?"

As head of security now, she couldn't be gone every other weekend. She had vacation. And days off, but they rotated.

"Bruce has to make the drive here, to my house, to see her. He can take her to his hotel on Friday night, or I said he could just pick her up and spend time with her, then bring her home…"

"Has he done that?"

Well… "Not yet," Harper said, closing the screen when she could no longer bear to look at it. "But he's an undercover cop and he's been on assignment. We knew going in that there'd be times, when he was on a job, that he'd miss his weekends. It happened up in Albina, too, but Miriam still got to visit with her."

She could hear her defensive tone. It wasn't that she *wanted* to be with her ex-husband anymore. If she did, her marriage might have lasted more than a year. But she couldn't see a good cop having his life ruined because he couldn't keep his pants zipped.

None of that mattered at the moment. "You should know, Miriam isn't fond of me," she told her boss. "Truth be told, she pretty much hates me." The rest of the staff had a right to know what they might be facing.

But if Mason and Bruce were working together, presumably they'd chosen the Stand because she was there. Because they trusted her to keep their grandmother safe while they did their bit?

Bruce knew where she worked, if not the actual address, the name of the shelter. And he was a decorated cop with cop friends, she heard Lila's words again.

"Why does she hate you?"

"I left her grandson." Miriam hadn't been subtle in expressing her opinion as to where the blame lay. But she'd reluctantly agreed to keep her opinions about Harper to herself when Brianna was around, as long as Harper never showed up in their home. Unless Miriam was discreet, Harper wasn't going to let Brianna stay overnight with them. Bruce had given her full custody of their daughter, without state guided visitation rights—probably to stay on Harper's good side—and that meant she didn't have to let Brianna stay overnight with him. He'd given her everything she'd asked for in their divorce, requesting only that they remain in touch. That she at least let him be her friend. He hadn't wanted the divorce and had repeatedly begged her for another chance. He'd said he understood when she'd been unable to do so. Deep down, Bruce was a good man. One who lived a deceitful professional life that sometimes bled into his personal morality.

Miriam Thomas was at the Stand. Brianna attended day care there. She played out on the grounds during set times. The two of them could feasibly visit each other. Brianna would want to see her great-grandmother. Miriam would no doubt insist on seeing Brianna, too. And maybe there was no reason she shouldn't. Maybe Miriam had agreed to stay *because* of Brianna. Maybe they'd be able to help Miriam help herself.

She wondered whether Miriam would let

Harper do anything for her. But she knew she'd find a way. It was her job.

All the Stand's residents were like family to her for as long as they were with them. She didn't have to like them. She didn't even have to know them. She'd vowed to protect them with her life—every last one of them. And she would.

Just as soon as she sorted out this new reality.

CHAPTER TWO

THE LAST THING Mason Thomas had ever expected, or wanted, was to need anything from Harper Davidson. Needing her—wanting his brother's woman—was something he'd been living with since the first night Bruce had brought her home. He took full accountability for his inappropriate reaction, had dealt with and paid for it. All of which was a hell of a lot easier when he didn't have to see her.

Fully aware that the last thing in the world *she* probably needed was to have him knocking on the door of her office, he hesitated in the hallway.

"She knows you're doing this?" He gave Lila Mantle his most commanding stare. "That you're bringing me to see her."

"I spoke to her twenty minutes ago."

"And she agreed to meet with me."

Lila frowned as she studied him. Up to that point, he'd felt her to be nothing but supportive. A colleague helping him out in a despicable situation.

"Is there a reason she shouldn't have?" Dressed in a dark blue suit with her hair up in a bun, Lila didn't seem the least bit intimidated by his six-foot-two-inch stature.

He shrugged. The reason wasn't as important as protecting Miriam. He'd taken a huge gamble that Harper would agree with him, but now that he was about to see her, he wasn't as confident. He'd dressed for a normal day's work out in the field, examining scenes. Khakis, button-down shirt rolled up to his elbows, black slip-ons. Seeing Harper hadn't figured into it. "I haven't seen her in five years," he said.

Which didn't answer the question. Lila's glance let him know she wasn't completely satisfied with his answer, but she didn't push. At least not yet. He was left with the impression that she might. He needed her on his side; without The Lemonade Stand, he didn't have much hope of saving his grandmother, let alone freeing her to enjoy some happy days in the years she had left. God knew, she'd earned them.

Lila knocked, ushered him ahead of her, said a few words and stepped out, closing the door behind her.

"Mason." Harper got to her feet, but kept her desk between them, a pencil in her hands. Her hair was shorter than he remembered, her eyes as blue, with the tinge of violet around the edges that he'd never forgotten. She didn't seem any happier to see him now than the last time he'd looked at her. The morning after...

"Harper." Hands at his sides, he stood there in a moment of uncharacteristic hesitation. Not sure what to do, how to take control of his interview. Hugging her was definitely out.

Mentioning the past...ditto.

"You look good." She wasn't quite smiling, but there was no chill in her gaze, either.

"So do you." He hoped to God the wealth of feeling in that statement didn't convey itself to her.

They'd known each other since Bruce had brought her home from work more than six years before, a new recruit who'd also been his new romantic interest, to have dinner with the family, but Mason had never taken much time to actually talk to her that night.

After his initial reaction to her—feeling like he'd been hit by a semi and liking it—he'd deliberately shied away from conversation. She was his brother's girlfriend.

The time for talk would've been when he found her on the beach in tears, sobbing hysterically, a week before her wedding. Unfortunately, he'd just come from one hell of an argument with his brother—cursing Bruce for having been unfaithful to her—and hadn't given any real thought to conversation. He'd wanted beer. As much as he could get, as quickly as he could pour it down his throat.

He hadn't left her sitting there crying, though. He'd made the biggest mistake of his life. He'd invited her along.

"I like your hair shorter," he said, mostly to remind himself that the night in question was long ago. To get his head out of the past and into his current situation.

Some women might have raised a hand to their hair. Made a comment. Smiled even. Harper just nodded.

Although he was having more difficulty than he'd expected holding her eyes, he'd refused to look lower than that pencil in her hands. But when she continued to assess him, his damned gaze dropped.

And noticed the gun strapped to her hip. The beige uniform hadn't surprised him. Both of the guards, her employees, whom he'd met the night before, had been wearing them. They'd been armed, too, but...

"I'm fully trained to use it," she said, seeing where his gaze had landed.

He nodded. "Graduated at the top of your academy class," he said, letting her know he remembered. From what he'd been told, she quit the Albina police force when she divorced his younger brother. According to his father, for the two years she'd served, she'd been a good cop. Good instincts. No hesitation.

It wasn't like she was hesitating now, either. She was...waiting.

He'd asked for the meeting. This was his call.

"My grandmother..." He stopped, met Harper's stare. In his line of work as an independent crime scene investigator, he saw a lot of gruesome things, studied horrific photos and picked apart heinous crime scenes down to the smallest detail. He'd learned how to compartmentalize a long time ago. He opened his mind, not his heart. And yet, he had to take a minute to stop the quiver inside him as he thought of the scene he'd come upon the evening before.

"I've been working in Alabama for most of the past month," he began. "Was on a serial killer job in Boston before that. With all the new DNA technologies, cold cases are coming out of the woodwork, and departments don't always have the manpower or the time necessary to study the evidence and pictures..."

She seemed fully focused on him.

"Anyway, you don't need me to get into that," he concluded.

She held the pencil in one hand now, while two fingers of the other moved up and down the shaft. She wasn't as composed as he'd thought.

His family wasn't hers anymore. Hadn't been for all that long anyway. Didn't mean she didn't care about Miriam. They were still her daughter's family.

He'd seen pictures of the kid a couple of times in the past four years. Cute. From what his grandmother—who chattered about her on a regular basis—had relayed, Mason figured the child might be a bit too inquisitive for his comfort, but smart. According to Miriam, the little girl had a great disposition, not at all whiny.

Harper wasn't the whiny sort. He couldn't imagine her being tolerant of it in her daughter.

She was still watching. Waiting for him.

"I make it a point to stop and see Miriam as soon as I return from a job. Especially since Dad's been gone…"

Harper hadn't gone to Oscar's funeral. Brianna had been there, but Mason only got a brief glimpse of her. In Bruce's arms. Clinging to him and burying her cute blond head in his shoulder as someone approached. Mason had spent most of his time watching over his inconsolable grandmother, and Bruce had left him to it. Keeping his distance from the older brother who'd betrayed him.

Miriam had taken her son's death much harder than her husband's, and Mason had his hands full. Back before his mother died, she'd always been at Gram's side, and then his father had stepped in. Now it was up to him.

"I was expecting to be in Alabama until next week, but I caught a break in the case and got an earlier flight out. Gram's been struggling a lot this year. Seeming to age right before my eyes…"

"Did you talk to Bruce about it?" He listened carefully as she mentioned his brother. Her ex. Trying to determine if the closeness his brother had alluded to truly existed. Her tone, her expression… She could've been speaking of a mutual friend.

"I did," he said, watching her even more astutely now, wondering again if she and his brother were as close as Bruce wanted him to believe. If maybe she knew more than he'd expected. Speaking slowly, choosing his words with care, he said, "More than once. Each time he told me I was imagining things. Says she's just getting older and that if I saw her more often I'd know that."

Harper's brow furrowed. "I thought…" She shook her head, looking perplexed, giving him cause to wonder for a second if she actually knew Miriam was there. Then he remembered that *he* wouldn't be standing in her office if she didn't know. Lila'd had to talk to her before Mason could see her.

"Thought what?"

"Miriam…you… Bruce…" She shrugged and he remembered how shocked he'd been the first time he'd realized how slender her shoulders were. They could carry a lot of weight. "I thought you and Bruce were working together here…running some kind of undercover investigation to figure out what happened."

Now he was the one who felt confused. And tense all over again. How exactly did a guy go about turning in the brother he loved? "Bruce has been abusing her, Harper. I thought… Lila said you knew."

The pencil dropped as Harper leaned both hands against her desk. "She said as much. I figured you guys were using Bruce as a cover, you know, so as not to alert whoever you suspect…"

She thought he and Bruce were a team? That they'd somehow reconciled? Which had to mean she and her ex weren't that close, after all. With Bruce it was sometimes impossible to tell exactly where he stood—even for Mason, and he'd had more experience resisting his brother's convincing charm than anyone else.

"Bruce still won't be in the same room as me if he can help it," he said. "Which is why I always make appointments to see Gram when he'll be away from the house."

"He won't be in the same…" She shook her

head again, alarm emanating from her expression, her posture, everything. "I really thought you were working together here…"

"The agreement didn't disappear just because your marriage did," he said now, glad he hadn't taken a seat in the chair across from the desk. He'd have had to stand up again. "He still has the goods on me, and I still don't want them spilled." That made him sound like a total ass, and while he was one, his reputation wasn't the reason he continued to honor his little brother's wishes. "I hurt him," he said now. "My presence still hurts him. Staying away is the price I pay for the choice I made."

"A-agreement?" She completely ignored the rest of it.

He might have been forgiven for thinking she was slightly daft. If he hadn't known her better.

"The *agreeement*." He drew the word out, certain that neither of them wanted to get any further into it.

"I'm sorry, Mason, I have no idea what you're talking about."

White-hot anger at the injustice of life shot through him and was gone as instantly, leaving calm in its wake. A level, assessing calm. With a reminder that just because something changed one person's entire life, that didn't mean it affected another's. Just because the agreement had hurt him irrevocably, didn't mean it had changed Harper's life at all.

"Bruce wouldn't go to Dad or Gram, or create any kind of family rift, as long as I never contacted you and stayed away from you. And as long as I gave him his space, stayed away from him as much as possible. He'd speak to me when necessary, but otherwise I wasn't to contact him."

One night with Harper had cost him the brother who'd once idolized him.

With more than a frown now, she shook her head. "What on earth are you talking about?" She wasn't calm anymore. If anything, she sounded pissed off.

Not that he blamed her. He'd screwed up all their lives because he'd been drunk and not thinking straight. Not that she hadn't consented. But she'd accompanied him to the bar that night, her fiancé's older brother and soon-to-be brother-in-law, devastated, her whole life falling apart, looking for compassion. For an explanation, a way to understand what Bruce had done. Not for alcohol-induced sex.

Bruce had been counting on him to help her understand...

"I mean it, Mason! Tell me what on earth you're talking about." Her hands, splayed on the desktop, were shaking with tension.

He hadn't seen her in five years. The last time he *had* seen her she'd been naked. And horrified to find herself in bed with him. Could he be blamed for feeling a little bothered here?

"After you told Bruce what happened," he said, "before you were married, he came to me. Said the two of you had talked and worked everything out." She'd told her fiancé that she'd slept with his older brother.

And Bruce had still wanted to marry her. Because his brother was that much in love with the woman. Even now.

She nodded. "That's right. We did."

He could understand why Bruce had forgiven her. After all, his brother had just slept with his partner.

And Harper had slept with Mason but afterward, even before agreeing to go ahead with the marriage to Bruce, she'd never so much as called Mason. Again, not that he blamed her. She'd owed him nothing. Her loyalty had been to the man she'd decided to marry, even after he'd hurt her so badly. The man she loved so deeply she'd chosen to forgive him for what he'd done. It wasn't as if Mason had done anything deserving of loyalty.

"So... I'm talking about the agreement the three of us reached..." he said slowly.

Which earned him another shake of her head.

"I haven't even spoken to you since... How could you possibly think we reached some kind of agreement about anything?"

"You didn't want to see me," he reminded her. "Bruce explained. Understandable. I suppose I could have insisted on hearing the words directly from you but frankly, at that point, I was just glad to be done with it all. And still be welcome in my family."

"Welcome in your... Mason, why on earth *wouldn't* you be welcome? It's not like Bruce was any saint—and if I was welcome, why wouldn't you be?"

"Let me get this straight. You're telling me you didn't know about the ultimatum?"

"About you staying away or Bruce would cause a stink?"

"Yeah."

"Of course not! I would never have agreed to such a thing. If you, or Bruce, felt it necessary to tell your father or Miriam what we'd done... that was up to you two."

Another question burned its way through the barriers he was trying desperately to hang on to. "Did you tell your parents?"

He'd only met them once. At the engagement party. But he'd spent more than an hour talking to her father. Had really liked both of them. They were farmers. Down-to-earth. Practical, not prone to drama. And yet, emitting a love that couldn't be missed.

"Yes. Eventually. Not at the time..." She picked up the pencil again. "This isn't getting us anywhere," she said. "I had no idea that Bruce had gone to you, or that you'd been warned to stay away, but it's all in the past. We have other concerns to deal with."

She was right to get the conversation back on course. But this was his interview. He'd requested it. And he had to know where she stood. Where they stood. His grandmother's life could very well depend on it at this point.

"Didn't you ever wonder why I wasn't around?" he asked.

For the first time since he'd come into the room she looked down. As though ashamed. Or embarrassed. "I figured you were mad at me for marrying Bruce."

He had been. More than mad. But... "And you thought that would be reason enough for me to miss my only sibling's wedding? You thought I was that much of a selfish ass? That I couldn't get over myself for an afternoon?"

Her gaze flew back to his. "Not because you couldn't get over yourself, no," she said. "I thought you weren't there because you couldn't witness something you felt was wrong."

It might have come to that—if he'd had a

choice to make. More likely, he wouldn't have gone because he'd still wanted her himself. But she'd loved Bruce. And Lord knew, Bruce adored her. No one had ever been in doubt about that. Including the other women his brother had slept with. "Bruce told me I wasn't welcome. Warned me that if I showed my face he'd let everyone know what a jerk I was, taking advantage of his fiancée a week before the wedding."

Her mouth twisted, and he remembered how it had tasted—a combination of beer and sweetness.

"He never would have done that."

Her defense of his brother didn't surprise him all that much. If the situation were reversed, he might do the same. Bruce had a way about him that compelled people to like him. To trust him. And even when, like Mason, you were forced to see his other side, you still loved him. Because he wasn't a mean or malicious man. He was, at his core, a needy one.

"On the contrary, he most certainly would have." And it wouldn't have been the first time he'd stabbed Mason. It just would've been the worst.

"He'd have had to out me, too. And himself."

Mason almost laughed, but not out of humor. "It isn't like he would've taken a mic and announced the news," he said. "Or even told the whole story. His version would've been more along the lines of an emotional aside to my father, where he was the total victim and where I got you drunk and then slept with you after you passed out."

"And you don't think I'd have stood up for you? Told the truth? You think I would have let it stay at that?"

He stared at her. "What I think is that you never would've known," he said. "You didn't know about the agreement…" Her stricken look bothered him. "My father certainly wouldn't have told you. I just wouldn't have been welcome anymore."

"Your father would never have turned his back on you, Mason. Even I know that."

She was right. To a point. "He'd see me, talk to me, sure. He'd definitely come running if I called in need." Just as he would for Bruce. It was their way. "But any family invitations… they'd have stopped. Him calling to catch up, or to tell me one of his infamous stupid jokes… that would've stopped."

If she didn't realize by now how insidious Bruce could be with his twisting of truths, maybe she never would. Maybe he wouldn't be able to rely on her for help. All he knew was, he had to try.

"And it wouldn't have ended with my dad,"

he said. "If Bruce needed support for something else, he'd drop a word in someone else's ear at the pertinent time." Bruce had been playing his parents against him since elementary school. Because Mason's footsteps had been too big to fit him. Because Bruce, growing up in Mason's shadow, had never felt he had a chance to become something great on his own. He'd developed a need to have everyone love him the most. A sense of competitiveness. Mason had understood that back then. And on the whole, Bruce's manipulations had been pretty harmless.

Until Harper. At least as far as he knew.

"How do you know he didn't do it, anyway? Tell people what we did?"

"I don't." At this point, Mason hoped he had. Hoped he'd be able to dig up enough proof of Bruce's duplicity to help Gram get healthy again. To either show her what was really happening…or to expose Bruce to the authorities. He'd prefer the former, but if he had to involve the authorities, then he would. He wasn't going to see his little brother kill his grandmother. Wasn't going to lose Gram that way. And most certainly didn't want his brother to be guilty of murder.

"I was sorry…to hear that Oscar died."

He nodded. He wanted to ask about her parents, but didn't.

He wanted to ask about Brianna, too. Wanted to know what the little girl had to say about visiting her father. The child was four—and precocious. She might have insights that would help them get the proof they needed to save Gram, and get Bruce the counselling he needed before it was too late. He needed access to Brianna, but had to get her mother on board first. He could only talk to Brianna if Harper approved.

"So...you're telling me this is for real? That you really think Bruce broke Miriam's arm?"

Among other things.

He nodded. "And I don't think it's the first time."

"Lila said as much. But if you thought this was happening, why didn't you do something about it sooner? It's not like you're not without power yourself, Mason. My God, you work with the FBI! With police departments and crime labs all over the country. You've got a hell of a lot more clout than an undercover cop in Albina, California."

He'd actually *been* FBI for a time. Until his skills had been needed in so many other places. He'd been offered the high government clearance he'd needed to work where he was needed as a private crime scene investigator—even when it meant rebuilding a crime scene from old evidence.

"In the first place, I didn't know about the previous injuries until last night. And in the second, Bruce has clout with Gram," he told her, "and she insists he's not hurting her."

CHAPTER THREE

HARPER NEEDED TO sit down. To have a few minutes without Mason's energy bouncing around the walls of her office.

But she had a job to do. That came first. And, at the moment, he was it.

"I'm just getting up to speed on this," she said now, needing to be done with personal conversation. She'd left the Thomas family. Other than accommodating Bruce's visitations requests, she couldn't allow herself to go back.

Brianna. She stared at Mason.

"You don't think he... I mean, if you really think Bruce did this..." She shook her head. "There's no way he could have."

Now she sounded like any number of their residents. Her career was in the domestic violence field. She was fully versed on abusers' needs to control their victims, and also understood abusers having the ability to mentally and emotionally control their victims even after their ability to do so physically had been contained.

"Up until a month ago, Brianna was in that house every other weekend."

Thinking of the little blond burst of energy who took up every single nonworking moment of her life, Harper panicked. What if…

No! She would've known. Bruce had never, ever shown any sign of physical aggression with their daughter. He…

She glanced at Mason. "He doesn't even spank her," she said.

"Has she ever shown any indication of distress when you get her back? Any falls or bruises or other injuries?"

"No, of course not!" She was a cop, for heaven's sake! Employed at a women's shelter. She knew what to look for. And even if she hadn't… She'd protect Brianna with her life.

Her baby girl *was* her life.

"How about emotionally? Is she more clingy? Does she have nightmares? Does she ever resist going back there? Or say she doesn't want to see her dad?"

She shook her head, but stopped to think, hard, in case she was missing something. Looking back over almost four years of visits… "She was only three months old when we got divorced."

Now was not the time to go into all of that.

"But…" She turned to Mason, still traveling back in her memory. "I mean, it's not like I can remember every single time I've picked her up, but she's always happy to see me, then hugs him goodbye, gives him her special daddy kiss on the cheek and tells him she'll see him later."

"What about when she misbehaves? Does she talk about him punishing her?"

"She doesn't really get into trouble."

He rolled his eyes and she shrugged. "I know, I know, the proud parent, right? But she doesn't, Mason. She's like this adult walking around in a little body. She tells you she wants to do something and you tell her no, and she looks at you and asks why. If you give her a valid reason, she says okay. I'm not exaggerating."

"Every kid has tantrums now and then."

"Yeah, she used to hold her breath until she passed out when she wanted to get her way. Back during the terrible twos." She grinned.

He looked horrified. "I'd say that's misbehaving! What did you do?"

"Panicked the first time. Then I called her pediatrician. He told me to let her pass out. He said she'd start breathing again and if I didn't make a big deal out of it, she'd soon learn that it accomplished nothing."

"Was he right?"

"She did it once more after that and never again."

His grin tripped up her insides.

"I'm not saying she doesn't get in bad moods, or get mouthy now and then. I'm just saying that if you reason with her, she almost always responds positively. Once she was pretty rough when she was playing with a dollhouse my mom and dad made for her. She wrecked it, and I was furious with her, of course. I told her that what she'd done was wrong. She looked at me and said, 'I know.'"

"Wow. She did it without conscience?"

"No, she's just that practical. I asked her why she'd done it, and she said she'd had a pretend fire, but didn't mean to hurt anything. She figured I could just fix it. I told her she had to have a time-out."

"What did she do?"

"She sat quietly in the corner, until I went to get her. Then she told me she was really sorry and started to cry."

"So, if Bruce has ever shown any signs of aggression...with anyone...while she's around, she'd probably be able to tell us about it."

Harper's breath stuck in her throat. "Not *us*," she managed. "But I'm going to get her in to see one of our counselors here at the Stand this morning." She picked up the phone, pushed the extension for Sara's office, made the appointment for an hour later, then hung up and glanced back at Mason.

"Like I was saying," she said, all business now. "I'm just getting up to speed here. I haven't even had a chance to finish reading all the reports. But you can rest assured that there's at least one guard aware of Miriam's whereabouts at all times. Today Lila called in an off-duty officer, but by noon I'll have a schedule made out for the remainder of the two weeks. Don't worry, Mason, I can promise you that if it's humanly possible, we won't let Bruce get in and we won't let her leave."

He nodded, hands in his pockets now, but didn't seem in any hurry to leave. She needed him to go. His familiar scent had wafted all around her and she needed her mind clear.

Was it likely that a guy would use the same soap for more than five years? Or the same aftershave? Or whatever it was that gave Mason the scent that just seemed to call to her? Tricked her into thinking that within him lay her security.

It was ludicrous. Laughable. She was the head of security. The filling of any *security* needs she might have lay firmly within her.

"I was hoping you'd talk to her." It took her a second to realize he meant Miriam.

Tapping her pencil against her palm she said, "I have no problem with that, but I don't think it would do any good. She's not particularly fond of me."

Now it was his turn to frown. "What do you mean? She adored you. And you were so great with her. She's never given me any indication that changed."

Trying to make light of something that had hurt her deeply, she said, "I don't know what happened. After the divorce Bruce told me she agreed not to bad-mouth me in front of Brianna as long as I didn't step foot in her house. I'm allowed to pull into the driveway, but have to wait for him to come out and get her from the car."

His hand flew out of his pocket and into the air with such force it was a wonder his pants didn't rip. "See what he does? He told me you said you couldn't bear to see me again, and he's told you Miriam said…"

Couldn't bear to see me again… His words seemed to have…emotion…attached. Something she'd have to revisit. Later.

"No, that wasn't the end of it," she clarified, and then continued. "The first time I brought Brianna over to see Bruce, I went in with her. This was before he was living with Miriam. I was sitting on the couch, watching Brianna play on the rug, trying to reach for a toy Bruce had bought for her. Miriam came in the front door, saw me sitting there and went off on me. Asked me was I satisfied now that I'd ruined her Bruce's life—and who did I think I was, invading his home after I'd hurt him so badly…"

"*How* did you hurt him so badly?" Mason's expression was quizzical and she saw the conversation going off track again. But she answered anyway.

"By leaving him. He couldn't believe I actually would. Especially with Brianna still a baby. He'd trusted me to always be there and then I wasn't." She got it completely. Knew how badly it hurt when people destroyed your ability to trust them.

When he seemed about to follow that up with another question—one she feared would be more in depth about the reason for her divorce—she barreled ahead. "Anyway, when I saw how much Miriam hated me, I told Bruce I didn't think it was healthy for Brianna to be around her. Instead, he talked to Miriam, and the rest you know. I don't go in the house. She doesn't bad-mouth me around my daughter. I can't explain why she didn't mention any of this to you, but my guess would be that she didn't mention me at all. She wasn't going to risk losing her access to her great-granddaughter."

"She'll want to see her."

Yeah. "We'll think about it."

"No, I mean today. It's how I got her to agree to come with me. And to stay. She gets to see Brianna."

Hackles rising, Harper said, "You had no business promising her that."

"I had no idea you and Miriam were on bad terms. I thought I was bringing her to family."

"Yet you didn't call me last night."

"You and Brianna are that family. I believed, remember, that you were part of the agreement that I never contact you again."

"And you brought her here anyway, and then had Lila arrange the meeting." In spite of his agreement not to contact her. Didn't matter that there'd been no such agreement. As far as he believed, it had existed.

"Like I said, I thought she was family to you. You'd been so fond of her, and she talks about Brianna every time I see her. I was sure you'd want her here…and that you'd tolerate me because I was the only one who could get her to agree not to go back home. Which was where she was headed when I got the call from Albina Urgent Care."

She dropped her pencil again. "I thought you went to the house when you got back to town." Hadn't he said so? Or only that he always went there on his first day back?

"When I got into town early, I called, but

Bruce was home, off work for a couple of days, she said, so I told her I'd see her later in the week."

"And you got a call from urgent care?" If she could have a damned minute to get to her morning reports she'd know these things.

"Yeah. She drove herself there—broken arm and all. And planned to drive herself home. They didn't think that was a good idea. So she had them call me. Thank God I'd finished the job early and let her know I was in town."

"So…if you weren't at the house, how can you be sure she wasn't telling the truth? That she didn't fall off the stepladder?"

"The doctor told me he noticed a pattern of abuse when he examined her. The X-rays confirmed it. There's a bruise on her arm, with finger marks, where the break is. Same with her chin. He tried to get her to tell him whose hand had been on her, but she kept insisting she'd fallen. So when I talked to her, I didn't ask the same question. Instead, I asked who she'd seen that day. She told me Bruce. Just like she'd said when she called. But she also said she hadn't called him to come and get her because he'd gone to the bar, and she didn't like him to drive any more than the block or so home when he'd been drinking."

The "cop" bar in town. A place where members of the force could hang out and unwind. Talk about cases. Support each other. Harper remembered it well. Had spent some good times there, actually.

Feeling almost giddy with relief, she had to point out, "Just because she saw Bruce doesn't mean he did this, Mason." There was still bad blood between the brothers. She'd hoped they'd joined forces to save their grandmother from harm. It would take something that serious to get Bruce to admit he needed his older brother, and maybe Mason was overreacting here...

As much as Bruce had idolized his brother, he'd also figured that people thought less of him because Mason was such a standout at anything he tried. His entire life, all Bruce had heard was what people expected of him because of the things his big brother had done. Harper guessed that was why Bruce had chosen to go under-cover. It was dangerous work. Hard work. And it came with a load of trust, freedom and respect from the force. It was also something Mason had never done.

"I called my brother," Mason said next. "I didn't tell him I had Gram with me, or that she'd been to urgent care. He thought I was calling to arrange a time for me to be at the house for din-ner with Gram. I told him she hadn't answered when I called. Asked where she was. He said at home, where she'd been all day. I suggested maybe someone was with her, and he insisted he was the only one who'd been there and that he'd been home all day."

"Still…you have no idea who could have gone there after Bruce left."

"According to him and to Gram, he left around 7:45. Gram checked in to urgent care at 8:01, and the bruises on her chin were already purpling."

Her chest tightened. For a lot of reasons. Most she couldn't stop to think about. "You know you have no proof at all. Nothing you can charge him with. Not without her testimony."

"Yeah."

His gaze met hers, and she knew why he'd asked to see her. What he needed. Her help in finding a way to charge his brother with elder abuse.

She just wasn't sure she had it to give.

CHAPTER FOUR

MASON WAS ANXIOUS to get back to Albina, to get started on finding out everything he could about his brother's life—and to stay the hell away from Harper until he could keep himself in check. But he hung around The Lemonade Stand for another hour that morning, sitting with Gram in a family visiting room in the main building. The rules he'd insisted on meant he couldn't take her out, and Harper had asked him to be present for her first interview with Gram. A perfectly reasonable request.

"I haven't seen my baby girl yet," Gram was saying, throwing a discard on the pile, on her way to beating him in a second game of gin rummy. The cast on her lower arm didn't affect her ability to pick and throw cards any.

"She's in a class this morning." He'd already told her so. Twice. But he didn't think she was having any trouble remembering that. Her problem was knowing she couldn't leave. She'd been bobbing her right foot under the table since they sat down.

Miriam Thomas was used to looking after her home, her family, her community. She wasn't good at inactivity. Never had been.

"Seems like they could pull her out of class to see her Gram. Especially since it's my first day here." There was no petulance in her tone, more like…suggestion. Gram's way of demanding—and every single one of her men knew to jump at that tone.

Mason drew a card. Threw one on the pile.

Brianna was in a counseling session—to see what she could tell them about her visits with her father—with Harper in attendance. When she was through, Harper was going to take her back to day care and meet him and Miriam at the card tables. Gram's visit with Brianna was going to have to wait.

The room they were in was a decent size and nicely appointed, with couches and chairs arranged in conversational areas with plenty of lamps for reading. A family living room atmosphere, though, for safety purposes, family members didn't generally visit the shelter. It took special permission and security clearance for anyone other than staff, residents and police to get inside. At the moment, they had the place to themselves.

Mason's high-level government clearance allowed him access to the entire facility. He'd

asked for Gram to be called to the main building. He wanted her bungalow to be a place none
of the Thomas men had ever visited. If they
were going to get her to admit that Bruce was
mistreating her, they had to break her belief that
it was her duty to serve her men.

"Gin." Miriam laid down her cards. He played
what he could. Tallied up the score, then gathered the cards and shuffled.

"I need to get home to Bruce." Statement. Not
question. In navy polyester pants and a matching tunic, with her short hair curled and styled
as usual, Miriam could have passed for someone on her way to a business meeting. Even at
seventy-five, she could've handled herself at one
just fine. Her strong will was part of the reason
he'd had to bring her to the Stand. She was determined that her place was with his younger
brother, whether it was healthy for her or not.

"He needs me." Probably. At the moment,
Mason didn't give a shit.

"Does he know where I am?"

Again, probably. His younger brother was a
damned good cop. Mason might have been ex-
pelled from Bruce's life, but he'd kept track of
him, relieved to see that his little brother was
doing so well. Had been proud of him, too. But
even if Bruce hadn't done well, Mason would've

watched out for him. He'd be the big brother until the day he died.

"I haven't told him."

"What *did* you tell him?"

He'd been waiting for the question. And wouldn't lie to his grandmother. "I told him I got a call from urgent care saying you'd been hurt, and your injuries were most likely caused by another individual. I said I was taking you someplace safe for a few weeks until you healed."

He hadn't accused his brother of hurting her. Not yet. But he hadn't not done so, either.

He was still holding out hope that he was wrong—not that he'd given Harper that impression. He needed her to believe it was possible that Bruce was guilty, so she'd help him find out, one way or the other.

He was holding out hope, but he didn't think he was wrong. No matter how much he wished differently.

Miriam drew. Rearranged the cards in her hand. Discarded. He waited for her to ask about Bruce's response and found it telling that she didn't.

"He'll find me."

"He won't get in."

Gram looked at him, her green eyes filled with the intelligence he'd known all his life. "He's a decorated cop with security clearance," she said clearly, easily. "They won't be able to deny him access."

It was his turn to play. He waited for her to look over at him, then held her gaze. "Yes, they will, Gram. You have my word on that."

She nodded. Didn't argue. But he knew she wasn't convinced.

Where the hell was Harper?

"You really think if it's Bruce against *her*, she'll come out on top?"

Her.

"I met with Harper this morning," he said. He'd been debating whether or not to tell her. To preempt the meeting they were about to have. But he'd decided to let things play out and observe the two women together because he wasn't truly convinced his grandmother had a problem with Harper. The older woman had adored her. Sung her praises every single time Mason called or stopped by to see Miriam and his father during the year of Bruce and Harper's marriage. She'd been certain that Harper Davidson would be the perfect cop's wife, just as Gram herself had been. And Mason and Bruce's mother, too, until the day she died.

"She thinks you don't like her, Gram."

"I don't."

They were both drawing cards. Discarding.

He had three aces and three kings. All he needed was a fourth to go out on her.

"Why not?"

"She took the easy way out. Bruce makes one mistake and she leaves him. He changed after that. Worked all the time. Volunteered for the most dangerous assignments. Nothing I could do or say would bring him around. You think your grandfather didn't make a mistake or two? Or your father, for that matter? You and I make mistakes. We don't turn our backs on each other because of them. We stick together. That's what family does."

He'd been raised on this rhetoric. Believed most of it. "What mistake did Bruce make?" If he'd been talking to anyone else, his nonchalance would've been persuasive, but Gram saw right through him. He knew it when she paused, hand halfway to the discard pile, and looked over at him.

"He didn't tell you?"

Mason stopped just short of rolling his eyes. "You think that's likely?"

He'd spent five years telling himself he didn't need to know why Harper had left his brother a year into the marriage she'd insisted on going through with. That he didn't care. And that it was none of his business.

All lies—except the last part.

But now…it felt like his business. So he pushed. "What did he do?" he asked his grandmother.

"He had sex with a perp. Her older brother was a gang leader involved in human trafficking. He recruited local kids to use as drug mules. Bruce had to get close to get enough evidence to make a conviction stick." Gram had spent more than fifty years living with law enforcement. There wasn't a lot she didn't know. Or that shocked her.

Mason's stomach dropped. He'd suspected. Hoped he'd been wrong. He'd hoped there'd been another reason for the divorce—maybe that they'd decided they didn't love each other enough. Something ordinary. Non-soul damaging.

"He told her right away, didn't try to hide it from her. Didn't lie to her. Or even expect to get away with it."

Which made him wonder, considering Harper's reaction the first time his brother had screwed around on her and considering how badly she'd been hurt, why Bruce had run home and confessed. Didn't seem like something his younger brother would do.

Mason reminded himself that what he was hearing could very well be the version of things Bruce had given Gram. A version of the truth colored by Bruce's need to look good to every-one, to always be the victim. To be perceived as the one who tried to do right and yet was wronged by others.

"He did what he did for the job, made the arrest because of it. She knew she was marry-ing an undercover, knew the job entailed some tough calls. And he was honest with her about what happened," Gram said, then added, "Gin."

Three aces, three kings and a four counted against him.

SHE WAS IN a tailspin, walking on familiar paths, smiling at familiar people and feeling as though she'd landed in a world she didn't know. On the surface, she was the same. But inside, Harper felt she'd changed irrevocably. In the space of two hours.

She didn't like the change, wasn't ready to accept any kind of new reality.

"Am I in troubles?" Brianna, her blond curls glinting like gold in the morning sun, wrinkled her nose as she looked up at Harper.

Giving the tiny hand tucked securely within hers a soft rub, Harper smiled down at her daughter. "No!" She put as much cheer and hap-piness as she could muster into the one word. "You've done nothing wrong at all," she assured the little girl, fully aware, even if others weren't, how much Brianna grasped from the adults living around her.

"Why did I hafta go to Miss Sara during my reg'lar day?"

Harper smiled down at her. She'd had no time to prepare for the meeting with Miriam and Mason. To avail herself of informational chats with the professionals around her. To gather facts.

"It's just like she told you, Brie." She kept her tone light and at the same time reassuring. "Gram's going to be staying here for a couple of weeks and we wanted you to know."

Brianna nodded. Just as she'd done in Sara's office. When the counselor had asked if Brianna had any questions, she'd shaken her head. Harper had been working at The Lemonade Stand since she'd left Bruce, which meant Brianna had grown up there, in day care, from the time she was three months old. How much the little girl knew about the Stand, about the work they did, no one could really tell. Sara had stressed from the very beginning of Harper's employment that the less the little ones knew, the better. She'd said that kids tended to see what they needed to see, unless someone else pointed out bad to them.

Even many of the younger resident children living with them didn't know why they were there. They might've been aware there was a fight if they'd witnessed it, or abuse if they'd suffered from it, but often they didn't know.

When Brianna had seemed unconcerned about her Gram being there, other than asking when she'd get to see her, Sara had sent Harper a glance and taken the child's cue.

The rest of their time together had been spent chatting about Brianna's visits with her dad. About the places they went, the games they played, what they ate and bedtime rituals when they were together. She got Brianna to ramble on about all kinds of things, watching for any sign of unrest. There'd been absolutely none— to Harper's total, weak-kneed relief.

"Is Gram mad at Daddy?" Brianna asked now, her voice concerned.

"No! Of course not!" she answered automatically, wondering if this was one of those signs Sara had been looking for. "Do you think she should be?"

"Nooo."

She'd never, for one second, thought Bruce was a danger to their daughter, to anyone. And yet Mason had managed to make her doubt. But the fact that Lila had believed him, that had thrown her. Lila wasn't easily fooled.

And for what purpose would Mason have done this? None that she could find.

She stared at the top of her daughter's head, feeling...lost. Unsure of herself. Not something she usually had to deal with—especially where Brianna was concerned. Motherhood had come naturally to her, maybe because she loved it so much.

"Why did you ask if Gram was mad at Daddy?" She had to check.

Even Brianna's shrug was reassuring; the little girl wouldn't be so casual if she was going through a traumatic moment. "Gram takes care of Daddy and she can't do that here 'cause it's a far drive in the car."

"Daddy's a big boy, Brie. He knows how to cook and do laundry and stuff."

"But...why did Gram leave him all alone?"

A small piece of the world righted itself. She was concerned about her father. That was all. Just like she worried about leaving Harper alone every time she went to her father's house.

"She wanted a little vacation. You know, like when we go to Disneyland. For Gram, this place, with the gardens and everything, is like her Disneyland. She can read and walk and do crafts with other ladies and not have to cook and clean. Plus, she wanted to be able to see you every day. With Daddy coming down to Santa Raquel for visits now, Gram doesn't get to see you as much."

"He said he could bring her."

"I know. And I'm sure he will, but he's on a job and she missed you!"

There was no way Miriam would tell Brianna anything different. According to Lila, the woman was adamantly protecting her grandson. And Harper didn't doubt Miriam's love for Brianna or ability to care for her in the slightest. With her hand in Harper's, Brianna swung their arms and skipped one step. "So can I see her today? When I get done with playtime?"

After-school playtime signaled the end of Brianna's day at the Stand.

"Maybe before that," Harper told her. "Maybe, just for today, you could miss playtime and play with Gram instead. Would you like that?"

"Yeah!" Brianna skipped again. "I would *love* that, Mommy. Can I? Can I, please?"

"I'll see if it can be arranged," Harper said, not promising anything until she'd met with Miriam herself. Which, she remembered with a knot in her stomach, she was on her way to do as soon as she dropped off Brianna at her preschool class.

"Yaayyy!" Brianna squealed. And then, looking up at Harper with an innocence that touched all the way to Harper's soul, said, "You're the mommy I always wanted. I love you."

"I love you, too, sweet pea." Harper's eyes

were uncharacteristically misty as she pulled open the door that led to Brianna's class.

You're the baby I always wanted. She used to tell her baby that—in the womb—and later, too, as she'd been starting a new life in a new town with a new job, and a three-month-old baby to provide for. All alone.

You're the baby I always wanted. She'd told the baby that to remind herself. And to make sure Brianna knew, that even though she was being raised by a single parent, she was wanted more than anything.

You're the baby I always wanted.

Brianna just hadn't had the father Harper had wanted for her.

CHAPTER FIVE

ONE OF MASON'S sought-after skills was his ability to home in on the smallest things. To see what the eye generally passed over. Like a tiny pencil mark on the wall. Or patterns that fallen cookie crumbs left behind. He had no magical powers, no special sense that others didn't have; he just paid attention.

To everything.

Growing up with a little brother out to stab you in the back did that to a guy. Especially when your folks expected you to protect that younger sibling. The cherry on top had been the fact that he truly loved his brother—and knew Bruce loved him, too. Mason believed, even now, that each of them would die for the other.

All of this made his current situation as close to untenable as it ever got for him. Mostly, he just moved on through, no matter what muck he might find himself standing in. Taking it on the chin was also one of his perfected skills. Or drawing the hurt—the contradictions—inside himself.

Six of one, half a dozen of another...

"There she is." Miriam's half-mumbled, somewhat ornery remark took him by surprise. He'd been watching for Harper for more than half an hour and yet he hadn't been the first to see her.

His skills seemed to desert him when she was around.

"Harper." He stood. Held out a hand to her, not to shake, but to guide her to the third chair he'd pulled up. Without touching her, of course.

That was a mistake he'd never make again. Touching her.

"Well, you must be pleased," Miriam said by way of greeting, and Mason frowned. What the hell? He'd never seen his grandmother be this downright ungracious. Vindictive. Mean.

I told you so was all over the look Harper sent him.

"Gram." Mason wasn't going to ignore the rudeness, regardless of the situation. "I can't believe you just said that. You know damn well that Harper doesn't want you hurt. And she doesn't want the father of her child in trouble, either." If he hadn't been sure of that before his meeting with her that morning, he certainly was afterward.

While he didn't understand it, couldn't dissect it and study it, he'd always been aware of Bruce's special charm. People gravitated to him.

Liked him. Stuck up for him. Their parents and Mason included. And, apparently, that charm even worked with ex-wives.

Gram's bent head made him feel a second of shame, and he regretted the harshness of his words, if not the sentiment. He recognized that he'd overreacted in his somewhat primitive male desire to protect a woman he'd once gone to bed with—

Nope. Not going there.

"You're right," Gram said before he could rectify what he'd said. She looked at Harper. "I apologize for my rudeness. But I don't think you're happy to have me here."

What?

"I'm not happy you're in this situation," Harper said, then sat forward, her hands on the table in front of her. Open. Not clasped. She had nothing to hide, he translated. "But how I feel doesn't enter into this," she continued, sounding like a doctor breaking bad news, or a reporter on television. Compassionate and yet...professionally distant.

He glanced away, but not soon enough. The serious look in her eyes, the softness of her expression, even the damned uniform—it was all a turn-on.

Which made him a creep.

Or a man who'd been without a woman for far

too long and unexpectedly saw one with whom he'd had a night of incredible sex.

Being turned on was preferable to giving in to the myriad of emotions vying for his attention. Fear for his family was at the top of that list.

If it took a sexual memory to get him through this...

"My job here, first off," Harper was saying, "is to verify that you signed the VNL freely and of your own accord. The voluntary no release form."

Chin tight, Miriam nodded. "I did."

"Then it's my responsibility to make sure you don't leave. And that no one gets in who could do you harm. I'll be assigning around-the-clock duty to you, which, at times, will include me. My officers and I will keep our distance, and do everything we can not to impinge on your privacy, but we will be present, at all times, as set out in the VNL. Are you in agreement with these terms?"

Gram's glance in Mason's direction seemed to waver for a second—almost to the point of vulnerability. He met her eyes. He felt a driving need to promise her that everything was going to be fine.

It was a promise he couldn't make, and the words caught in his throat.

"I am in agreement." Gram turned back to Harper.

Mason had to hand it to Harper. Her gaze remained straightforward, her face unsmiling. There was no sign of victory, or even of satisfaction in having Miriam agreeing to do as she said. Of having Miriam in a position of needing her.

"I'll make this as painless as I possibly can," Harper said. "Including keeping myself off your detail as much as I can."

"I appreciate that. You being around as little as possible."

Wow. Gram wasn't letting up on her obvious dislike of Bruce's ex. In all his years, Mason had never seen his grandmother behave this way. He wondered, for a second, if she was starting to lose her faculties. Bruce had assured him she wasn't. Mason's earlier concern about Gram's aging hadn't had anything to do with her mind; it had been due more to her lack of energy. Emotional and physical.

"That's all I need, then." Harper stood. "If you have any problems, if something alarms you or bothers you, even a little, don't hesitate to speak to my team. Any time of the day or night. That's what we're here for."

"Thank you." Gram stood, too, and Mason saw the move for the power play it was. Miriam was going to stand up to Harper every step of the way.

With a nod toward Mason, Harper turned to leave. "Wait." Gram's voice, calling her back, filled Mason with a sense of relief. His grandmother was going to make this right.

And he wanted Harper back, too. They hadn't spoken about Bruce yet. He'd hoped the two women would talk. That Harper would convince Gram to tell them what had happened. Convince her, too, that it would be best for Bruce in the long run if they could get him help.

When Harper had turned back, Gram said, "What about Brianna? When do I get to see her?"

Wow, again. This was so *not* the way to get what you wanted, by speaking with antagonism toward the person who could provide it. Or not...

"I told her she could see you during her afternoon playtime. Would that work for you?"

Gram blinked and Mason almost smiled. Except that it would be a result of seeing his grandmother put in her place. He didn't want that to happen. He just wanted her rudeness to stop. Mostly because it was so out of character. And maybe, a little, because it was directed at Harper. Unfairly.

"That would be fine," Gram said.

"One of my officers will deliver her to your bungalow and stay there while she's with you, in addition to the officer who'll be on duty assigned to you." Harper named a time. "If that's okay, Brianna can stay with you until I'm ready to head home. At that point, her officer will deliver her back to me."

"That's okay with me, as long as you aren't the officer." Gram wasn't giving an inch.

Harper had just given miles.

And Mason had no idea where to go with any of it.

HARPER WAS UNUSUALLY off her mark for the rest of the day. Other than the hysterical crying bout she'd suffered five years before, after discovering that her fiancé had been unfaithful to her shortly before their wedding, she'd never had drama moments in her life. She just wasn't the sort.

And yet, all day Tuesday, she was…jittery. She'd seen Mason. The sky hadn't fallen in. She hadn't died, or melted into a puddle on the floor. She hadn't even been filled with rage at the callous way he'd disappeared from her life without so much as a phone call in five years' time.

Not that she could blame him, she supposed. She hadn't called him, either.

But now, her not calling seemed…worse, because the only reason he hadn't contacted her was that he thought it was at her bidding. He'd been honoring a request he'd believed had come from her. Whereas she hadn't contacted him because she'd simply chosen not to. Most of the day she managed to avoid thinking about that revelation. Lives depended on her ability to focus, and she gave her job every ounce of herself when she was on duty. Tuesday was no different. Cameras provided around-the-clock surveillance at all times. And every single unidentifiable individual who lingered too long on the block that fronted the Stand, or frequented any of the Stand-run shops there on numerous occasions, was quietly and efficiently investigated. Rounds were done on a regular basis. Gates, locks and bungalows were checked at least once an hour, although residents were never disturbed unless necessary. She ran regular background checks on anyone who was employed by, volunteered at or visited the Stand. She also had daily meetings with the Stand executive staff, so she always knew what events were coming up and could ensure they'd be properly guarded. Those meetings also allowed her to know—and to let her officers know—which of their residents might be having a particularly hard day, which ones had recently had contact with family members, and those whose abusers were known to be agitated or on the hunt. At every shift change, she had an update meeting with her own staff of fifteen. That afternoon, she passed around Miriam's guard schedule and disclosed, to the few who were still unaware, that the woman was her former grandmother-in-law. Without criticizing Miriam, she disclosed that the older woman wasn't all that fond of her. She gave instructions that Miriam was to see Brianna every day if she chose, but only with an officer assigned to Brianna present at all times.

Maybe that last part was overkill. Until a month ago Brianna had spent the night in Miriam's home every other weekend without any guard detail at all. But that was before Harper had learned that Miriam was being abused and lying about it. Whether Bruce was her abuser, or she'd had someone else in their home without his knowledge, the fact remained that Miriam was protecting someone who'd hurt her.

After her last meeting she could've packed it in, called for Brianna, gone home. Instead she cleaned up the small pile of paperwork from the in-box at the corner of her desk. Watered her plants. And then texted Alissa, the guard she'd assigned to her daughter for the afternoon, asking her to bring Brianna up to the main building.

The rest of the evening, until Brianna's bedtime, would be consumed by her chattering, her constant questions and observations. It was the lifeblood that kept Harper going. The source of her true happiness.

Maybe they'd go out for French fries. Not healthy, not something they did often, but a treat they both loved. She was thinking about Uncle Bob's, a beachfront restaurant not far from their town house. There were sandboxes for kids to play in while waiting for their food; that would distract Brianna, giving Harper a few minutes to think her own thoughts. Or at least a few minutes during which Brianna wouldn't notice her mother's preoccupation.

She'd just received an affirmative response from Alissa that they'd be along shortly, when her cell rang. Her stomach lurched as she saw Mason's newly programmed name flash on her screen. She'd given him her private number but she hadn't expected him to use it.

"Yeah, Mason, what's up?" she answered. Straight to the point. All business. Racing right by social niceties like "hello" and "how are you?"

"I'd like to stop by tonight. I have some questions."

"What kind of questions?"

"An official interview of a suspect's ex-wife." She heard no emotion in his delivery. Oddly enough, instead of calming her, that seemed to put her more on edge. "I've been asked by the Albina police force to pursue this case quietly, to protect my brother, whichever way it goes."

"I don't have anything to add to what I told you this morning."

She was a cop. If she were Mason, she'd be after the interview herself. So why was she prevaricating?

"The interview is official, Harper."

Heart thumping, she sat behind her desk, watching the door for her daughter to burst through. "Bruce has been charged?"

"No. You remember Clark O'Brien?"

"Captain O'Brien?" As in her boss's boss's boss when she worked for the Albina PD. Which had made it awkward for her when he'd shown up for dinner at her former father-in-law's home. The two had been like brothers.

"Yeah."

"I called him right after I left you this morning. I knew the department would probably be receiving a doctor's report from urgent care."

She nodded and stood up, grabbing her keys, thinking she'd meet Brianna and Alissa outside, intercept them on the way from Miriam's bungalow.

"You wanted him to intervene." She understood now. Mason had Bruce's back.

"I wanted to forewarn him. Who knows how Bruce is going to react when this hits."

Locking her office door, she headed down the hall. "Don't you think, if he did this, he'd already be reacting in light of your call to him last night, telling him she was hurt? And that she'd been to the clinic?"

"What would you expect him to do?"

She gave it a second's thought. And then had to say, "He'd go on as normal." But in her experience, he also admitted his crimes. He hadn't tried to hide his infidelity from her. He'd just lied when he'd said it would never happen again.

Also in her experience, he wasn't a violent man...

The door leading to the resort's secure grounds wasn't far ahead of her.

"So is he suspended?"

"No. Clark asked me to conduct a private, preliminary investigation, apart from the PD."

Her breath of relief made her feel heady for a second. Sunshine on her face felt good, too.

"So his reputation won't be ruined if it turns out he didn't do this."

"Yes. But he did it, Harper. And if we prove that, we can handle this quietly, help him, rather than ruin his entire life."

"Shouldn't you be keeping an open mind, since you're conducting the investigation?"

"What cop did you ever know who didn't work with suspicions? With gut instincts? It's what guides us to the truth."

He was right, of course. But...

"Does Clark think he's guilty?"

"I don't know what he thinks, other than that he's not happy about it. Any of it. He's known Miriam for forty years. And Bruce and me for most of our lives. Out of respect for Dad, he wants me to find the truth. And, I guess, he's hoping I find something other than Bruce has been abusing our grandmother."

"So...about this evening..."

She had Brianna to consider. Still, Mason was Brianna's uncle—not that they'd spent any time together.

"How about if I meet you?" Her thoughts came quickly. Brianna and Alissa were approaching, only a football field's distance away. "At eight...at The Cove." A beach bar about a block from home.

"What about your daughter?"

"That's past her bedtime." She was panicking. For no reason. "I'll call a sitter for her," she said, thinking on the fly. "If I brought her along, the chances of us having a conversation without an inquisition from her would be nil."

His brief chuckle warmed her. Which brought its own bout of panic.

"Okay, I'll meet you at eight," he said.

"You know where The Cove is?" It wasn't as if Santa Raquel was all that big. Or he'd spent any time there. Not her problem.

"I'll find it."

Of course he would.

CHAPTER SIX

SHE'D DRESSED UP for him. In skintight black pants, a long, figure-hugging white shirt and a black denim vest trimmed with white lace, she knew she looked good. She'd spruced up her hair with enough spray to give it the sexy just-got-out-of-bed look her stylist had left her with the day she'd cut it. And put on eyeliner, too. She didn't kid herself. A perverse, lesser part of her wanted Mason to regret never having called her after the night she'd spent in his bed. She wasn't proud of the feeling. She also wasn't fool enough to deny it was there.

The much bigger part of her, the rational part, dressed up to give herself confidence. And to prove that she wasn't afraid of her sexuality in his presence. He could come on to her or not. She'd have no problem resisting him. Mason was a little too...much for her tastes. Taller than Bruce, broader than him, he'd always seemed larger than life to her. Gorgeous. But somewhat...intimidating. Both of the Thomas men, with their thick dark hair, swarthy coloring and striking green-gold eyes, had the ability to stop women in their tracks. Bruce had longer hair—and unrulier than Mason's more military cut. She'd always preferred hair she could run her fingers through.

Like the night she'd run them through the thick patch of curly hair that covered Mason's chest...

She shook that thought away—far away—as she entered the bar fifteen minutes ahead of schedule. She was going to have a beer in front of her before he started shooting questions at her.

Happy to find the back booth clear, she slid in, facing the door, and looked out the window beside her, imagining she could see the ocean she knew was mere yards away. She could see the beach, but The Cove's outside string of lights didn't penetrate enough of the darkness for her to delineate waves. If the moon had been out...

He slid in across from her before she'd had a chance to order. The last time they'd been together in a bar, the only other time, they'd sat side by side on stools.

Pulling a small, leather-bound pad from the back pocket of his jeans, he flipped it onto the table and settled in.

"Did you order?"

"Not yet."

Glancing around, he signaled the waiter. "You still drinking the same kind of beer?" He gazed in her general direction, but not directly at her.

"Yeah." She said nothing else, knowing she was challenging him to remember, sure that he wouldn't. And didn't really care either way. Being perverse again, which seemed to be something he brought out in her. She'd have to rein in her lesser self when he was around.

Her hands folded on the table, she noticed that his hair was longer than five years before, and still as thick. Not as long as Bruce's, which usually fell past his collar, since he worked undercover so much of the time. She'd also noticed that Mason had not only changed into jeans, but the black shirt was different from the one he'd had on that morning, too.

It was unbuttoned down to midchest.

She stared down at her hands. And then out toward the ocean again.

Why was his shirt unbuttoned? Surely not for her? Had she told him she liked running her fingers through the hair on his chest? Parts of that night they'd spent together were a blur.

Other things she remembered as though they'd happened yesterday.

He was talking to the waiter about beers on tap and specials. Her preference was neither on tap nor on special. She waited.

He ordered a tall dark lager for himself. And the light beer, bottled, that she'd always preferred.

"You changed your clothes," were the first words out of her mouth when the waiter left. She wished she'd bitten her tongue.

He nodded. "I was up most of the night and hit the sack as soon as I got home."

And then he'd obviously showered when he got up. That was why the musky aftershave he wore was reaching her nostrils so clearly. He'd just put it on.

"Where are you staying?"

"At home, why?"

"You drove back to Albina this morning?" And then another two hours to meet her for questioning?

"Yeah."

"You going all the way back tonight?"

His shrug distracted her. Those shoulders... She had a mental flash of tanned, smooth skin. And a strength that allowed him to support his own weight, and hers, too, as he'd moved them together into the most incredible physical experience...

"Depends on how much beer I drink," he said, not quite smiling, but she thought he might have if their situation had been different.

"Well, don't let me keep you." Their beers had

arrived. She took a long cold sip before he could tip his mug to her bottle—something he'd done with each and every drink they'd shared that long-ago night. Their toasts had grown more and more ridiculous as the night had worn on. If she was remembering right, they'd tipped their glasses to see-through bras and boxers at one point.

He opened his pad before he took a sip. Got out a pen. Asked a series of questions that she knew were designed to put her at ease. Did she and Bruce purchase their house together? Had she liked it? Did she help choose the furniture? Yes, to all of the above. He wanted to know how she liked Santa Raquel. She liked it fine. Did she miss Albina? Not really.

She missed being closer to her parents, but since he didn't ask, she didn't reveal that piece of information.

It dawned on her, as she sipped twice as fast as he did, that he'd been driving for the past couple of hours. "Did you have dinner? They have great bar food here."

His weakness. She knew that from Bruce.

Funny that she'd only ever seen the guy a handful of times in her life and yet knew so much about him.

Knew him intimately…

She took another sip. Her limit was three.

He'd better be done with his questions by then because that was when she was leaving.

"I made a sandwich and ate it on the road." He glanced at the tables around them, presumably to see what others were consuming, and she reached for a menu, placing it in front of him.

Her tentative theory was that if he was busy eating, he couldn't be worrying about getting information for that pad he'd yet to write on. She really had nothing to give him that could in any way prove that Bruce had hurt Miriam. She had proof of him not keeping his word. Proof of unexplained absences. She'd caught him looking at normal adult porn on the internet once in the year they'd been married.

None of that added up to anything worthy of an investigation. Or anything criminal, either.

It just added up to a man she couldn't accept as her partner in life. And one she tried to keep from disappointing her daughter.

"I think I'll have this combination platter," Mason said, looking up from the menu. "Will you share it with me?" He was getting fried green beans, onion rings and barbecued chicken niblets.

"I'll have an onion ring or two. If you don't eat them all." She'd shared an appetizer platter with him once before. Really late at night, when she'd been too drunk to be aware of what was on it.

Or so she'd told herself.

In actual fact, she'd been tipsy enough not to care, enough to deaden the pain, but she hadn't been too drunk to know about the choice she'd been making. She'd known, when she went to bed with him, exactly what she was doing. She simply hadn't cared how wrong it had been.

Not until she woke in the bright light of day and found herself naked in his bed.

Mason ordered and tacked on another round of beers to be delivered with his dinner.

"Everyone has some kind of temper. Everyone gets angry." His gaze met hers with total focus now.

"Yeah."

"What did Bruce do when he got mad?"

She wanted the truth as badly as he did, so she met his eyes. Tried to recall a time when her husband had been in a bad mood, or upset about something. Other than when she'd told him she was leaving, of course. That had been a once-in-a-lifetime bad morning for both of them—inarguably the worst of her life. She'd said things, called him a loser, with colorful language attached. Her only comfort in the whole situation was that at three months old, Brianna had been too young to understand her words. Or remember them.

"You know Bruce," she finally said. "He's always so self-assured, so confident. If something doesn't go his way, he looks for the bright side, sure he'll find one, and then convinces everyone else that the darkness is gone, too."

"I asked about his anger."

She had a flash of the time a prosecutor had refused to press charges after Bruce had worked six months to make an arrest. She explained the circumstances, then said, "He sat for over an hour with this…chiseled look on his face, staring at a blank television screen. His jaw was clenched. Whenever I walked by the room, he'd still be sitting there, staring. Eventually he got up, told me he was going out for a while, and he left. When he came back, he was more subdued than normal, but still easy to get along with. He helped me make dinner."

Mason's expression was intent. "Do you have any idea where he went? What he did when he was gone?"

She shook her head. "I assumed he went in to work. That's what he normally did when he had something to sort out. He'd talk to Clark or other people at the precinct."

"But you don't know if he did that day?"

"Like I said, it was my day off, so no, I wasn't there to witness his presence or conversations."

"Do you remember anyone ever mentioning that he'd been there? Or hearing anything about the conversation?"

She shook her head again.

"What about the case? The prosecutor? Did anything change? Were charges eventually pressed?"

"Not for dealing. He got him on possession, though—with enough drugs to put him in prison for a while." That was how Bruce worked. He found a way. "If something prevented an outcome he needed, he came at it from another direction."

Shouldn't be news to Mason.

"What about at work? Did he have a reputation for getting physical with his perps?" He frowned. "Roughing them up, I mean."

"No. He's tough, you know that. He's not afraid to stand up to anyone if he believes the action is warranted. He doesn't shy away from danger or back down. He'd blast a guy with words. But I never heard of a single instance of him doing anything more than not putting cuffs on gently. You know, maybe lift a guy's arm a little high on his back, or put the cuffs on tight. But nothing compared to some other cops. He never shoved or struck anyone that I ever heard of."

His food arrived and she sat back, figuring they'd relax now. She really wasn't aware of anything that would help him. If she'd had any concerns about Bruce having anger or violence issues, she'd never have left Brianna with her father overnight. Or unsupervised.

"And at home? When he got angry at home, what did he do?"

"He didn't mince words in letting me know I'd pissed him off. He raised his voice sometimes. Then he'd usually leave for a while and when he got back, he'd have calmed down enough for rational conversation. We'd talk about it, and things would be fine."

"Where did he go when he left? Did you ever ask?"

Harper shrugged. "Not really. I wanted to give him his space." She paused. "I got the impression that he drove around for a while. Or, if it was evening, that he went up to the bar for a couple of beers. So I didn't ask." Truth was, she'd been glad that Bruce had taken his anger out of the house. He'd always been ready to talk fairly when he'd returned.

"Would he come home drunk?"

"Bruce handles his alcohol, you know that."

"Would he come home drunk?" he repeated.

"I'm not sure I'd recognize it if he had. I once saw him put down eight beers at an after-funeral gathering with the force, and he didn't act any differently than if he'd been drinking tea. He didn't argue when I announced that I was driving home, though."

"Did he ever come home smelling of alcohol?"

"Sometimes. Slightly. He hangs out at the bar with off-duty officers. Again, something a lot of them do. Something I occasionally did, too, before Brianna came along. It's good to unwind with other people who get it." Surely Mason socialized sometimes when he was working with departments around the country.

"I went by to take a look through the house today before I headed back here." He picked up a couple of fried green beans, put them in his mouth, then pushed the plate toward her. "If there'd been a fight, Bruce would've had plenty of time to clean up, but you never know what a scene can tell you. His truck was there, so I didn't stop."

He really seemed convinced that Bruce had done this.

"What about the house the two of you shared?" he asked. "Was anything ever broken? A knickknack that got shoved? Maybe a door opened with enough force to push the knob through a wall?"

"Of course not! Don't you think I'd remember something like that? And have concerns of my own?"

He didn't answer. Instead, he loaded his fork with sauce-smeared chicken niblets and ate them.

Still managing to keep her hands off the onion rings, and to nurse her second beer, she leaned forward. "Look, if you're trying to convince me that Bruce would manipulate the truth to make someone look bad, maybe, given time and enough examples, you could get me to see that. I know that he struggles, and sometimes fails, to keep his work distinct from his personal life—in terms of separating a carefully concocted pretense from reality. But I also know, for a fact, that he owns up to his mistakes. Before he's caught. Not afterward. Like that time he did a line of coke to prove to a dealer that he was trustworthy. He went to the captain the second he was off duty and volunteered for daily testing the rest of the time he was on that case. He never touched the stuff again."

"Bruce doesn't like to give up control. Nor does he have the ability to relax enough to enjoy the high. That's why he's never had trouble staying away from drugs."

Her head cocked, she studied him. "What about you? You know how to 'relax and enjoy the high'?"

It sounded like that was what he'd just told her. But...

"Nope. Which is why I understand and how I recognize the same trait in my brother. It's also why neither of us drinks anything stronger than beer."

"I've never so much as taken a drag from a joint," she felt compelled to tell him. And then wondered why she'd felt that need. "Or a puff on a cigarette."

His grin made her insides flip-flop. "I've met your folks," he said. "They're pretty straightforward, down-to-earth people. And with you being an only child, I'm guessing they kept you too busy on the farm, and too aware of the effect chemicals have on the body, to leave you with much opportunity, or desire, to experiment with substance abuse."

Her parents' all-organic fruit and vegetable business hadn't made them rich. But it kept them comfortably warm, clothed and fed. "I know more about holistic treatments and remedies than I do traditional medicine," she acknowledged, returning his smile. "And I also know that the world is what we make it—each of us, with our individual choices."

She'd had a great childhood, and didn't take that lightly. Or for granted. She felt a huge responsibility to give Brianna that same sense of purpose, of healthy living and societal contribution.

"I'm telling you, like I've already told you several times today, that if I had any suspicions about Bruce, any knowledge that would be of concern, I'd be calling Captain O'Brien myself."

"I don't think you're deliberately holding anything back," Mason said, picking up an onion ring and handing it to her.

It would be churlish to refuse. She had to accept it. And it would be equally rude just to sit there and hold it or throw it away. Especially with him watching her. She took a bite. Closed her eyes while she chewed.

He was grinning again when she opened them. "Good, isn't it?"

It was good there was only one left on his plate. "Mmm-hmm," she said and finished the onion ring, then took a sip of beer.

And promised herself that she'd be heading home within minutes.

CHAPTER SEVEN

MASON WAS BROUGHT up short when he realized he was enjoying himself. He wasn't there to have a good time. Nor was it appropriate that he do so with his brother's ex-wife. Particularly when he was investigating that same brother.

No one would be happier than he would to find that Bruce had never had anything to do with hurting their grandmother. But his gut was telling him Bruce had done this. And it had to stop.

Period. For Gram. And for Bruce, too.

"Things aren't always what they seem." He was beginning to suspect that these days, with Bruce, they almost never were. It used to be only when he'd tried every other means to get his own way that Bruce would resort to manipulating the truth. But in the past few years, through things Gram had said, he'd caught his brother doing it for seemingly no reason at all—as though he'd been undercover for so long, he'd lost perspective on the difference between lies and truth.

None of which meant he'd turned violent. Or hurt Gram.

If Mason was going to find the truth, he needed help. Fast. And Harper, with her ties to Bruce and her current proximity to Gram, was the most obvious choice. Gram had given him a couple of weeks with her agreement to stay at the Stand. Two weeks before she'd insist on going home to Bruce.

Her hands on the table—Mason didn't miss the open body language—Harper frowned. "What do you mean, things aren't always what they seem? You trying to tell me something?"

He'd been debating, since seeing her again that morning, whether or not he would. Whether or not it was necessary.

Whether he dared bring up the night that had changed his life forever—and not in a good way.

He had two weeks.

"That night I found you crying..."

The atmosphere around them changed completely. Electricity singed the air he breathed. Leaving an unmistakable stench of acrimony.

"What?" Harper's hands were no longer on the table. She'd put on her "cop" face, which she was remarkably good at. He couldn't read a thing she was thinking.

Which left him with only the surface beauty he'd never been able to get out of his mind since

the first time he'd laid eyes on her. It occurred
to him that she might know full well the effect
she had on him—especially after he'd noticed
the leggings that sculpted legs he could still feel
around him if he closed his eyes and allowed it
to happen. Noticed the makeup drawing attention to blue eyes that had been haunting him for
five long, lonely years...

She'd been bereft that night, and he'd taken
advantage of her. He'd betrayed his own brother.
Slept with the woman Bruce was in love with.
He was a jerk and he paid the price every single day.

And here he was with her again, possibly
building a case to put his brother in prison. Betraying him in the worst possible way. The irony
of it wasn't lost on him.

"What about my crying?" Harper's tone was
colder. As if he was a perp she didn't trust.

She'd steered away from the latter part of that
evening, and he was grateful.

Curious, too.

Slightly miffed.

And yet he didn't blame her.

"You've said, more than once today, that
Bruce owns up to his actions."

"That's right." Her frown cleared. "And he
did that day, too. I told you back then. As soon
as he'd slept with that woman, he told me. He'd

been pretending to be her guy for over a month. She'd come on to him and would've gotten suspicious if he turned her down. He couldn't risk her feeling rejected and breaking up with him. Almost eight weeks of infiltration into the rent scheme she and her brother were running would've gone down the drain and thirty senior citizens would have ended up broke and homeless."

Mason had heard a couple of versions of the story. Including the proven fact that Bruce had saved thirty elderly citizens from financial ruin and eventual homelessness when they no longer had the money to pay rent. As, one by one, they had to move into government housing, the brother and sister who owned the building would've rented the vacated apartments to other fixed income social security recipients. They would've slowly drained their bank accounts, too, with hidden costs and fees, with suddenly broken plumbing, or electrical issues for which their rental agreements held them accountable.

Bruce had slept with the woman, just like he'd said. But...

"Bruce started sleeping with her on their second date."

Harper shook her head. "He took her on a dinner cruise and was home before eleven."

Home to Harper's apartment? Officially his

brother had been living with his father before they were married, while he waited for his and Harper's house to close.

"He took her for a picnic on the beach and had sex with her." Mason lowered his eyes to his plate as he said the words, using the last onion ring to wipe up what was left of the barbecue sauce.

He'd gone through various scenarios when he'd considered the pain he'd be causing Harper by telling her the truth. He'd weighed that against the need for her to see his brother as he really was. It might change how other things from the past looked to her. Or help her remember events she might not currently consider relevant.

The decisive factor for him had been the number of times she'd so adamantly told him that Bruce always "owned" his mistakes. Unless he was grossly mistaken, she was a woman who'd want the truth.

He glanced up to see a mixture of shock and confusion on her beautiful face. She didn't smile enough.

The thought came unbidden and he instantly pushed it away. Harper Davidson's smiles were none of his concern.

"After…that night—" more accurately, after seeing the look of horror on Harper's face when she'd woken up in his bed the next morning "—I asked Clark if I could see the files from Bruce's investigation, to confirm what I already knew, to confirm that he'd had sex on the second date. I was still FBI then and I had concerns about federal monies being misused by the landlord."

That had been the official story.

He'd been checking up on his brother because he'd been hit like a ton of bricks by his brother's fiancée.

"Bruce keeps meticulous records when he's on a job," Mason reminded her.

"So…that day he told me…the night before hadn't been the first time he'd had sex with her. But at least he admitted it. He told me what he'd done before we got married, so I could call it off if…"

She was still seeing his brother for a better man than Bruce was. Mason was not proud of how much that irked him.

And yet, he admired her for it, too.

So much that if he weren't on the job, if he didn't have a vision of Gram's face, her cast, so clearly in his mind, he might have left Harper to her version of truth.

"He'd had sex with a woman the night before, exactly as he told you. It just hadn't been with *that* woman." He tried to keep emotion out of his voice, and yet tempered the words, the tone, the way he would with any other victim deserving of compassion.

Her mouth fell open. She lifted her beer bottle, seemingly nonchalant, until he noticed her hand trembling.

She swallowed a gulp of beer, and then, with a nod toward him, asked, "Then who did he have sex with that night a week before we were married, if it wasn't a perp?"

Certain that she didn't want to know, Mason paused, wanting to be elsewhere. Her marriage had ended because Bruce had been unfaithful a second time. He'd blamed both times on cases. What harm did it do to have her continuing to think so? Except that he needed her to see how his brother re-framed truths.

"His partner."

"*Gwen?* He had sex with Gwen? But…she was at our house all the time the year we were married. She was like a sister to me. And treated Bruce like a brother. There was no way there'd been anything physical between them. I'd have noticed something. A look. Tension. *Something…*"

"It only happened that one time before you were married." He hoped the news softened the blow some. Probably not much. Because his brother had also been sleeping with a perp before he married her, too, just as he said. Just not the night he claimed.

"It wasn't like they worked together all that often," he droned on because he had to fill the silence before he slid around to her side of the booth, plied her with beer and took her in his arms to soothe away the hurt his brother had caused.

Been there, done that. Never again.

"They only rode together when he wasn't on an undercover assignment," he said.

She sat up straighter. "He was on an assignment at the time. I know he was, because I was still working at the department." Her entire demeanor seemed to take on strength. He almost let her have this one.

"The night he told you he was with the perp... It was the night of his bachelor party."

"He didn't have a bachelor party. I didn't have a bachelorette weekend, either. We agreed to save our money for..." He knew before her voice faded that she was getting it. Her expression seemed to freeze.

"She was at his bachelor party. Said she'd been one of his guys longer than most of them and couldn't not be part of the big send-off."

"He slept with Gwen." It was more statement than question. Mason nodded anyway, taking no pleasure in confirming it.

After a long swig of beer, elbows on the table, she folded her hands together. "And the perp, he did it with her multiple times."

As often as it had taken to get the indictment he'd been after, according to the report. Undercover work gave a cop more leeway, and Bruce took advantage of it. Mason knew his brother well enough to realize Bruce would see his actions as some kind of sacrifice for the job— proving to his superiors that there was nothing he wouldn't do to bring down the bad guys.

"I hope to God he wore a condom."

Half choking on the swallow of beer he'd taken, Mason put down his mug, motioning to the waiter for one more. "It was a long time ago," he said. He tried not to think about the woman *he'd* slept with, the woman sitting across from him—and how much he wanted to do it again.

Wasn't going to happen. No matter how everything played out. Bruce was family. And still in love with his ex-wife. His brother had mentioned, more than once, that he was planning to renew his relationship with Harper. Mason wouldn't take his own happiness at the expense of his brother's.

Harper wouldn't have Mason again anyway, he was certain of that. The memory of that look on her face…a man didn't forget something like that.

"I'm sure he wore a condom," he said now, needing to arrive at the truth about Bruce, get Gram settled and get out of town. "But if you'd caught an STI from him, you'd have known long before now."

"I'm sure you're right." Harper stood, grabbed her purse. "Listen, I have to go home," she said. "Kelsey from next door came over to stay with Brianna while I'm gone, and it's a school night for her. I promised I'd be back no later than ten."

It was quarter to. She lived about three minutes away. He'd purposely checked on his drive in. But he nodded. "I'll be in touch in the morning," he told her. Because he needed her help.

She nodded. Reached for her wallet.

"I've got this," Mason said. "I'm going to order a soda to go and then head home."

"You're going back to Albina?"

If he said he'd rather not, would she offer him a night on her couch? He wanted to know. Badly.

"I'll be home by midnight," he told her, figuring the drive would do him good.

He had work to do.

And very little time to get it done.

CHAPTER EIGHT

BRUCE HAD SLEPT with Gwen. In the larger scheme of things that mattered not at all. Miriam's injuries were what mattered. Brianna's well-being, too.

It wasn't like she and Bruce were still married, or even had feelings for each other, except mutual respect where raising their daughter was concerned.

And there was little reason for shock where his infidelity was concerned. It wasn't like he'd been faithful after he'd "come clean" the first time about the night he'd slept with another woman. He'd promised her then it had been a one-time thing. The only time. He'd said work had gotten away from him.

She hadn't stuck around long enough to hear anything else. Devastated in a way she'd never experienced before, feeling such an overwhelming chaos of emotions that were new to her undramatic life, she'd taken off. She'd ended up at the beach where she'd run until her calves ached. And then kept on running.

She'd trusted Bruce. With her heart. With her life. The idea that he'd been unfaithful to her—and a week before their wedding—she hadn't known how to cope. With all the crap that cops saw on the job, they had to be able to trust each other. Implicitly. And when a cop was the man you loved, your partner in life… His disloyalty had been unfathomable to her.

And still…she'd loved him.

By the time Mason had found her, her calves had given out. She'd been sitting on the beach with her head on her knees sobbing so hard her ribs hurt.

Now, sitting in the same position on her living room floor sometime after eleven, Harper picked up the phone.

"Yeah?" Not surprisingly he answered on the first ring. He'd still be driving.

"How did you find me that night?" Back then, she'd given no thought to the way he'd shown up on the beach. She'd been too far gone to question much of anything at that point.

But during the years since, she'd wondered a million times, with no one to ask. Her night with Mason was the one subject she and Bruce couldn't handle. And never, ever mentioned. As time passed, and her relationship with Bruce ended, Mason's sudden appearance that long-ago night had seemed to take on new meaning.

Almost as though he'd been led to her...

"Bruce."

She shook her head, confused. "What?"

"He called me, completely distraught. He knew you wouldn't talk to him and said he'd never seen you so upset. Truth is my little brother was scared to death. He told me that you liked to jog on the beach. I knew where you'd been when you left him, went to the closest beach access, saw your car and followed the female-sized tennis shoe footprints."

"Bruce sent you."

He'd been on an errand for her brother and then he'd taken her to bed.

"Yep."

"No wonder he was...no wonder he acted like he did when he found out what we'd done."

"I didn't expect you to tell him."

"You didn't know me well enough." And yet, it felt as though he had. That night... She'd probably built it up into way more than it had been. For one night she'd felt...cherished. As if she had absolutely no reason to worry about anything.

It was a result of the amount of alcohol she'd consumed. She knew that.

"For what it's worth, I've spent every day and night since regretting what I did to him," Mason said in a low voice. "And to you."

"I feel the same way."

"You were hurting beyond belief, he'd just been unfaithful to you and you thought your relationship was over." He paused. "I don't think you did anything wrong."

"I came on to you."

"I should never have responded."

"As I recall, you didn't."

"The facts contradict your recollection."

"You watched over me all night, never left my side, made sure I was safe. You even took me home with you, all the while managing to avoid my attempts to get you to do more. Even after we got to your place, you gave me the bed and went to sleep on the couch," she told him. Yeah, some details of that night were hazy, like how many bars they'd actually visited and what time they made it back to his place—in a cab. She remembered that much. Actually, some of her memories were completely clear.

Like the way she'd felt, leaving his bed dressed only in one of his T-shirts, and going out to the living room to convince him to come to the bed with her.

"I shared the bed with you." His tone was droll. "In the end, that's all that mattered."

She disagreed, but didn't see how belaboring the point was going to get them anywhere.

They couldn't go back. And they weren't going forward, either.

"You're positive Bruce was with Gwen that night?"

"Yeah."

There was only one way he could've been positive. He'd seen them together.

"Because you were at the party, too, weren't you? You knew he left with her."

"Yep."

Which meant he'd known, that night they'd barhopped together, that the story his brother had given her was false, and he hadn't said a word. He'd had sex with her, instead. With the lie right there between them.

He'd spent the night with her, never telling her that Bruce had sent him.

Oh, God, what a mess they'd all made.

BANG! UPRIGHT IN a second, reaching for the gun beneath the pillow next to him, Mason surveyed his room. Listening.

The sound came again. More of a pounding than any kind of blast. Someone was at his front door at—he glanced at his clock—two in the morning. Pulling on the jeans he'd worn to meet Harper the night before, he slid his gun into his back pocket and headed down the hall.

His doorbell rang.

Resisting the urge to yank open the door and share a few choice words with whoever was out there, he reined himself in long enough to look through the peephole.

Gwen Parker?

What the hell was *she* doing there?

Oh, God. *Bruce.*

Skin cold and heart pounding, he opened the door. "What is it?" he asked. It had to be about Bruce.

"How bad is it?" Did he have time to get to him? To try to make things right between them? To tell his brother how much he loved him?

Stepping up to him, nose to nose, Gwen, still in uniform, slapped his face.

Hard. *What the hell!*

"Your brother is the best cop I've ever known," the dark-haired woman hissed. A little shorter than Harper, and larger-boned, the woman was…a great cop.

And ordinary-looking.

Not the type Bruce had gone for. At least not publicly.

"Why in God's name are you hell-bent on destroying him?" Gwen wasn't backing down. At all.

It occurred to him then that the night of the bachelor party might not have been the first time

Bruce had slept with Gwen. That it was possible he still had sex with her on occasion.

He smelled alcohol on her breath and figured she'd gone straight to the bar after her shift. She'd had a few hours to tie one on.

"Did you drive over here?"

"Of course not! I've been drinking. I took a cab." She gestured wildly behind her and he saw the taxi across the street.

"You might want to get back out there," he said softly, hoping to disarm her anger enough to get her out of his home. They could deal with their situation in the morning at the station, after she'd sobered up. "You're running up quite a tab."

"It's worth it," she hissed. "I don't care how much it costssss." This was the first time she'd slurred a word. And spat on him, too. "What you're doing…it could ruin his life. You know how many lives would be hur-hurt by that?"

She swayed a bit, stepped on his bare toe as she caught her balance. The stench of alcohol turned his stomach.

How she'd come to know what he was doing, he had no idea. And he wasn't any happier than she was about word getting out, damaging Bruce's reputation. Once he had enough proof to do something, he hoped the matter could be resolved quietly.

O'Brien wanted the same thing. Had insisted on it, actually. So…

"You're ju-just jealous…" Her vituperative tone had faded to basic disrespect.

Now was not the time to ask her how she'd come about her knowledge. Or to defend it, either.

"Let's get you out to your cab," he said, with a hand at the small of her back. "I'll meet you at your convenience tomorrow, when and where you like."

She nodded. Looked toward the door and then, suddenly pale, looked up at him. "Bathroom?"

He pointed.

And prayed she made it in time. Cleaning up puke wasn't on his agenda.

Going for a shirt and shoes, Mason paid off the cab and got his keys. The second his unwanted guest came out of the bathroom—luckily leaving it in the condition in which she'd found it—he handed her a barf bag, ushered her out to his car and drove her home.

Thankfully, she made the trip without saying another word.

TASHA, A DOMESTIC abuse survivor who'd gone through the police academy and was one of Harper's top agents, met Harper at the door to her office the next morning. Tasha had another hour on shift and would've been out on the grounds unless she had a matter of possible importance.

"You asked us to keep you apprised of Miriam Thomas's actions." Tasha had been on Miriam's detail until four that morning. Each member of her staff was doing four-hour rotations.

Unlocking the door to her office, she preceded Tasha inside, dropped her satchel and keys on her desk. "I want to know anything out of the ordinary. Any change in her demeanor. Any friends she makes..." She'd do whatever she could to help Mason get the information he needed to protect his grandmother.

The officer was nodding, her expression pained. If Tasha had made a mistake, at least she'd come to her.

Still, they'd have to deal with that. Mistakes in their business could cost lives.

"I had a stomach upset last night and had to use the restroom. Miriam was in bed asleep and I called Allie over to the bungalow to cover for me. I waited until she arrived and then I hurried on my way. I didn't double-check Miriam's room before I turned over my duty."

That was it? Relief flooded her. For Miriam's sake. And for Tasha's, too. She was the best young officer, the most committed, the most clearheaded and the least hesitant, she'd ever had.

"I did the check as soon as I got back," the officer continued, her concern no less. "Miriam wasn't there, ma'am." She met Harper's gaze head-on.

Immediately on alert, Harper withheld her sharp rebuke at the fact that she was only now hearing about this.

"Allie radioed it in immediately and stayed at the residence while I went out on the grounds. As soon as I stepped outside I saw her, just a few yards from her place, coming up the sidewalk."

Miriam was fine. Harper took a deep breath. "She walked outside and neither of you saw her?"

The officer looked at her, offering no defense.

"Tasha?"

"I only left my post for those few minutes, ma'am, and I know for certain she didn't walk out that door while I was there." That sounded like Tasha. "So you think Allie left the post?"

"I can't say that. She was there when I went off and she was there when I got back. She swears she didn't leave the post, either."

"Where is she now?" Why weren't the two officers reporting in together?

"She's on Thomas duty now. Since Mrs. Thomas was fine, just out for a short walk because she couldn't sleep and was on her way back to the bungalow when I saw her, we didn't wake you. But I knew you'd want to know the second you got here."

Nodding, Harper told the officer they'd talk more about the incident later, thanked her for reporting it right away and sent her back to work.

FIVE MINUTES LATER, after a brief knock, Harper was opening the front door of the bungalow Miriam was sharing with two other women. All three were in the main room, the scent of bacon wafting from the kitchen.

"Miriam, can we go outside for a few minutes, please?"

"I'm making breakfast."

"We'll cover for you!" Nancy, a forty-year-old lesbian who'd been abused by her partner, spoke up, motioning toward their housemate Laura, a twenty-year-old who'd run away from an abusive boyfriend, but who'd also been abused as a child.

"I'm making breakfast," Miriam said again, and then, looking toward Nancy, she added, "But thank you, dear. I appreciate the offer."

"Ladies, will you excuse us?" Harper spoke to Nancy and Laura.

"Let's go to the cafeteria for breakfast," Nancy said to the younger woman, who nodded.

With a harrumph, Miriam went into the kitchen. As soon as the other two were gone, Harper followed her.

"You want to tell me how you got past my officer last night?" She wasn't going to play games with her. She hadn't asked Miriam to come to the Stand. Hadn't asked her to sign a VNL. She was bound by duty—and also because she truly cared—to protect Miriam. But she would not go to war with her.

Miriam said nothing. With a fork in hand she expertly turned the bacon frying in the pan, not even slowed down by the fact that she was working with only one arm. Bacon that would be too much for the one person it would now feed.

So they could have bacon, lettuce and tomato sandwiches for lunch.

"If you're trying to make me look bad by proving that my staff is incompetent, it's not going to fly."

Again, Miriam ignored her. With the hand of her casted arm, she pulled two pieces of bread out of a bag and popped them in the toaster, resealing the bag.

Harper tried not to think about the times the older woman had made her breakfast, chatting the whole time, treating her like a beloved member of her family. Never having known either of her grandmothers, Harper had taken Miriam as her own, glad to have a relationship with her. She'd thought, if nothing else, they'd developed a trust in each other that wouldn't be broken.

What she made herself think about was the fact that Miriam was a victim. One look at the still-purpling bruise spreading to the middle of her chin brought much-needed clarity.

"I'm trying to help," Harper said softly. "If Bruce didn't hurt you, then let's clear his name."

The only response she received was the sound of eggs cracking.

"If one of my officers made a mistake, I need to know about it and I need to know how."

Miriam pulled the bacon out of the pan, laid it on a paper towel and, picking up the bowl into which she'd cracked eggs, she poured the mixture into the bacon grease.

Maybe not the healthiest breakfast, but Harper knew it would be delicious.

"Other women's lives could very well depend on my staff doing their jobs well."

With the same fork she'd used for the bacon, Miriam whipped the eggs in the pan.

"You want me out of here, then give me what I need," Harper said, wishing she could comfort Miriam, not piss her off. "I'll gladly leave you in peace, but I can't. Not until I know who you got past last night and how it happened."

Harper continued trying to get through to Miriam, watching while she dished up her breakfast, sat down and ate every bite, then cleaned up afterward.

All to no avail.

She was going to have to discuss the incident with Lila. To put herself and her two officers on report.

But first, she was going to talk to Mason. If being at the Stand was making Miriam defensive, he might have to try something else. They needed her to open up, to tell them what had happened to her—not to challenge the plans they had in place to protect her.

Or maybe Harper should step aside for a couple of weeks, stay out of Miriam's world. But if she did take time off, Brianna would also be gone from the Stand and according to Mason, the ability to see her great-granddaughter was what had convinced Miriam to stay.

She was already listening to the ring of his cell phone as she headed up the walk toward her office.

It had been a long day and the morning wasn't even half over.

CHAPTER NINE

MASON DIDN'T GET to speak with Harper Wednesday morning. He'd been in the shower when she called and had listened to her voice mail. The last thing any of them needed at the moment was for Gram to be causing Harper and her staff problems. He'd known he was asking a lot in requesting her help, but he'd never considered for a second that he could be putting her job in jeopardy.

Not that she'd said so, but it couldn't be good for the head of security to be considering a break from work just a month into her new position.

He'd get back to Harper. But not until he had some answers to give her.

He'd been planning to spend the morning canvassing Miriam's neighborhood to find out if anyone had noticed anything unusual in the past few months. A visitor who was there when Bruce was not, for instance.

He wanted to know if anyone had noticed any change in his brother's behavior or heard Bruce raise his voice.

He also planned to visit the grocery store where Gram regularly shopped. Plus her hairdresser. And her retired officers' wives group. If he was going to figure out what had gone wrong in Gram's life, he had to build a clear picture of what that life had become.

Instead, he found himself back on the freeway to Santa Raquel. If Gwen called, ready to meet with him, he'd have to put her off, too. Just until he got back to town. That was one meeting that couldn't happen too soon.

Gram was in white capris with a blue short-sleeved shirt when she came up to the main building to meet him. She'd never been overweight, but she seemed to be getting smaller. Thinner. Like she was shrinking in on herself.

Could be his imagination, of course. Or guilt. He'd ripped her from the one thing that had always mattered to her—looking after her home. Her family.

He'd taken away her purpose.

"Did you enjoy your time with Brianna yesterday?" he asked when she took the seat opposite him at the same card table they'd shared the day before. The little girl was Gram's family. A child who could benefit from a daily dose of her great-grandmother's loving care.

"She asked me why I had a bruise on my chin and had a lot of questions about the cast," Gram said. Her short silver hair was curled and styled as usual. She was wearing makeup, too. Something she'd always done.

"From what I understand, she's about as precocious as they come." He tried not to think about the child too much—other than to assure himself that she was well cared for. Although she was his family, too, she was off-limits to him. Didn't do to build a yearning for what would never be.

"I'm sure her mother put her up to it," Gram said in a truculent tone of voice that was not like her. Or hadn't been, in his experience, until the past couple of days.

"Harper wouldn't use her child, Gram."

He received a long look from watery green eyes. "Yes, she would."

"Brianna loves you. Of course she'd have a lot of questions when she saw your cast. I hear she has a million questions about everything she notices."

"She told me her mother said I'd been hurt."

"Because Harper wanted her to be prepared. She didn't want her scared or worried. She wanted her to know that you're safe. And that you're going to be fine."

His words garnered him another long look. If he didn't know better, he'd think she wasn't sure she could trust him.

Which was downright ludicrous.

And a little scary, too.

What had Bruce told her? About him? About Harper?

Had his brother effectively isolated their grandmother so that he was her only champion? The only one she trusted?

It fit the typical pattern of abuse. Fit Bruce's own pattern, too, in that he had a history of manipulating the truth to make others look bad— and to make himself look better by comparison. To keep others from thinking less of him about something he'd done. Or to minimize the price he'd have to pay.

"You're on her side," Gram said, her words ramping up the tension inside him.

"I'm on *your* side," he told her, covering her hand with his. "I love you, Gram. It's the reason you're here. Because you've been hurt, more than once, and I have to make sure you're protected." Leaning forward he looked her straight in the eye, finding it difficult to speak for a second or two. "You know me," he continued when he could. "You know how much I love you and you know I can't ignore this."

Her lips trembled before they formed a smile. She nodded. And then said, "I fell off my stepladder."

Mason wished he could end the meeting for

the time being. That he could take his grand-mother out to lunch, to the mall, to the beach. To hear her laugh and tell him stories from when he was little. Or, even better, from when his father was little. She'd been quite the dynamo back then.

"I need you to tell me what happened last night, Gram. How you got out of your room."

He expected her to pull her hand away. To see a return of the almost belligerent expression she'd worn the day before when Harper had joined them. Instead, she nodded once more.

"You aren't going to like it."

He'd already figured that much. His gut tight, he waited to hear how bad it was going to be. She was safe. Bottom line was still good.

But if she was going to risk her own safety to sabotage Harper, he'd have to waste valuable time finding a new place for her—and lose Harper's help, as well.

He'd also lose his one advantage, the one thing he'd had to convince Gram to stay here at all—the promise of daily visits with Brianna.

"I can't make a move without someone watching me."

He nodded. Held her hand in both of his on top of the table. The surveillance was for her own good, but he understood how hard it had to be for her.

"I'm an independent woman," she said next, raising her chin a notch. "I had to be, with your grandfather out there risking his life every day. I always knew I had to be prepared to handle things on my own if something happened to him. And then when your dad and you boys went into the business, you needed to know you had a home. It's what keeps cops safe. Helps them make those instinctive, split-second decisions that keep them alive."

He didn't disagree. Her gaze held his, as strong as it had ever been.

"It felt like I was losing my independence."

"What did you do last night, Gram?"

"I climbed out my bedroom window."

His mouth fell open. He closed it. Opened it again. Not sure if he was going to smile or rant.

"I thought about it the first night I was here. How I could climb out the window if I needed to. How you all might think I'm old and helpless, but I'm not..."

Instincts on alert, Mason almost challenged her, denied that any of them considered her helpless, but the casual way she said the words held him back. He filed them in his mind, knowing he had to mention them to Sara, Gram's counselor there at the Stand. And maybe to Harper, too. Just to keep her in the loop, since he'd dragged her into this.

Pulling her hand from his, Miriam folded her arms, cast on the inside, and stared at him. "I got out as easily as I knew I could. I took a walk. Enjoyed the gardens by moonlight, and then I came back. If that guard Tasha hadn't come looking for me I'd have been back in through the window without anyone knowing. It's low enough that I could sit on the sill and slide down without having to use any arm strength even. And I go up and downstairs every single day."

The grounds were locked. Safe. She'd put herself in no real danger.

Still, she could have found a way out, which scared the hell out of him. The Stand was nearly impossible to break into, but it wasn't as difficult to leave. It wasn't a prison. Which was why they had the voluntary no release system, assigning round-the-clock watch over women who considered themselves a flight risk. And Harper's team would have no way of knowing that a seventy-something injured woman would try to climb out her bedroom window.

"It's at the back of the house, you know," she said, as if that somehow changed things.

"You gave me your word you'd cooperate."

She glared at him, and he almost took her on. Until he saw the hint of vulnerability in eyes that were growing old—their fire undimmed.

"The officers are here to keep you safe, not

make you a prisoner. If you want to take a walk, anytime of day or night, you take a walk. Just let them know, okay?"

"They're there to see I don't leave," she said in as strong a voice as ever. "I signed the voluntary no release form, Mason, in essence making myself a prisoner."

"The choice was yours."

"I had no choice! If I didn't stay here, you'd find someplace else."

No point in denying it. "This is a nice place, Gram."

"It's not home."

"It's only for a couple of weeks."

"I have work to do at home. The place doesn't stay clean by itself. And Bruce needs to eat better than he does when he's alone. He won't iron his shirts, and he leaves clothes in the dryer. He doesn't change his sheets. And he'll dump his dirty dishes in the sink until he runs out."

He was sorry to hear all of that. A bit surprised, too. He'd had no idea his younger brother was such a slob. From what he'd heard, at work he was meticulous about every detail—from the way he filled out his reports to filing. The few times he'd gone into the precinct to see him in the past, before Harper, he'd found Bruce's desk to be almost OCD neat.

He thought about offering to hire a housekeeper for her so she could relax during her time here, but stopped himself at the last second. Taking away Gram's sense of purpose would not serve any of them well. Especially her.

"Bruce is a grown man. If he wants to wear wrinkled shirts, that's his choice." He told himself not to belabor the point. Gram needed to be needed. "I know it's not ideal, Gram. I know it's causing more work for you on the other end. But I can't let you go back there until I can guarantee you're going to be safe."

"You planning to take away my stepladder? Force me to stand on a chair?"

The doctor had shown him the pictures from his grandmother's scans. Explained about bones and types of fractures. "The break in your arm was not caused by a fall."

"I fell off the stepladder."

He wasn't going to put her any more on the defensive. "Do I have your word that you'll exit your bungalow by the front door, or do I need to pay to have officers on all four sides?" he asked now.

The thought of Gram climbing out a window in the dark still made him want to grin. And to cringe, too. She could so easily have fallen— broken something else. She could've lain out there in the dark.

But not for long. Harper's staff had found her missing within the hour, based on their reports.

"No more guards than I already have," Gram said. "Please."

"Then you'll play by the rules you volunteered to follow?"

"I will." She didn't seem very happy about the idea. But he believed her.

"Thank you."

She met his gaze again, looking more fragile. "I don't want Brianna to think I'm weak. Or unable to care for myself."

"Oh, Gram, she's not going to think that!"

"You have no control over what she thinks. She was patting my cheek and telling me everything would be okay."

He was out of his area of expertise. So far out of it, he felt like a prisoner in his own scenario.

"Did it ever occur to you that maybe she's a mini you?" he asked as the idea occurred to him. "You're a nurturer, Gram. The best caregiver ever. It comes naturally to you. That's not something everyone has. Or does well. But Brianna…she's a natural, too. Some of that had to come from you." He'd never even met the kid.

"Don't try to charm me, Mason Thomas."

Don't confuse me with Bruce turned into "I'm not the charmer in the family, Gram. I'm just thinking that during these two weeks, with you right here, maybe you could teach her to cook a few things. And maybe give her some tips on how you do what you do around the house. She's a bright one. I'll bet she'd pick it up fast. And if I'm right and she's a little version of you, she'll probably love every minute of it."

He was coming up with aces all over the place.

"She'll go home and tell Harper I'm making her clean toilets and then Harper won't let me see her anymore."

Another statement that Mason tucked away for Sara.

"I'll talk to Harper," he assured her. "Leave it to me."

For the first time that morning, Gram's smile made it to her eyes. "Thank you."

He got up to go. Gave her a hug and a kiss on the cheek. "Love you, Gram."

"I love you, too."

He was halfway to the hall—on his way to see Harper before heading back to Albina, when he heard her say, "Mason?"

He turned.

"I fell off my stepladder."

CHAPTER TEN

"SOMEONE'S GOING TO have to go." Harper, in her uniform with her holster at her waist, sat behind her desk, facing the woman sitting calmly in the chair on the other side.

Lila, in black capri pants and a black-and-white floral print top, didn't express disagreement.

"Whether she was trying to make me look bad or not, it's clear that my staff and I failed to do our jobs. But if she's bent on showing me up, I'm not going to risk her safety or her life by staying here. I'll just go. Whatever you and Brett choose to do in the meantime or even the long run is your call. I'll abide by whatever it is. I just can't place a resident at risk."

"Brett and I choose to work this matter out in another way," Lila said.

Harper's breath caught. If Lila had already talked to her son, their silent founder, she obviously considered the matter of utmost importance. Even in this new world where Lila interacted with all her family members, she still ran the Stand as autonomously as always.

"You've talked to him?"

"I wanted his opinion."

That didn't sound good. In a day that already stank.

She loved her job. Loved helping these women, protecting them. Loved being able to have Brianna on the premises all day. Safe and secure and close by.

"I've spoken to Sara, as well." Sara Havens Edison, the Stand's top counselor. Lila would have filled her in, for Miriam's sake.

"None of us will even entertain the idea of you stepping back, so please let's get that off the table now." When Lila's eyebrows rose, something she'd never seen before, Harper found herself nodding before she'd even had time to think.

"Good. As soon as Mason Thomas gets here, we'll see what he has to say and go from there…"

Harper nodded again. "Tasha's really beating herself up about this," she said. "She wants to quit. She thinks she let us all down. I assured her that she hadn't, but she was still pretty upset when she left."

"Survivors are sometimes still affected by the way their abusers made them feel—as though they aren't good enough," Lila said, watching her. "It's not uncommon for them to revert to victim mode—where they retreat, rather than stand up and fight for themselves."

"She'd fight with every ounce of her energy for any of these residents," Harper said. Tasha was tough. Emotionally strong. "I'd bet my own life on her."

Lila's nod told her the other woman had something on her mind. You might not always know what she was thinking, but you could count on the fact that she *was* thinking. That she saw more than she let on.

"And so would all of us here," Lila said. "Is she scheduled back this evening?"

"Yes."

"I'll have Sara call her in for a chat before her shift. We aren't any more eager to lose her than we are to lose you."

Lila's glance seemed to carry more than her words were saying. But if there was a message for her there, she wasn't getting it. Before she could pursue the matter any further, or even decide if she wanted to, there was a knock at her door.

As Harper stood, Lila let Mason in, indicating the seat next to her as she sat down again. He glanced at her, and then away, exchanging a polite "how are you" with Lila as Harper sank back into her chair.

He looked…so good. His short, thick hair a little askew, as though he'd been scratching his head, his strong features with their permanent honeyed tan, the polo shirt that hugged muscles she knew intimately, and…well, she didn't need to look at his khakis. Didn't need to look at any part of him.

"My grandmother wasn't trying to make the Stand's security look bad," he said, starting right in. "She needed to prove to herself that she still had her independence, that she was still capable of being her own boss. Unfortunately, in order to do that, she chose to act like a child. I suspect the way I initially handled this might have made her feel like one. She climbed out of her bedroom window. She'd intended to climb back in, but Tasha found her first."

Harper's heart was pounding in her chest. Her knees were weak, and she felt a sudden need to weep. None of which made any sense.

"Because our security measures are good," Lila said, turning to Harper. She nodded. The strange moment passed.

"I have to admit, a seventy-five-old woman climbing out her window was not something my staff or I considered when we discussed how best to keep Miriam safe on the premises." Somehow, she came out sounding one hell of a lot more professional than she felt.

"She gave me her word that she'd follow the program from here on out," Mason said.

Lila stood. "Good, we've got things resolved here. I'm going to have a chat with Sara and then I'll be in my office if either of you needs me."

And just like that, a meeting Harper had expected to be painful was over in less than five minutes and she found herself alone with Mason. Again.

He'd made a four-hour round-trip because his grandmother had climbed out a window and Harper and her top-notch team hadn't known a thing about it.

"I'm sorry," she told him.

"I was about to say the same thing. You all have so much to do and you've wasted your time on what turned out to be a childish prank. I'm embarrassed."

"As you probably know from your time with the FBI, Miriam's sense of a loss of personal power is a key element of abuse," she explained. "A victim's power is taken away a little at a time, whenever her abuser lashes out, whether physically or verbally. It's a slow process, because there are usually times of love and kindness between the incidents, and because the abuse comes from someone the victim trusts, so she's often not aware that it's happening until she finds herself feeling completely powerless."

She was giving him basics—a very elementary version of what she'd learned during her victim advocate training with The Lemonade Stand.

He watched her. "I know I didn't help when I all but kidnapped her and gave her an ultimatum to make her stay."

"From what Lila told me, you tried to explain it to Miriam. To get her to see reason—even just to give you a little time to clear Bruce's name. But she couldn't or wouldn't see the reason."

"It's so unlike her."

"But not an unusual reaction for a victim. Whoever's hurting Miriam has convinced her that the breakdown is her own fault."

"She continues to insist that she fell off a damned stepladder. If I hadn't met with the doctor, seen the physical evidence in the images he showed me, I'd believe her. She's convincing."

Harper's stomach dropped. "I've seen that kind of behavior before," she told him. "In some of our more severe cases here. But I'm not the expert. You really should talk to Sara. It could be that Miriam's been manipulated to the point that she *believes* she fell off a ladder…"

Then something else occurred to her. A thought she kept to herself. It was awful.

"What?"

She shook her head. She had no expertise

whatsoever when it came to this part of the
Stand's business.

"You know something you aren't telling me."

"No, I don't."

"What were you just thinking?"

His gaze held hers and she had the strongest
urge to give him everything he wanted.

Had to be left over from the night she'd felt
like dying and he'd found her. Taken her with
him, rather than let her sit alone in her misery.
He'd been kind to her that night. A good friend.

A good brother.

She was the one who'd turned the evening
into something completely different.

"Please, Harper. I'm out in the cold here, I'm
doing this one solo. I'd like to know what you're
thinking."

"I have no professional experience, just basic
training so I can protect our residents."

"I understand. Full disclaimer noted."

"We had a resident one time, an older woman,
older than Miriam. She'd accepted the abuse because she'd been afraid that if she said anything,
she'd end up in a nursing home. Her abuser, a
niece, threatened her, telling her she'd ship her
off if she didn't mind her p's and q's." P's and
q's. Harper could remember the woman's tone of
voice. "What made me think of it now is…this
resident confided the whole thing to me late one

night. She'd called security for a chaperone so she could take a walk. She'd been crying, feeling completely powerless. She was petrified that when she got out of the Stand her family was going to put her in a home."

"Did they?"

"I honestly don't know. I didn't ask." And she had to admit, "I didn't *want* to know. I couldn't do anything to help her, couldn't do anything about the outcome. I have a job to do. I have to maintain a certain distance, keep boundaries, so I don't miss something."

The compassionate look in his eyes reminded her again of the night they'd shared. Maybe the problem was that it was the only real memory she had of him. The few other times they'd seen each other had been brief. With Bruce running the show. Somehow, that explanation soothed her.

"What I do know is that Lila and her staff are the absolute best and have only the health, happiness and interests of our residents at heart. If it had been at all possible to keep her out of a home, they'd have helped her make that happen."

"I have another favor to ask you."

If he kept looking at her like that, he could have anything he wanted.

She shook her head, denying herself that

thought even as it came to mind. Mason Thomas was so far off-limits, he could be on another planet. For a lot of reasons.

Many of them starting with Bruce. She was not going to risk his ire, creating problems that could directly affect Brianna. They'd managed to divorce and stay cordial enough to raise a happy, secure little girl who loved both of them. And who didn't have to choose between them.

"Could you at least hear me out before you refuse?" He was kind of grinning, but not really.

It took her a second to realize that she'd shaken her head—although she'd directed the gesture at herself.

"I'm listening."

"Miriam's entire life has been centered on her role of family caretaker. She's feeling like a failure here because she's not taking care of her home—which, these days, means her house and Bruce."

"I completely agree. What's the favor?" She kept a clean house, but could always use a little help. It wasn't as though Miriam could move in with her, though. Or would, even if she could.

"It occurred to me that if she could spend her afternoons with Brianna teaching her the art of nurturing, of caretaking—you know, as if she was passing on her family traditions and values—then she'd settle in to being here. She'd quit fighting us. She might even *want* to stay."

His idea had some merit. For Brianna, too. "She's definitely a little ruler of the house," Harper told him. "She's always underfoot, wanting to help sweep and mop and—" She broke off. "What kind of things did you have in mind?"

"Stuff like that." He nodded. "I thought we could leave it up to Gram. But maybe, cooking and baking, too."

She remembered the Miriam she'd known and the older woman's eagerness to teach Harper family favorite recipes. And she thought of Brianna, who wanted to know how to do every single thing Harper did. She imagined the two of them, Miriam and Brianna, with hours to spend together every day Harper worked over the next two weeks…

"I have to confess." Mason interrupted her thoughts. "I might have already mentioned this to her. As a matter of fact, of course I did. It just came to me and I blurted it out because it seemed like such a miraculous idea."

"What did she say?" He wouldn't be there talking to her about this if Miriam had refused.

"She loved the idea." He glanced down at the shoe he'd crossed over his knee.

"And?"

"She was convinced you'd have a problem with it. I told her not to worry about you. That I'd handle it." At least he had the guts to look at her when he confessed that last part.

"You'd handle *me*, you mean."

"Yeah. That's pretty much what I told her."

Her stomach warmed when it should be knotted and slightly cold. Or getting ready for lunch. "Just out of curiosity, how did you plan to go about 'handling me'?"

"I hadn't worked that out yet." She was sure she saw a glint in those green eyes. Mason had seemed to enjoy their time together that night so long ago. Even when they were just acting like brother and sister. Or platonic friends, she amended. He'd never been a brother to her. She'd never spent enough time with him for the familial bond to develop.

Because she wanted to continue baiting him, she stood up to end the conversation more abruptly than she might have done. "I have no problem with the plan at all," she said. "I think it's great." Brilliant, she might have said, but thought that might lead them down a path she didn't want to travel.

She could assist Mason. She could care, from a distance, about his family. She could even fantasize about him in private—although she didn't recommend that to herself. She was simply acknowledging that it might happen. What she could *not* do was tease him. Joke with him. Or in any way let him inside her personal boundaries.

She walked to her office door and he joined her. "I don't mean to rush you off, but I've got a full schedule this morning," she said, pulling the door open.

She was meeting with the managers of all of the Stand's public businesses out on the strip adjacent to the property in half an hour.

And she had no room in her schedule, or her life, for private conversation with Mason Thomas.

CHAPTER ELEVEN

MASON WAS BACK in Albina by midmorning on Wednesday, canvassing the neighborhood where his father had grown up, and where Bruce now lived with Gram. His brother's truck wasn't in the garage, but it was clear he'd been home, judging by the dishes in the sink. Mason had Gram's key and her grudging permission to look through everything in the house. He still felt like dirt doing it.

Gram had said she'd fallen while trying to get some liqueur out of a top cupboard for a parfait recipe that was one of Bruce's favorites. The stepladder was in the kitchen. Empty parfait glasses still sat on the counter. But the doctor had been insistent that the break in Gram's arm could not have come from a fall. The bruises on either side of her chin were very unlikely to have come from a fall, either. And the previous breaks...

He was a crime scene investigator. It was his job to look for the signs that weren't obvious. For the small thing that might tell the true story.

He didn't find it in the kitchen. Yes, Gram could have fallen. But the fall didn't break her arm.

At her age, however, she should've had other bruises from such a fall. The doctor hadn't reported any.

Removing the phone from his pocket as the thought occurred to him, he redialed his most recent call. And when Harper didn't answer, he left a message asking her to have someone check Gram for other bruising, just because the littlest thing could point him in a different direction. A small circular bruise on the leg would at least indicate that she'd taken physical pressure somewhere else. Even just a little bit of it. He got off before he could introduce a personal note into the recording.

He'd spent much of the drive back from Santa Raquel fighting a mind that insisted on hanging out with Harper. Replaying conversations. Thinking far too much about the past.

About what he'd done. And hadn't done.

About her.

Remembering the softness of her lips. The passion in them. The way her tongue hadn't been shy at all about tangling with his.

Remembering the soft moans...and the lack of shyness in the way she'd asked him to love her harder.

A box of tapioca was on the counter where Gram did most of her meal preparation. Behind an empty cereal box. He found an unused mixing bowl with a couple of used cereal bowls on the counter. A used plate and glass were in the sink. One set.

Just Bruce, eating and leaving his mess, just as Gram said he'd do. Not even bothering to put away Gram's unfinished business.

DISAPPOINTMENT FLOODED HARPER when she saw she'd missed a call from Mason. Stupid, senseless emotion that had no place in her current situation. He'd left a message. She knew what he needed, called Lynn Bishop, their resident nurse practitioner to look in on Miriam—not an unusual occurrence when a resident came to them with injuries—and erased the thought that now she had Mason's voice on her voice mail.

She'd saved the call. She took her lunch of veggies and a bagel out to the Garden of Renewal and sat alone, thinking about listening to the message again, trying to justify a reason for doing so. She deleted it instead and watched her phone on and off all afternoon in case he called again. She was on patrol for part of the time, and had a break from thinking about Mason while she focused on the Stand and its residents. But in her office, with paperwork in front of her, she started checking her cell again and saw the text come in from Alissa, telling her that she and Brianna were with Miriam.

A moment later, she saw Bruce's number pop up. Grabbing the phone, she willed the alarmed pace of her heart to slow—a habit she'd adopted sometime over the past five years. She was no longer married to Bruce. His infidelity was not a threat to her well-being. She had no cause to get riled when she heard his voice.

"Hey, there," she said, keeping her own voice calm—and filled with the compassion she'd always felt for him. The man did a hard job very well with no thought to himself. He saved lives. Even more, he truly cared about the lives he saved. As a junior officer at a crime scene, she'd once seen him with tears on his cheeks as he held a young boy in his arms while the boy bled out...

"Hey." His tone was soft, too, reflecting the easy familiarity he'd adopted very early in their relationship. His "bedroom voice" she'd once teased him about.

Her turn again. She had no idea what to say. Bruce hadn't been told where his grandmother was. He'd have no legitimate reason to be calling Harper to ask about her.

Mason didn't want Bruce to know anything. He thought Bruce was the bad guy they were out to get, and for the life of her, she couldn't understand it. From the day she'd met Detective Bruce Thomas, she'd admired him. His skill on the job. The respect in which he was held by the other officers—officers who'd worked with him for years.

"How's Brie?"

Oh. Right. Of course. He had reasons, other than Miriam, for calling her. What the hell? Her mind was so wrapped up in Mason, in his hunt for Miriam's truth, she'd missed a step.

"She's fine. She was telling me last night that houses should have screens in every room that would let you order food. That way she could have a snack in bed whenever she wanted it."

His familiar chuckle calmed her. "Did she think the screen would prepare and deliver the food?"

Harper was smiling now, too. "She said workers would do it. The people who owned the screen business." No matter how much her time in the Thomas family had changed her, hurt her, she'd come out of it with Brianna and having that little girl was, hands down, the best thing that had ever happened to her.

"I was going to try to make it down to see her at the end of the week. I expect to be wrapping up this case tomorrow or the next day, but…"

Now that she was no longer at the department, she wasn't privy to the details of his assignments. His words sent a jolt of panic through her. Deep breaths, focusing on slowing her heart rate, weren't helping.

"Just let me know when, and we'll meet you someplace." He could *not* show up at The Lemonade Stand. Technically he didn't know where the shelter was, or what shelter she worked for, but with his cop skills, she could never be sure what he did and did not find out.

As a cop, he'd have the clearance. But now that he was, based on Lemonade Stand paperwork, a possible abuser, he'd be arrested if he came anywhere near the place.

He'd be charged, too, if it could be proven that he knew his grandmother was there.

It wasn't right, arresting a guy when all he thought he was doing was picking up his daughter. And yet, she couldn't tell him Miriam was there. The whole point was to keep her safe from him.

Or from whomever had hurt her.

On the edge of her seat now, literally, Harper forced her mind into work mode. Did Bruce know more than he was saying?

Would he tell her that Miriam was away? That she'd been hurt?

Did he know she'd been in touch with Mason? That his brother had contacted her? She could

just imagine what *that* would do to him. Silent
fury would build until he walked out without a
word…

She shook her head. He couldn't walk out on
her anymore. Not ever again. She'd left him.

"The thing is," he continued, "I caught a
break this afternoon, found myself with some
free time so I'm here in Santa Raquel now. I was
hoping I could take her for a couple of hours this
afternoon. Maybe the three of us could have
dinner together before I head back tonight. I'd
like that a lot…to have some time with my girls.
Maybe you and I could have a few minutes to
talk…"

She'd had so much fun dating Bruce. He'd
do things just like this, surprising her with a
plan out of the blue, and every single time she'd
loved it. They'd enjoyed each other's company.
He liked to have fun and had a way of helping
others enjoy themselves, too.

They weren't dating anymore. Harper wasn't
one of his "girls." Brianna was with Miriam, and
taking her away from the older woman would be
like putting gasoline on a fire. Telling Bruce *no*
wasn't a great idea, either, for so many reasons.

He didn't like to have his surprises falter; he
didn't cope well when his plans were thwarted.
Try to do something nice for someone and…

She'd heard that more than once during her year of marriage.

And even though he didn't know *she* knew he was without Miriam at the moment, he probably figured that his brother suspected him of abusing their grandmother.

And if he *did* know how much she knew…he was playing a very dangerous game with her.

Something Undercover Bruce might do.

So what was his endgame? To get to Miriam? To convince Harper that he hadn't hurt his grandmother? Press her for information?

"Harper?" He was waiting for her response. "I'm about a mile from the part of town where you said you work. Give me an exact address and I'll meet you outside."

"I'm…actually…not there right now," she said, heart pounding again as she lied to him. She was about to invent some kind of professional meeting, until she realized that he'd want her to have someone bring Brianna out to him.

Not that she was going to give him the address of the Stand.

With his police resources, he probably already knew it. She'd assumed that years ago, although he'd never attempted a visit before. As far as she knew he never came to Santa Raquel at all.

"Give me a second and I'll see what I can arrange," she told him. "I'll call you right back."

She wasn't handing Brianna over to him. Not without backup. And not without Mason's knowledge.

She still wasn't sure she should risk taking the little girl away from Miriam. It wasn't like she was going to tell Miriam that Bruce was there.

She wasn't afraid for herself. She could handle whatever came her way in the danger department. But the case wasn't hers, which meant the right to make the decision wasn't hers, either.

Hanging up, she called Mason and prayed that he'd answer.

IN THE MIDDLE of a conversation with a friend of Miriam's, Mason felt his phone vibrate against his thigh. When he saw the caller's name, he excused himself from her living room and stepped outside. Five minutes later, after a second quick call, he'd said his goodbyes to Miriam's friend and was in his car, calling Harper back.

He'd asked her to stay put. To give him five. He hoped to God she had.

And breathed a sigh of relief when she answered immediately.

"Go ahead and call him back," he instructed her. "Arrange a meeting someplace away from the Stand. Tell him you'll bring Brianna to him."

"You want me to meet him?" She sounded incredulous.

"Of course not. I just want you to tell him you will. If he suspects you're helping me, he's going to do what he can to get to you—mentally if nothing else. If these were normal circumstances, you'd do what you could to accommodate him, which is why I'm asking you to call him back and say you'll meet him."

He had more to say. But he needed her to make that call first.

"I'm on my way to Santa Raquel now," he said. "I'll talk to you when I get there."

"You're coming back? I hardly think this is worth another trip down. I'm a cop, Mason, and I'm living in a town with a top-notch police department. We can keep Miriam safe. I just didn't know how you wanted me to play it. If I want Bruce to think everything's normal, I'd take Brie to him. But then I'd have to go get her from Miriam right after I agreed to let Miriam have her every afternoon. I'm sure you don't want me telling her that Bruce is in town. And then we have to consider that if Brianna does see her father this afternoon, she's going to mention it to Miriam tomorrow. And will tell Bruce that her grandma is staying at mommy's work."

"Bruce is going to be getting a summons from O'Brien in another ten minutes or so, calling him back to work. Which is why I wanted you to call Bruce now. You won't have to see him, but it'll look like you were willing to."

"I still don't get why you're coming here, but I'll call him now."

Mason wasn't going to relax until he knew his brother was in Albina. And probably not even then. But he took an easier breath at Harper's compliance. He liked the idea that they were on the same team, working side by side.

Maybe he liked it a bit too much.

HE GOT A room at a cheap Santa Raquel inland motel, dropped the satchel that was always packed in his trunk inside the door of the room and, back in his SUV, called Harper. He felt better just being there in town. Knowing that Bruce had been in Santa Raquel, while Mason was almost two hours away, had not sat well with him.

She'd texted half an hour before to say that, as expected, Bruce had called to cancel his time with Brianna due to being needed at work. Mason was still waiting for confirmation from O'Brien that his brother was, indeed, back in town.

It was part of the deal they'd made. The captain would keep an eye on Bruce, and Mason would find out what the hell was going on. O'Brien's plan was that Mason get some counseling for his grandmother and convince her to talk to them. He wanted to know who'd hurt her, to take action against that person, first and foremost. But the administrator also wanted to know that one of his top officers was in the clear. Albina PD relied heavily on Bruce's expertise in the field.

Miriam *was* talking to them. And Mason was beginning to realize that his grandmother truly believed what she was saying. He just had to figure out why. Why she was saying it. *Why* she believed it, even when faced with radiology film that clearly showed something different, and medical opinion that said the bruises on Miriam's chin could not have come from a fall. Miriam had been shown the films, had heard the doctor's assessment. They'd asked her to tell them the truth. Unless her chin had hit something that had bruised both sides of it, there was no way she'd hurt herself falling off a stepladder. He'd found nothing in the kitchen to prove otherwise. Someone had grabbed her chin hard enough to bruise her.

And had broken her arm, too. More than once.

Harper picked up on the third ring. She was already at home with Brianna but would be leaving soon to take the little girl to her beginners' dance class. It was the first Mason had heard that his niece was taking dance. A tug at his gut, and the moment was gone. Like so many others over the past four years.

"Can we meet afterward?" he asked, an investigator on duty needing to interrogate his key witness further.

And a man who wanted to see an old friend who could very well be under the manipulative influence of the brother he loved—and distrusted. Some of the things he'd heard that day...

His suspicions hadn't been laid to rest. Still, he could recite facts to refute them, too.

He wasn't forming any more judgments yet. But he felt this compelling need to speak with Harper. Spend a little more time with her. It was the only way to get a feel for what might or might not be going on between her and Bruce. Mason knew she wasn't out to deliberately trick him; that much was clear. The fact that she'd called when Bruce showed up in town was proof enough of that—not that he'd really needed proof. Some things you just had to take on instinct.

"It's Brie's bath and bedtime by then, and I don't want to call a sitter again tonight. I need to keep to our routine as much as possible. She jabbers about her day, her life, anything that pops into her head when we go about our normal day. I can't miss that. Particularly while she's spending time with Miriam."

Because his grandmother might bad-mouth Harper? Or in case Brianna repeated something Miriam had said that might help them? Or perhaps something about Miriam's situation, her behavior, upset the little girl. Or confused her. Defending her father, for instance. He could see Miriam doing that, and Brianna having no idea why.

"I visited several of Miriam's friends today—all separately, in their homes. I'm questioning her neighbors, too. I'm in a hotel in Santa Raquel tonight because I need to see Gram first thing in the morning. I've got an appointment at eleven in Albina." With Gwen. He'd yet to connect with the woman who'd shown up drunk at his door—and he suspected she'd been avoiding him.

Not too smart considering he could report her. Her word against his, of course. It wasn't like he had any wounds to prove that she'd struck him; a slap in the face could be considered assault but he wasn't pursuing it. And puking in his john wasn't a crime.

He wasn't out to ruin her. Or anyone. But he wanted answers.

"I also need to speak with you." His time was limited. Twelve days and ticking. He had to get to the truth. Anything else driving the need to meet with her in person was irrelevant.

"I turned the third bedroom in our townhome

into a minigym so I can keep up with my physical conditioning without taking time from Brianna. I work out several nights a week and I've already missed one of them. If you'd like to join me in the gym, you're welcome to do so."

She'd just invited him into her home? To work out?

"What are the chances Brianna would hear us and wake up?"

"Slim to none. Her bedroom is upstairs beside mine. The gym is downstairs, in the den. Why?"

"She's four. I don't think it's a good idea if she knows I'm in town. Just in case she sees or speaks with her father."

"I'm thinking it's best that I find a way to keep them apart," she said. "She's going to mention Miriam to him otherwise. But as far as you're concerned, she's not going to know who you are, Mason. You never see her."

And it wasn't like his brother kept pictures of him around the place. Even the one his grandmother used have on the mantel in the living room disappeared when Bruce moved in.

His niece had no idea he was alive. He'd figured as much. Funny how a guy could care so much and be nonexistent at the same time.

"I put her to bed between seven thirty and eight. Give us until nine, since she might take a while to get to sleep."

He had all night. And he *had* to talk to her.

If he only had a minute, and no need to meet with her, he'd still go. He wanted to see where she lived. To be in her home. Just so he'd no longer have a reason to wonder where she was and how she was doing.

"What equipment do you have?" If he was going there, he might as well make use of the gym.

Or rather, he should definitely make use of the equipment. He needed to spend time with her. To observe. And to ask her some questions. Not to get turned on.

"I have a dual-cable home gym—up to five hundred pounds, plus an elliptical trainer and a treadmill."

"I'll be there at nine."

Starting his vehicle, he backed out of the lot as she hung up. He'd need dinner. And had to stop somewhere to purchase exercise wear. O'Brien had left a message while he was talking to Harper, letting him know Bruce was on the job and accounted for.

Mason would see Harper that night, Gram in the morning, and head back to Albina with time to spare.

The investigation was going as planned.

CHAPTER TWELVE

HARPER RECOGNIZED TROUBLE the second Mason, in black basketball shorts and a white T-shirt, stepped into her home. She'd thought expending physical energy and mental concentration in the gym would distract her from lusting after him.

She'd neglected to consider the attire factor—other than to choose baggy sweats and a too-big T-shirt for herself, rather than the leggings and short bra top she usually wore to work out. She'd turned up the air so she didn't get too hot.

There was no air conditioner that could dissipate the heat that Mason gave off. It was that way five years ago, too. What had been left of her alcohol-infused brain had known it was wrong to sleep with her fiancé's brother even though for those hours, she'd considered the engagement over. She'd returned the ring. She'd also been very aware that Bruce had refused to accept her declaration and had said he'd hold on to the ring for her. But her body's message had been much louder than anything her head was telling her.

She'd blamed it on the alcohol.

She'd had nothing but water this evening.

Her plan to take him straight to the gym room was thwarted when he stopped to look over the easel with painted and colored artwork in a corner of the living room, a corner that was decorated like a children's playroom. It was neat, but filled with colorful child-sized furniture and a toy box, plus shelves with books and toys. And the easel.

"Wow," he said, looking at the picture Brie had drawn while Harper cooked some macaroni and cheese with peas in it for dinner. Her daughter loved peas. "She did this herself?"

"Yeah." The colorful drawing of a house and orange trees was impressive—at least in her admittedly biased opinion.

"That's pretty incredible for a four-year-old, isn't it?"

His words brought home to her how little he knew of his own niece. The lapse seemed suddenly criminal, so she led him into the kitchen to get a look at the refrigerator covered with various art projects. "She's precocious intellectually, and she's testing right-brain gifted, as well," she told him. The whole idea scared her; she had no experience raising *any* child, let alone a gifted one, but she wasn't about to reveal that.

Brianna was her daughter. She'd do what she had to do.

According to the psychiatrist who'd done the testing recommended by Brie's teacher at The Lemonade Stand the previous spring, Brianna's drawings showed an understanding of depth perception that most children didn't have.

Harper liked to focus on the shapes that were still babyishly not straight, or true to form. The coloring that was outside the lines. She'd also put Brianna in art lessons at the Stand with Julie Fairbanks, who was getting married next month.

Julie had just asked Brianna to be her flower girl. Joy Walsh, an eight-year-old Brianna idolized who'd lived at the Stand for a while the previous fall, was going to be junior bridesmaid. The wedding would be a lavishly beautiful society event—another thing Harper had to be nervous about. She loved Julie. She'd never been to a society…anything in her life.

Mason didn't make any other comments about Brianna's work. Didn't ask any questions about his niece. But he took his time looking at every drawing, every photo of Brianna at different stages and all the toys, even studying book titles.

His job centered on taking in his environment. He was there because he figured her for a key witness in the case he was working. No other reason. Her insides squirmed anyway.

Every nerve in her body was on alert.

She didn't dare stop him, didn't want to inadvertently draw him into any conversation except the one he'd come to have with her. About Bruce and Miriam. About whatever Miriam's friend had told him. Harper would help if she could.

There just wasn't much she could do. She really hadn't seen Miriam in the four years she and Bruce had divorced. She could only attest to the fact that, to her knowledge, Bruce had always been wonderful with his grandmother. He'd made a point of having family dinners with her. Of calling her. Stopping by any chance he got. Anyone could see how much he loved her.

Brianna had nothing to do with any of it.

And Mason had nothing to do with Brianna. Messing with the status quo wasn't a good idea.

The thought occurred to her that he might venture upstairs, but she quelled that twinge of fear with the denial she could give him without question—she didn't want to wake her daughter.

As he neared the end of the room that led down to the gym, Harper was there ahead of him, leading the way as quickly as she could. Her all-in-one gym machine beckoned. She'd do some seated chest flies first. Knowing that as a former FBI agent, Mason would be fully versed in working out, she went straight for the all-in-one gym and left him to look around and determine a course for his own workout.

"I usually listen to music," she told him, nodding toward the portable Bluetooth speaker on the small table in the corner. "But since you're here to ask questions…"

Sitting, she spread her arms, placing them against the pads. The machine was set at the twenty-five pounds she was doing this week; she wanted to work her muscles, not build them. She wished he'd get on the treadmill. His back would be to her then, and she'd just have to avoid the mirrors. With him just standing there by the watercooler she'd purchased secondhand for a song, watching her, her breasts felt completely exposed. She pulled the pads together with ease. Held them for a count of ten.

He hadn't moved. Was still watching her. She had to spread her arms wide again. Slowly. Or the weights would bang down and give away her agitation.

She could feel her nipples hardening. Thank God she'd had the wherewithal to put on the oversize shirt.

If he was trying to get a reaction out of her, he was succeeding, but she wasn't going to let him know that. She did another rep. As she began the third, he crossed the room to the free weights, picking up a set she'd never used due to their size, and started with some curls.

She'd had mirrors put up on one wall of the room, since she worked out alone, so she could pay attention to her form and know that she wasn't causing damage by doing an exercise improperly. Unfortunately, that meant that from where she was seated she could see every move he made. Front and back.

The baggy shorts gave his front some of the same camouflage her shirt provided her. But she didn't remember him being so well-endowed that he'd fill out the fly of his pants to the extent she was seeing, except when... Pulling away her gaze abruptly, Harper caught him looking at her in the mirror—watching her watch him.

"Speaking of that night," he said, sounding as though he was doing nothing more strenuous than sitting on the couch.

No! That night was exactly what she *didn't* want to speak of. Especially not now that things were closing in on her.

Her sexual attraction to him was a huge mistake. One she'd rectify somehow. And the rest... the aftermath...it did neither of them any good to go there.

He hadn't called. That whole day after she'd left his place, he hadn't called. By the next day, when Bruce had come looking for her at her apartment, she'd never been more ashamed in her life. She'd thrown herself at his brother, and the incident had meant so little to Mason that he hadn't even called to assure her there were no bad feelings, or that if there were, they'd work through them. She'd given him her number. Asked him to call…

"I know when Brianna was born, Harper. I've left well enough alone, but now…with this…if Bruce is abusive…"

Her weights clamored and she swore out loud. Could have been a reaction to the way he was maiming the reputation of her daughter's father, right there in their home.

"Brianna was born nine months after I married Bruce." She squeezed again. Holding her count. Released slowly. Another couple of reps and it would be time to move on to leg lifts. A quarter of the way around the machine. Putting her closer to where he was standing.

"You married Bruce six days after you and I had sex."

"You wore a condom." At least, for the past five years she'd been praying he had. It was one of those details she couldn't remember. The room had been dark. They'd been under the covers. There'd been a lot of movement. Mostly, there'd been Mason, touching her so expertly.

Everywhere. Giving her more pleasure than she'd ever had. Before or since.

He hadn't stopped in the process of climbing on top of her. He'd just kept working his magic. What he'd done to himself with his other hand… she'd just assumed…

Hoped.

Prayed.

"No, actually, I didn't. I didn't expect to have sex that night. And contrary to popular belief, not all guys carry condoms around in their wallets. You said you were on the Pill."

"We were at your house." In his bed, next to his nightstand. Where else would a guy keep his box of condoms?

"I don't ever bring women to my house." The news made her heady for a second. If only she'd known… All those times over the years that she'd brought herself down by thinking about him in that bed, sharing such a glorious night with another woman.

She'd wanted it for him. Just not *there*. Which made no sense whatsoever, as she'd told herself each and every time her mind had strayed.

"Where do you keep your condoms?" She was done with her reps. She had to move. To keep moving. All those years, she'd prayed he'd used a condom. Had somehow convinced herself she remembered movement under the covers that meant he'd put one on.

In the middle of butterflies now, Mason didn't even grunt as he said, "In my glove box."

Okay, well.

"Bruce didn't use condoms, either."

She changed her routine and got on the elliptical, grabbing the hand bars and starting her climb. Refusing to let these thoughts creep in. Refusing to panic.

"And yes, I was on the Pill."

"So you went off the Pill when you got married."

She could lie. She had to lie.

To do anything else would compound the mess they'd made. And yet…lying would be wrong.

"No, I got pregnant while I was on it."

He froze. "You…but…how?"

"I'd been on an antibiotic. According to my ob-gyn, they sometimes make the pill less effective."

"When did you start taking the antibiotic?" He still wasn't moving. And the look he was giving her was intense enough to burn.

She took a shaky breath. "The week before you and I…before Bruce…before…"

They could not be having this conversation! It had been avoided for five years, had been unnecessary all that time. He'd used a condom. She'd needed to believe that.

The idea of messing with their status quo unhinged her a bit.

"She's not yours." Her gaze met his in the mirror and she was surprised to see a hint of relief on his face. A softening of his features.

"He had her tested? With brothers, it's better if you have DNA from both, but as long as you had his, yours and hers, the test should've been conclusive."

There'd been no test. She'd begged Bruce, completely certain that Brianna was his. She *couldn't* have conceived with Mason. She'd only had sex with him once. Bruce had taken her to bed at least once a day back then. Sometimes more.

But he'd refused to have DNA tests done to prove his paternity, saying the test didn't matter. Brianna was his. She'd wondered at the time if he'd been afraid of the minute possibility that she *wasn't* his and had let it go. They were related by blood in either case. She'd told herself that was all that mattered.

"You seem relieved." She certainly hadn't expected him to worry about the situation. Or even consider the outside possibility. Especially since she'd told him she was on the Pill and she'd been so sure he'd worn a condom.

"For the past four years I've been working hard not to think about the possibility that I could be missing out on every aspect of my daughter's life." He was on to reps of lifting the weights straight up from his shoulder. "To go with the fact that you'd said you were on the Pill. To trust that you'd been telling the truth."

She started to say he could have called. Then remembered why he hadn't. He was a man of his word. A man who'd done what he thought he had to do to keep his family together.

Still, that first day, or even the next, before she'd told Bruce... There'd been no supposed agreement then.

Climbing an elliptical mountain, one that threatened to be too high for her to scale, she was reeling at the idea that he'd been mourning the years he might have missed of his child's life. His *possible* child. She wouldn't have wished that on anyone, least of all Mason.

"I'd have sent you pictures, whatever, if I'd known you were interested. You're her uncle. She should know you..." It felt like too little too late.

Putting down the weights, he stood for a couple of minutes, watching in the mirror as she climbed and got nowhere. She'd never had another person in the small gym with her. Mason filled the space, much like he'd filled her entire world that one night—like her own personal dark and very private fairy tale.

When he bent to pick up the weights again, to begin another rep of curls, she got an eyeful of his backside—and quickly looked away. She couldn't tell if he'd caught her again. She was too busy pretending it hadn't happened.

"So…"

When no other words followed, she looked over, catching his gaze in the mirror. She raised her eyebrows in question, rather than speaking. He might not be getting winded, but she was. More than normal.

"You never confirmed. Did you and Bruce have paternity tests run?"

Harper swallowed. Got off the elliptical. Considered forgoing the rest of the night's workout. Considered lying to Mason. What would he do if he knew the truth? Keep wondering what he could be missing? Or, God forbid, force a paternity test?

Panic overwhelmed her at the thought. Bruce would hate it if she allowed the testing. He'd feel threatened and blame her. Not completely without merit. She was the one who'd slept with his older brother. And if she told Mason that there'd been no definitive proof regarding Brianna's paternity, she'd be partially at fault for any action Mason might take as a result.

Ready to say she was done for the night, she glanced at the man who was now into his second set of butterflies.

She never shortchanged her cardio.

"No, there's been no testing done." On the treadmill in front of the mirror, her back to him, she started a slow jog.

CHAPTER THIRTEEN

MASON LIFTED HIS ARMS. Focused on his form. You didn't dick around when you were dealing with hundred-pound weights.

Nothing had changed.

He wasn't a father. He just wasn't *not* one. Been that way for over four years. He lived with it.

Seeing those drawings, the toys, the books— the kid had to be reading at the third-grade level—he knew more about his niece. That was all.

But his gut wasn't buying it.

There was a reason he'd been content to stay away from Bruce and Harper and Brianna. He couldn't and wouldn't try to claim his brother's family, steal it away from him.

And he couldn't trust himself to ignore his need to find out if he was a father. The father of a very special little girl. He already knew how dangerous being around Harper was to him.

Moving on from curl to shoulder push-ups he counted. Welcomed the sweat dripping down his back. And tried not to watch Harper run. He couldn't clearly make out the shape of her breasts under the tent she was wearing, but he knew how they fit his palms. Knew how responsive her nipples had been to his touch.

He could imagine...

No! He couldn't imagine. Harper was as off-limits now as she'd always been. Even more so as he investigated his brother for elder abuse. People might suspect that he was out to get his brother. Anyone who thought he wanted to prove that Bruce had hurt Gram was 1000 percent wrong.

Bruce was the kid brother he'd always watched out for. It would be a mammoth blow if Mason was the one to bring him down. And he dreaded coming up with those findings, but knew that if he did, Bruce would be forced to see the truth. To accept the consequences, get help. Gram would be safe again. And there'd still be hope of a future for their family.

But there'd be absolutely no chance of ever having any kind of relationship with his brother if he took Harper, too. Because that was how Bruce would see it if Mason got involved with her.

Not that he was saying she'd have him. But he had a pretty good idea that he could tempt her into...something.

Nothing. He couldn't tempt her at all.

And there'd be no more talk about testing with Brianna, either. Bruce was a responsible father. He loved the little girl, who, by all counts, was doing very well. Growing up healthy and happy.

Mason knew his place. He'd accepted that he was paying for the mistake he'd made in allowing himself to have sex with the woman his brother loved. And where Brianna was concerned, he was out.

Putting down the weights, he moved to the all-in-one machine. He looped his feet under the steady bars, lay back with his head toward the floor and did a hundred sit-ups, followed by leg lifts.

He'd just walked over to the opposite side of the circular machine, ready to add weights to the arm presses, when Harper finished her run.

Even with her sweat-soaked hair, the woman was gorgeous. So beautiful that when she smiled at him, he was instantly hard again.

"You done with leg lifts?" she asked.

Plopping down onto the arm-press bench, he nodded. Adjusted himself.

And thanked the Lord that she moved on to leg lifts—around the circle from him. Anything he might see would only be in the mirror and he wasn't looking there. He wasn't sure how much more temptation he could withstand without embarrassing himself.

"I heard today that you were a browbeaten wife." He'd meant to lead into it slowly, with words that were a little less...descriptive.

Harper's chuckle sounded completely natural. "Who told you that?" she asked lightly.

"One of the people I questioned."

"One of Miriam's friends?"

He'd mentioned that he'd spent the day interviewing Gram's friends. "Yes."

Including one who'd been close enough to see the inner workings of the Thomas family during the year Bruce and Harper were married.

"You're talking about Grace Parnell."

Right on the mark. He pushed one hundred and seventy-five pounds of weight together at chest level.

"Wow. I thought Grace was a friend..." He'd like to think the break in her voice was due to exertion but she'd released her feet from the leg-lift bar and was sitting still on the bench.

Finishing his rep, Mason went over to the seat next to hers. "She considers you a friend," he said. "In fact, she asked about you and when I said you were well, she not only wanted confirmation, but details. She said she thought of you as a surrogate granddaughter and that she misses you."

Harper's sideways glance held doubt. Distrust.

He couldn't blame her. Especially considering the possibility that Bruce had been mentally manipulating her for years. He'd occasionally wondered, but after speaking with Grace, real suspicion had set in.

"She said the two of you would talk about something—even something simple like where to go on vacation or what to have for dinner. According to her, you'd have solid ideas about what you wanted or didn't want, and then you'd talk to Bruce and suddenly you were doing the opposite. Sometimes they were things you'd said you wouldn't do. Like the time you went to an adult resort with topless bathing..."

He hadn't intended to mention that. He couldn't stand the image of his brother parading Harper around topless. Some things were meant to be private—and enjoyed that way.

"The only topless bathing was on the beach. And we didn't go down there. We stayed up at the pool."

So...good to know. Not his business or relevant to this conversation. "But you went."

"Grace used to tell me that I let Bruce control me, but I don't and I never saw it that way." Harper looked him straight in the eye. "She's been a widow a long time, living alone a long time. She didn't understand, as I did, that in a healthy relationship both parties' needs and wants have equal importance. And that means compromise. So I didn't always get my way."

Mason waited a second before responding, not sure which part of that to address first. Or at all.

A marriage that only lasted a year didn't indicate a healthy relationship. But he saw no point in belaboring the obvious.

"So you feel that your wants and needs were equally considered? That you got your way 50 percent of the time?" He felt slimy, like some kind of voyeur, digging for a look inside his brother's marriage.

Harper nodded. Mason wished he was convinced.

"Grace says that when you left, Bruce started doing to Miriam what he did to you."

Her instant frown—without any sign of alarm—told him her confusion was real. That didn't mean Grace's perception was any less real, only that Harper didn't see what Grace, an outside observer, had noticed.

"I have no idea what you're talking about," Harper said slowly, as though searching her memory. His dread grew. Was it possible that Harper really was a victim of Bruce's manipulation and didn't even know it?

Mason had grown up a victim of it, but at least he'd been a knowing participant; he'd given in by choice, not because he'd been controlled. In the early years he'd hoped Bruce would mature, find his own sense of worth, that his jealousy of Mason—and his hero worship, too—would ease. He'd wanted to protect his little brother from himself.

Instead, he was beginning to see that he might very well have helped enable a monster.

"He spins a picture of the truth in such a way that you feel empathy for him. He plays on people's sincere desire to care for each other, to be compassionate, and he does it so effectively, he gets whatever he wants. He uses love as a means of control."

She shook her head. "What are you, some kind of behavioral analyst now? I thought your skills were more in gathering evidence for the lab."

"I'm not the science guy. Or the behavioral analyst. I'm the guy who can find a needle in a haystack and who can figure out how it got there. My skills are observation, paying attention, listening. When I'm at my best, taking it all in, the pieces fall into place and I can see the complete picture. The lab guys and the behavioral guys and the arrest warrant guys take it from there."

It was a completely elementary explanation—

beneath her—and yet, he had a feeling that at the moment, it was exactly what she needed.

Was she looking for something from him that would give her confidence? Kind of felt that way. Or he could just be kidding himself. Lord knew he wasn't at his best on this one. Far too close to the situation. And yet, with O'Brien's willingness to watch Bruce and allow Mason time to find the truth without damaging Bruce's reputation, he had to do everything he could. Bruce was family, and going above and beyond was what family did.

"So…" She was still meeting his gaze, and yet seemed not to be as…vibrant as she'd been when he'd first sat down. "As the observation guy, can you give me an example of what you're talking about here? I mean, it seems like you think Grace was right in her impression."

In one way or another, Mason had traveled shaky ground more times than he could count. He couldn't remember ever being nervous about it. Until that moment.

"Okay, an example. He'll tell you why he can't eat asparagus… Because it reminds him of the night our grandfather died. He'd been in trouble for not eating it. That same evening, Grandpa had a heart attack and died. Bruce hasn't been able to touch the stuff since."

Harper nodded. "Yes, so? It's true. Asparagus

was a trigger for him. He couldn't tolerate even the smell of it. So because I loved my husband enough to understand that and not serve asparagus, I'm somehow being manipulated and he's an abuser?"

As though a bomb full of shrapnel had gone off, Mason felt blasted by stinging pellets. She'd loved her husband—not Mason, her husband. Mason had known that, and yet he'd allowed himself to believe, for one night, that she'd felt something for him, too. *Ping*, went the first hit.

He'd pulled the asparagus scenario out of his past—not repeating anything he'd heard from Grace. Expressly so Harper wouldn't feel any personal connection and get defensive. *Ping*.

Her tone told him he was losing her. *Ping*.

Bruce's manipulation had worked on her, too. *Ping*.

She'd loved her husband… *Ping. Ping. Ping.*

"Our mother used to insist that you sit at the table until you finish your dinner. Bruce used to get away with not eating asparagus by cramming it in his mouth and holding it long enough to get upstairs and spit it out in his dresser drawer." He knew because when his brother had forgotten to dispose of the dried mess one time, Mason had done it for him, thinking Bruce would realize he had his back, that he wasn't out to show him up in front of their parents.

"The night our grandfather died, Mom wouldn't let him leave the table until he showed her he'd swallowed his asparagus. He wouldn't, so he was sent upstairs to bed. Our grandfather, Mom's dad, was at home with his third wife. He did die that night, but we didn't hear about it until the next day. So, yeah, it's possible that Bruce somehow came to associate Grandpa's death with the taste of asparagus. As a kid, he got away with the story. He never had to eat asparagus again."

Harper's shoulders were sinking. "That's one possible explanation," she said. "I'll admit that the way he told it to me was somewhat different, but we form perceptions as children that we sometimes carry with us into adulthood. Who's to say what connection Bruce made between not eating asparagus and his beloved grandfather dying? Maybe as a kid he somehow thought it was his fault—payback for being naughty."

Either she was more clearheaded and forgiving than anyone he'd ever met. Or Bruce had done a number on her.

"We hardly knew the man," he said now. "Mom's dad left them when Mom was in high school. She lost contact with him after that, and although they were in touch later, it was a visit every few years, that type of thing. He'd stay for a couple of days, with occasional phone calls between him and Mom between visits. Some years we got Christmas cards from him. One year, I got a model airplane. Bruce didn't get anything."

His grandfather had figured Bruce would be too young to know who the present had come from, so it wouldn't matter; Mason had overheard his mother tell his father, who'd been noticeably upset. They'd taken the plane away from Mason and gone out and bought both of the boys presents—Mason's being another model airplane.

"Maybe he thought he was a bad boy and that was why his grandfather didn't like him. Maybe he decided that he'd no longer have a chance to show his grandfather that he was a good boy."

Was she for real? Or playing devil's advocate? His best self should know the answer to that question.

"Bruce holds things over people. Reminds them of some grievance he's got against them, something they've supposedly done to him. That way, they're more prone to make amends. His charm keeps them on his side."

Again, Harper shook her head. "I really think this is all a bit much," she told him. "It feels like you're digging too deep here."

Because he was hitting a vulnerable place? Or because Grace had been overdramatizing? She'd always been the calm, nurturing one of

Gram's friends. The one Mason had most enjoyed talking to. The one whose opinion he'd most respected.

"So you didn't ever feel you had to make amends?"

"Of course I did! But everyone feels that way about their partner—or should feel that way if the relationship is going to survive."

There it was again—that reference to a lasting relationship. They were speaking of a marriage that had only survived a year. So were Bruce's references to him and Harper getting back together actually based in some truth?

"No one's perfect," she continued. "I'd make mistakes, say things I didn't mean, especially when I was pregnant and tired."

She'd been pregnant through most of that one-year marriage.

"I'd be an idiot if I didn't apologize and try to make amends."

"Did Bruce apologize as often as you did?"

"I don't know. I didn't keep track."

"Do you feel like he did?"

She'd looked away, brought her gaze back to his. "I truly don't know, Mason. I feel I apologized a lot, but people always notice their own apologies more than another person's. Because, if the apologies are sincere, it hurts having to give them, so you feel them more acutely."

"Grace says he seemed to keep you in a state of constant guilt. You were always trying to appease him, rather than please him. Her words, not mine."

Harper had little reaction to that. Showed no confusion. Didn't frown. She just sat there, as though she was thinking seriously but unemotionally about what he'd said.

With her arms behind her on the bench, she scooted back and rested against the bars of the machine. Her nails were well-groomed. And short. Preferable, in his opinion. Less chance of hurting a guy when her hand was on his...

She should smell like sweat. He caught a whiff of something that smelled more like soap. A residual scent from her shampoo? Maybe the spray she'd put on her hair?

His training, which had taught him to notice the smallest detail, didn't *always* serve him well.

He didn't know which was worse. Dealing with his inappropriate sexual arousal or listening to her talk about her marriage to his brother. Defending his brother.

"I have no idea how Grace would have known, but I suppose I did feel a sense of perennial guilt where Bruce was concerned. But it wasn't because he barraged me with anything. On the contrary, the guilt came from within me."

His discomfort took a turn, but was no less difficult to deal with.

"You're certain of that? He didn't hold anything over you? Didn't expect things of you because you'd done something to displease him?"

Her frown had returned. Lifting her feet onto the bench, she hugged her knees to her chest. He didn't miss the closed body language in that one.

"What if you'd contacted me, for instance?" He'd told himself their night five years ago was off-limits. Anything to do with that night was off-limits. But he'd already blown that all to hell with the whole Brianna-testing thing.

He was beginning to see that there was no way to delve into her relationship with Bruce— or to gain a true understanding of his brother at all—without looking at how that night had changed life for all of them.

"Did you ever think about it? Ever think maybe I should be invited to Christmas dinner and then try to approach him about it?" They'd only had one Christmas as husband and wife. "Or since the divorce…you've never called to ask if I'd like to spend some time with my niece."

"That would be disloyal to Bruce. I don't want to be married to him, but he's still the father of my child."

There wasn't even a hint of hesitation over

that. And chances were pretty good that she was right—that Bruce *was* Brianna's father. Bruce had been with her a lot more than Mason had— and after the antibiotic would've had more time to interfere with her birth control. But still…was he the only one who'd spent four years wondering what he might be missing? Years that he'd never get back?

He couldn't really blame her for not calling. Or blame Bruce, either. She was being loyal to the man she'd loved—as had he all those years. Both of them understanding that they'd wronged Bruce. Both of them trying to make amends.

"And you knew it killed him to find out we were together."

"Of course," she said.

He'd known, too. Because Bruce had made it plain to him just how much Mason's defection was costing him, how much pain it had brought him.

"But Bruce didn't hold that night over my head, Mason. We spoke about it the one time and then made a pact that it would never be mentioned again. I brought it up once, after Brie was born and I didn't want there to be any doubts that she was his. But when he refused to take the paternity test, I let it drop. I always knew that night was there between us somehow, but not because of him. It was because of me. It was my own shame that ate at me."

The words were a kick in his gut, but Mason moved past that.

"You don't think he understood that? And capitalized on it?"

"He never gave me the feeling that he didn't trust me. He knew it was a one-time thing."

"Which was why he banned me from all family life, other than private visits with my father and Gram?"

"He didn't want the reminder of that one time." She sat up straighter as she spoke.

Mason did, too. "How would you know that if you never spoke about that night again?"

"I'm not sure." She shook her head. "But I'm positive that was why."

"Because he let you know in insidious little ways. Like, for instance, saying he no longer believed in people as he once had. That life had taught him nothing's certain."

She stared at him. And a moment later said, "He was always referring to cases when he talked about…losing his faith in people."

"That's what he said on the surface. But he knew the message he was sending you." Mason had spent a lifetime dealing with Bruce.

"How did you know he said that exact thing?"

"I heard it, too." He'd recognized it for what it was.

So maybe he *was* the one to get this job done. Because he could see what others might miss.

"We did him wrong, Mason."

He didn't disagree. Not on his part. He was Bruce's brother, and family was far more significant than the sometimes unreliable wiles of sexual desire. Not only that, he'd been there that night on a mission for his brother. But it was different for her…

"You'd given him back your ring," he reminded her. "You were no longer engaged."

"I threw it at him in anger. He'd said he was going to keep it for me until I wanted it back."

"Manipulation."

"Or the faith of a man in love."

For her, thoughts of their night together obviously evoked shame. The knowledge rankled. A bothersome but futile nuisance.

"The point is, he was unfaithful first, Harper."

"He confessed to me the very next day."

"But he *lied* about the circumstance, making it sound like his motive had been clean and worthy, although the act itself was dirty. He told you he'd been with a perp that night and he'd been with Gwen. He also told you sex with the perp happened only once and it was multiple times."

Her silence spurred him on. "He had no business coming down on you for something he'd already done."

"Two wrongs don't make a right."

"Agreed, but two wrongs should cancel each other out."

"What he did—it didn't hurt me nearly as much as what I did to him."

Sound alarms went off all over his head. He stared at her. "How can you say that? I know how devastated you were! He betrayed your trust in him in the most elemental way."

"He had sex, yes, but for him it was emotionally meaningless—and at the time I slept with you I still thought I didn't know the woman. That she was the perp..." Her voice broke, but she drew a breath and continued. "I didn't have any kind of relationship with her." She paused for a moment, then stated the bigger betrayal. "And Gwen... I didn't know about her, about what they did, until you told me. Even though we were friends, I'm sure they slept together out of...expedience, after too much booze at the bachelor party." She took another deep breath. "For me...the night...with you...you were... you..."

She broke off again, as though she'd said too much—at a time when he needed more. Desperately needed more.

In true Harper style, she looked him in the

eye. "I couldn't tell him you meant nothing. That the night meant nothing. Add to that, the fact that I slept with his brother, knowing he idolized you, knowing that if I wanted to get back at him, that was the way that would hurt more than any other."

Whoa. Hold on. "Are you telling me that you came on to me that night, that you kept coming on to me…because you knew how much it would hurt him?" The idea had never occurred to him. And stopped him in his tracks. Maybe with some other woman, he'd have caught on. But… Harper?

"Of course not!" Dropping her arms to her sides, her feet to the floor, she sat up straight. "I would never, *ever.* Something like that wouldn't even occur to me. My brain doesn't work that way and—"

The hurt in her voice pierced him. Mason reached out to her before thinking about what he was doing. He touched her arm. Lightly. With the backs of his fingers. Once there, they rubbed softly, just taking in the feel of her. And how she felt moved him to the point that he didn't draw back as quickly as he should.

"The thought never even entered *my* mind until you mentioned it. I was… Well, let's just say I'm glad I wasn't wrong." She hadn't come on to him to hurt Bruce.

He pulled back. There were places they absolutely could not go. They'd go where they had to…but stay away from the rest.

Like touching. Not again. Period.

To force them back on track, he focused and came up with, "Bruce said it, though, didn't he? He placed guilt on you for hurting him in the worst possible way, making your indiscretion seem much worse than his."

Once more, Harper shook her head, her eyes filled with pain. "I don't remember him saying that specifically. It's been five years and that talk wasn't something I wanted to replay on a regular basis."

"But you did, didn't you?" He knew how it worked. He'd been living with it all his life. He'd just been stronger than Bruce's attempts to get at him. Immune to the disease. He'd somehow understood that his job was to love Bruce, to be there for him, waiting for the day he finally grew up.

That day had never come.

But the love hadn't disappeared.

"You didn't see him that night, Mason, but I saw a Bruce I'll never forget. He was crying. *Crying.* Not pretending. It was like…all his confidence, the bravado, just…left. He begged me not to give up on our lifetime of happiness because he'd messed up and gotten carried away by his need to bring in the bad guys."

"Sleeping with his partner after his bachelor party makes *him* a bad guy."

"The point is, he was really scared of losing what mattered most to him. And profoundly shaken because of what we'd done. We were the two people in his life he revered. And we'd let him down. Both of us."

Mason couldn't deny the truth of that one. So he took a minute to settle in with it.

"To know that what we did brought down tough-guy cop Bruce Thomas… I can still feel his body shaking as I held him, still hear him begging me to marry him. To forget you and give him the chance to spend the rest of his life proving his love to me. He said he didn't blame me for my infidelity—that he'd brought that on himself by his own actions. He told me I was the only woman he'd ever loved—and that he'd been sure his love for me was the forever kind from the moment we met. I believed him. And felt like I owed him that second chance. I was so confused, ashamed of what I'd done, and kept telling myself that until Bruce was unfaithful, I'd wanted nothing more than to marry him."

Mason did believe that Bruce's love for Harper was the forever kind. Bruce still loved Harper that way. Which was a huge part of the problem between the brothers. Because Mason had never gotten over her, either.

CHAPTER FOURTEEN

"I'M NOT DENYING there are good sides to Bruce." Mason chose his words carefully. The thin ice he was treading was melting beneath his feet. "I love my brother. He's a great cop. A straight-up one. Completely dedicated to the job." Bruce had always had wonderful qualities, which was one reason people were so drawn to him, to protecting him when his dark side got out of control. His parents had been the same way.

And so had Mason. Right up until the beginning of the week when he'd seen the cast on Gram's arm, the bruises on her face. And had been told that there'd been other previous hair-line fractures.

Did he dare hope Bruce hadn't done it?

"I'm convinced he needs help, Harper. Believe it or not, I'm trying to get him that help before he does something he won't be able to recover from."

She watched him silently and he wished to God he knew what she was thinking. Did she understand what he was saying? Was she under Bruce's mental control? Would she protect him at all costs—and hurt him by doing so?

Vacillating between anger at his brother and a deep love for him, Mason wasn't sure how to proceed. If he took himself off the case, O'Brien would be forced to make it public within their department. He'd had a report from urgent care. He had to follow up.

The only way to protect Bruce was for Mason to find out the truth and then—if Bruce *was* guilty—quietly get his brother help. It wasn't as if Gram was going to press charges against him.

O'Brien could. Bruce could lose his job.

He was hoping to prevent both of the last two scenarios.

Turning to Harper with renewed purpose, he said, "Looking back, can you see how Bruce came out of that whole situation the victim, with you beholden to him? You slept with his brother, and he made that seem worse than the fact that he destroyed the trust between the two of you. Worse than him lying to you about who he slept with that night. Beyond that, he *had* slept with the perp, Harper. You were unfaithful once, during the two days you guys were broken up. He was unfaithful multiple times."

"For the job, except that one time with Gwen."

He held her gaze for a few seconds. "Does that make it okay?"

She didn't answer.

HARPER KEPT HER mind open. The evidence had to speak for itself. She understood what Mason was saying—to a point. Life wasn't as easy, as black and white, as he seemed to need it to be. Emotions weren't weighted based on the components that had sparked them. They were all part of the whole person, the whole package. She'd always been one less prone to drama.

Bruce lived—and loved—big.

"Did you know Grace hasn't seen Miriam in over a year?" Elbows on his knees now, Mason faced her from his perch on the bench. His white tennis shoes looked brand-new. Hers were a year old. And black with fluorescent pink—Brianna had picked them out. She'd had a pair to match but had grown out of them.

Shoes didn't matter. But they were easier to focus on than the rest of the conversation Mason seemed hellbent on having.

"Did you hear me?" he asked.

She nodded. "I just… I can't believe it."

Grace and Miriam no longer friends? "What happened?" They'd been friends since childhood. Almost seventy years. Through school, and through both of their marriages. Through

Grace's grief when her husband was killed on the job; he'd been a truck driver, not a cop...

Grace had never remarried. Never had kids of her own. She'd emotionally adopted Miriam's.

"That's one of the things I need to speak with Gram about in the morning. I'm shocked, too. This morning was the first I'd heard there was a problem between them and I think it's important to know what happened. It could all be part of this same issue. As you've said, abusers isolate."

"Grace wouldn't tell you what happened?" The two had always had a fierce loyalty to each other.

His shrug, accompanied by a grim expression, put another knot in her stomach. She rocked forward and then back on her bench, trying to ease the pressure of the hard surface against her butt. She had more comfortable places to sit—places for conversation. She wasn't taking him there.

"She says that after you left, Bruce's control got much worse. Her theory is that you were the first person who loved him who was able to walk away. You were the one person he couldn't totally control. Everyone else—family, other women, Gwen—they all hung on, stuck around. Except for the women he dumped, of course, but then he was doing the walking away."

Harper just wasn't getting it. Something must have happened to turn Grace against Bruce. She was clouding the facts with resentment or some other emotion.

"Grace has known Bruce his whole life! When did she suddenly start thinking he was such a control freak?"

Mason's studied glance sent tension spiraling through her. But there was no real reason for her to feel that way. It wasn't like he could convince her of anything...or would even try. He was talking to her for confirmation—or not. Investigating. Not judging.

"Bruce has had...issues since he was a little guy," he told her. "We all want people to like us, but Bruce seems to be obsessed with it. Even when he was accepting blame, he somehow came out the victim so he didn't get into as much trouble. So he got sympathy instead of trouble. The thing with the asparagus wasn't an isolated experience..." He'd taken a breath as though he was going to say more, but stopped, seemed to change his mind about whatever had been on the tip of his tongue.

Harper wanted to call him on it. And yet she didn't want to know. Deciding he knew best what information she needed, she let it go. This wasn't a personal conversation. She was a witness being interrogated.

Mostly.

"Anyway, Grace, as well as Gram and my

parents, knew that he had a need for things to go as he thought they should. He'd have tantrums, and they'd work through them."

"I can't imagine they gave in to them." The Thomas family played by the book. Good cops, all of them.

"Of course not. But they sympathized with him, too. And there were times they didn't know he was manipulating them."

She wanted to know about those times. In detail. Again, she didn't ask.

"We all thought he'd grow out of his insecurities as he got older. Instead, he just grew craftier at his manipulation."

She shook her head, shivering when her sweat-moistened T-shirt brushed against her skin. "If this was such a big issue, why didn't I ever hear about it?"

Mason seemed to be struggling for words and Harper couldn't help wondering if he was seeing something that wasn't there, if his perception of his brother was so unclear, it was difficult for him to recognize the truth.

"We all wanted to believe he grew out of it," he finally said, and she had to know what he wasn't saying.

"Including you?"

Mason's shrug looked painful. "Like the rest of the family, I wanted to believe that, too, but I don't think I ever really did. Maybe for a while. Look at the supposed agreement I've been acting under for the past five years. No contact with you. I believed him when he told me you'd asked for the agreement—and that you were fully on board with it."

Okay, that was one example. But the situation had been untenable.

"My brother's had very little to do with me since then," Mason reminded her. "We talked on rare occasions. I saw him, briefly, a time or two. That's it. I kept up with him through Gram. And sometimes O'Brien and I would talk."

"You're telling me Gram doesn't see this side of him."

"Not that she's admitting."

"Did she ever?"

Another shrug. "I thought so. It seemed like we all knew. But I can't give you, or even myself, any concrete evidence that she did. I don't remember it ever coming up with her there, although I'm sure it must have. She was around all the time."

She had to be honest with him.

"I was with him for over two years, Mason, and I never saw it."

"Bruce was always on his best behavior when Gram was with us. He adored her and wanted her to think he was perfect. Maybe it was the same with you."

Apparently Mason had an answer for everything. What remained to be seen, however, was which one of them was seeing the real Bruce.

The man *wasn't* perfect. Clearly. She'd left him after only a year of marriage. But…

"The undercover work he does—he's gifted at it—but that takes its toll, too," she said. "Maybe you need to figure that into your opinions." He'd asked her for the truth. Could be it was up to her to clear Bruce so Mason could focus on finding out who had really hurt Miriam.

If it wasn't Bruce.

That last thought trickling in bothered her. Surely she wasn't going to let what Mason said play with her mind.

Like he'd accused Bruce of doing.

"He enacts different personas and his life depends on his ability to believe them enough to act them out. Sometimes he gets so involved in the person he's playing, he forgets to drop the guise when he's not at work. Maybe that's what you're seeing."

It was the reason her marriage had broken up—because she couldn't trust Bruce to be faithful to her when he left for work every day.

"According to Grace, your leaving, Bruce losing someone he loved and needed, seemed to make him more adamant than ever about controlling Gram. He couldn't lose her, too. Gram was getting older and, one by one, she dropped activities from her schedule, saying that Bruce needed her."

"It makes sense, if you think about it," she said, gaining strength in her mission now to give Mason her side of the story so that he could see it all clearly. He needed her piece of the puzzle. "She'd been living alone, having family dinner once or twice a week, but otherwise free to spend all the time she wanted with Grace. Then, suddenly, Bruce moves in with her and she has family to care for again. As you said, caring for family has always come first with Miriam. It's what she lives for. Bruce gave her the purpose she'd lost. But still, she wouldn't have the energy to keep up a full schedule and still cook and clean for him every day. Maybe Grace was jealous or put out because she lost her time with Miriam. Maybe she resented Bruce."

That made complete sense to her. It didn't explain why Grace had said Harper had pandered to Bruce—but you saw what you looked for. And bits of the truth strengthened perceptions, too. In her case, there'd been some truth in the fact that she'd tended to be more compassionate, often letting Bruce have his own way because she'd felt guilty about ripping his heart out. Felt guilty about the person with whom she'd been unfaithful.

I'd had nothing to be faithful to that night. The words came to her unbidden. Before she could follow the reasoning, Mason spoke again.

"It wasn't just her time with Grace. Gram still called her, they still saw each other most days, until about a year ago. Grace said that Bruce was gradually sucking the life out of Gram by stopping her from doing chores she was perfectly capable of doing. Like carrying the laundry downstairs, for instance. She said it started out with little things like that, and Gram would gush about how great it was to have a chivalrous and caring man in the house again. But then it became less helpful and more controlling. I guess one day he got home from work and saw her on a ladder changing a lightbulb and lit into her. Grace was on the phone with her at the time and heard the whole thing, but Bruce didn't know that. Gram had been talking on the Bluetooth Bruce had bought her, so she could answer the phone anytime he called, and could always call for help if she fell or got into trouble. Grace's theory is that after you left, Bruce fixated on Gram and was petrified of losing her, too. Over time, he continued to curtail activities until she started to feel like she wasn't capable of doing very much anymore. Grace in-

vited her to a retired cops' par three golf out-
ing, and Miriam said that she'd never make it
around the course. Didn't want to tire herself,
or risk putting a strain on her heart."

"Miriam loves golf!" Harper had meant to
listen from a safe emotional distance. By the
time she'd interjected she'd been completely
pulled in.

She didn't blame Bruce. She understood.
And, unlike Mason, saw a pattern of loving,
not abuse.

"It sounds more to me like maybe Miriam's
getting older, has less energy and wanted to con-
serve it, just like she said," she added. "We both
know how much Bruce loves her. I can see him
being overprotective—"

"The final blow between Gram and Grace
came last year, when Gram suddenly announced
that she couldn't drive across town to Grace's
house anymore. She said Bruce didn't think her
reflexes were quick enough and she could get
in an accident."

That was a little much. Unless... "Did he have
reason to think so? Had she had any accidents?
Any fender benders or near misses?"

"Apparently not. Grace had ridden with her
the week before, in downtown rush-hour traf-
fic, and said Gram had maneuvered like a pro.
Like she always did."

"She's a strong-minded woman. There must be some reason she didn't stand up to him."

"Grace is certain that he beat her down so much, she'd lost all confidence in herself. And when she tried to tell Gram, she said Gram hung up on her. They talked again a couple of times, but Gram said she wasn't going to listen to Grace maligning Bruce anymore and Grace couldn't watch what was happening to her friend and say nothing. Eventually their phone calls stopped."

The sadness that momentarily consumed her…for both women…had to be pushed aside. This was business.

Harper looked Mason in the eye. "Miriam just climbed out a window to preserve her sense of independence and control. Don't you find the idea of her giving in to Bruce due to a loss of confidence a little hard to believe?"

His lack of an answer was an answer in itself.

He'd come to her for the information she could give him. Harper felt the responsibility acutely. She said, "Look, Mason, I see some of what you're saying. Bruce can be a bit controlling. Maybe he does embellish to elicit sympathy sometimes, but there's got to be more going on here. Miriam not seeing Grace for a year… That can't just be because Bruce was getting

overprotective. Grace has known Bruce all his
life! Why not talk to him?"

"Grace said she tried. He gave her a heartfelt
testimony of his love for Gram, insisting that he
only wanted what was best for her. He said he
hadn't told her not to do her volunteer work, that
she'd sworn she wanted to be at home, caring
for him." He paused, looked down at his hands,
then back at her. "She claimed he had tears in
his eyes when he said it."

"But you just said that, according to Grace,
Bruce *did* tell her not to do volunteer work."

"Another reason I need to speak with Gram
in the morning."

She didn't miss the "tears in his eyes" reference, reminding her of the night Bruce had
begged her to marry him. She even experienced
a second of discomfort, until she realized that of
course Bruce would have been emotional. His
grandmother's oldest friend had accused him
of mistreating her, doubting his devotion to her.

"And none of this even remotely hints at
Bruce hurting Miriam. Her arm's broken. Those
bruises on her face…that's not mental manipulation or emotional abuse."

"Grace said that that one time Miriam was
changing a lightbulb and Bruce got home… His
tone of voice was not loving or kind. He asked
her if she'd lost her fucking mind. Called her an

idiot. Grabbed her around the waist and lifted her off the ladder, dropping her in her chair. Grace could hear most of it and Gram filed in the rest, insisting that Bruce was just worried and trying to keep her safe. He'd gone in to shower right after, never knowing that Grace had been on the phone the whole time."

Nausea didn't visit her often. But when it did, it came abruptly. Harper took a deep breath. Relaxed her stomach muscles. Went to the cooler for a paper cone of water.

She'd given Mason the facts she had to give him. As Grace had. There was no more she could do.

"I can't comment on that, Mason. I wasn't there," she said when her stomach settled, needing him to leave.

He approached her slowly, stopping a foot away. The urge to hold him hit her as suddenly as the nausea had. Water wasn't going to settle that one.

If she had to use Bruce as a barrier between them, she'd do it. For all their sakes. "Clearly, I'm not a victim of Bruce's manipulations," she told him. "I'm here. I left him. As Grace put it, I was the only one who didn't let his love control me." Or something to that effect.

Again he looked as though he wanted to say more. He studied her instead. If he wasn't going to leave on his own, she'd show him out. Heading to the door and to the hall, her unfinished workout didn't matter anymore.

Mason stopped her just short of the front door, turning her to face him.

"Please be careful," he said, his expression reminiscent of early morning hours in the moonlight, giving her the false impression that nothing mattered more to him than she did.

"I'm armed every day," she reminded him. "And I'm always careful."

"Be careful with Bruce. Don't accept things at face value. If your leaving changed him, just think what losing Gram could do to him. He has no idea she's protecting him…"

"If he didn't do this, he won't figure she'd need to protect him."

"But if he did do it…"

She'd hate to imagine the walking and staring he'd be doing. The walking out and returning hours later. Except, who would he walk out on? And return to?

"You don't really think Bruce is going to do something as stupid and bold as to try to get into the Stand? To Miriam or me?" *Or Brianna?*

Her vision reddening around the edges as fear engulfed her, Harper felt weak in the knees for the second it took rational thought to return.

"Not unless he thinks he's on the verge of

being reprimanded—if he was suspended from work, for instance—but he wasn't. Still, because he's shown up in Santa Raquel for the very first time right now, while all of this is happening, I can't just put his presence here down to coincidence."

"My job changed a month ago," she pointed out, facing down the fear his words were raising within her. "We've recently agreed that he'll visit Brianna here."

"I know. And he hasn't been to see her once in those weeks, until two days after I brought Miriam to you."

She had no argument, so she promised to be careful, looking at his lips as she told him goodnight.

And felt his gaze linger way too long on hers before he opened the door and let himself out.

CHAPTER FIFTEEN

AFTER A RESTLESS night in a nondescript motel room, with a bed like many of the others he'd slept in around the country, Mason was eager to unwrap his little bar of complimentary soap and jump in the shower Thursday morning.

Three days ago, life had been...predictable. Fine. Just the way he'd established it. Normal.

That morning, other than the leather satchel that served as his bathroom cabinet and dresser, he hardly recognized anything. Least of all himself.

As a guy who moved through life analytically, he wasn't prone to emotion. Or spending nights lying awake in the dark, questioning himself.

Was he wrong about Bruce? Had five years of suppressing questions gotten to him while he was busy with other things? Was his perception so clouded by an unrequited desire for the one woman he could never have?

Was he Brianna's father? Missing out on the most incredible experience he'd ever know?

Was he after his brother because, only by

proving that Bruce wasn't worthy of his family, could Mason step in and claim what was his? Or rather what he *wanted* to be his?

But Harper wasn't, and never had been.

The family, though... Gram... Brianna... Bruce.

Bruce was his family. His closest family.

The one way his brother would come through this without a smudge was if Mason proved his innocence before anyone else knew about the report sent from urgent care and started asking questions.

Shaking the water out of his hair as he left the shower, he determined to realign his thinking. Darkness was gone. The light of day had arrived.

And with it came sense. Clarity.

Gram had been abused. He hadn't conjured up that fact. His job was to find out who'd hurt her and make it stop.

An hour later, he was at the Stand, already sitting at their usual table, with coffee and doughnuts he'd brought in from a shop down the street, when Miriam came in at seven, just as they'd arranged. Hair and makeup done, wearing white capris and a short-sleeved light blue cotton top he'd never seen before, she looked small walking toward him. And yet putting on a good face. Her below-the-elbow cast caught his eye, renewing his anger at whomever had hurt her. He stood, pulled out her chair and set her coffee—black and mild as she liked it—in front of her.

"I brought you old-fashioned plain. Your favorite," he said, taking a doughnut out of the box and putting it on a napkin.

"You're a good boy, Mason." She didn't quite pull off a smile, but it looked as though she'd tried.

She nibbled a little of the doughnut. Mason watched, figuring the bagel he'd purchased for himself would wait until the drive to Albina.

"It's my turn to make breakfast at the house this morning," she said, when he mentioned her lack of appetite. "I've got to be back soon."

He didn't know whether to celebrate the fact that she seemed to be engaged with her temporary life circumstances, or to point out that they didn't have long to talk. He'd let her know the day before that he needed time with her. She could have rescheduled breakfast duty.

She was using it as an excuse, flimsy at best, not to have to talk with him for long. Watching her, he wished his father was alive and could translate Gram's actions for him.

"How did it go with Brianna yesterday?" He started there to put her at ease.

"Great." Her smile was genuine this time, and she met his gaze. "We made chocolate chip cookies for her to give to the kids in her class today. She insisted on doing all the measuring herself—said her mom showed her how—and needed very little help in getting it right. We just had to increase the ingredients because we were doubling the recipe."

A four-year-old who grasped the concept of measurement? He felt the news with a sharp stab of—

No. This wasn't about him. It was about taking care of his family. Taking care of Gram and Bruce.

"I should've been teaching her when she visited on weekends, but I didn't want to take her away from Bruce. She's his only child and he has so little time with her..."

Instincts on full alert, Mason said, "I had a chat with Grace yesterday."

The doughnut captured Gram's full attention. Fingers picking at it, she was creating a small pile of crumbs.

"I was shocked when she told me the two of you haven't spoken in almost a year."

More crumbs. No words.

"She misses you."

"She knows my number."

"You know hers, too."

Gram's nod wasn't encouraging. It disclosed nothing of what she was thinking.

"Don't you miss her, too?"

That got Gram's attention. "Of course I do," she said, bringing some crumbs to her mouth.

"So...what happened?"

Gram shrugged. Ate another small piece. "People change."

"Almost a whole life of being friends, and now, in your seventies, people change?"

"She wants me to be like her—free from family responsibility, doing whatever she wants when she wants it."

"Grace has never seemed like a selfish person to me. As far as I can tell, she still spends most of her time volunteering at church, and with the women's auxiliary."

Gram nodded.

"You used to love doing those things, too."

"I have a home and family to take care of."

"Bruce is a grown man who lived on his own long enough to know how to take care of himself."

"It's a big house."

"So hire some help."

She shook her head, frowning, and he knew he'd overstepped on that one. Gram would never be happy with someone else running her home. She liked things done her way.

"She says Bruce wouldn't let you drive at night anymore. Is that true?"

She'd driven herself to urgent care.

"He gets nervous. And I don't like to be out alone at night. My eyesight isn't what it used to be."

Leaning his elbows on his knees, Mason bent toward her, wishing he could take her hand in his and not have her pull it away.

"*Did* he tell you not to drive at night anymore?"

"I don't like to be out at night alone."

Yet she'd climbed out a bedroom window to take a walk in the dark. Alone. To prove her independence.

Because Bruce had stripped her confidence in herself—maybe even without meaning to? Or had he purposely replaced a sense of independence with fear as a way of controlling her?

"Did he forbid you to go out at night, Gram?"

She didn't answer.

"Look at me, please."

A few seconds of silence passed, accompanied by another few crumbs of doughnut going to her mouth, and then she looked at him.

"Did he forbid you to go out? At night or any other time?"

"I'm a grown woman! No one can forbid me to do something."

"Did he try? Did he ask you not to drive at night anymore?"

Her gaze dropped as she shook her head and Mason knew she'd just lied to him.

HARPER WASN'T EVEN out of the shower when Bruce called Thursday morning. Brianna answered the phone and came into her bathroom.

"Daddy needs you!" she called through the steam.

Fear shot through Harper and she yanked at the shower curtain and peered out. Brianna stood there, still in her short-sleeved princess nightgown, hair all askew, holding Harper's cell phone.

Thank God. The phone.

Had she really thought the man had shown up at her house and that Brianna had let him in?

She was letting Mason get to her. That had to stop.

Grabbing a towel, she dried her hand, wrapped herself and took the phone, an eye on her daughter as she did so.

What had Bruce said to Brianna?

The four-year-old seemed as happy as always.

"I'm sorry about yesterday," Bruce said to her, his tone affable. Kind. "I got called back for a job. Looks like I'm going to be on it all week. But…it's been too long since I've seen my little girl. Is there any way you could bring her up here? Just for a few hours, if that's all you can spare." He suggested hours during each of the next three days, saying he could be free from his assignment then.

"We could do something, the three of us," he continued. "Maybe have a picnic on the beach."

Picnic on the beach. That was what he'd done on his second date with the woman he'd been sleeping with for weeks before they were married. Mason had said that Bruce's report stated he'd slept with her on their second date— during a picnic on the beach.

"Harper?"

"I…" *Have Friday off.* The next day. With Miriam at the Stand, she'd been planning to go in—so Brianna could spend time with her great-grandmother. To keep Miriam satisfied and to give Mason an opportunity—to…clear Bruce?

"Sorry, I was just getting out of the shower," she told her ex-husband, trying to focus. To think.

What should she do?

Taking Brianna to Albina was better than having Bruce back in Santa Raquel. Near Miriam.

She'd have to come up with some explanation to give Brianna to make certain the little girl didn't mention seeing Miriam to Bruce.

What would Mason suggest she do?

She could see her parents. Time with them always put life in a more manageable perspective.

"I think I can do tomorrow afternoon," she heard herself say before she'd consciously reached that decision.

He seemed delighted, which always made her feel better.

But she hung up with a pit in her stomach.

Dressing, tending to Brianna's morning preparations, she couldn't seem to shake the feeling of unease. She didn't want to call Mason— although she had to let him know about the meeting—until she knew why she was feeling that way.

She wasn't afraid of Bruce.

So what was it?

GRAM'S MAKEUP COMPLETELY covered her bruises, but Mason couldn't look at her without remembering they were there.

She'd resorted to lying to him. How on earth was he going to help her?

Half of her doughnut gone, she'd pushed it aside. "I really need to get back," she said, her hands on the table as though getting ready to stand.

Placing a hand on one of hers, he said, "How about if I bring Grace down here to visit you?"

The idea had just occurred to him, but he knew it was a good one. "She really wants to see you…"

Gram's hesitation didn't seem to be caused by fear, but she was frowning. "I don't know, Mason…"

"Just for a few hours. You've been friends for practically your whole lives. What could it hurt?" Unless she was afraid that Bruce would find out? "She'll only be able to come if she agrees not to say anything to anyone."

Gram didn't seem convinced, but she was no longer shaking her head. "It's just…she wants me to do things…"

Finally. "Like what?" Get away from Bruce? Grace had already told him as much.

"Skydiving, for one."

"Skydiving?" He studied her. Was she losing her mind?

Gram nodded, her lips pursed with disapproval. "She read an article on the internet about a woman who went skydiving for her ninetieth birthday and she couldn't let it go. She said we had to do it together. Kept going on and on about it…"

Grace had never mentioned skydiving. Mason shook his head. "So…if she promises not to talk about skydiving?"

Another few seconds passed and then Gram's eyes lit with decision. A look he recognized from when he was a kid and was about to be told what to do.

Funny how some things lost no effect at all as you aged.

"I'm okay with her coming if you'll do something for me."

He felt a surge of relief flood him—more emotion that didn't normally invade his days. "What?" He'd pretty much do anything for her. She had to know that.

Unless it involved contact between her and his brother…

"My car's due for an oil change. I was scheduled to take it in yesterday."

And she couldn't ask Bruce to do it for her. She still saw to her own car maintenance. As the independent woman she was.

She was thinking ahead—about driving and living an active lifestyle in the near future.

"Of course I'll get your oil changed," he told her, pleased that he'd gotten off so easily.

"There's a coupon in the glove box," she said, seeming more relaxed than he'd seen her in recent days. "It's good for half off and expires this week, which is why I don't want to wait."

Gram was counting pennies? The woman had enough money to live two lifetimes.

Unless…whoever was hurting her had been taking her money, too?

CHAPTER SIXTEEN

MASON'S MEETING WITH Gwen was completely unproductive. She swore, looking him straight in the eye, that Bruce had nothing to do with her showing up at his house the other night. Swore that she and Bruce had not spoken in over a week.

She also assured him, quite insistently, that she wasn't going to tell him how she'd found out about Gram's abuse and his private investigation. He could guess, though. O'Brien had probably called her in for a talk, on the QT. As Bruce's only regular partner when he wasn't on undercover duty, she'd be the one most likely to know if there'd been changes in his behavior. O'Brien would have to be certain that he wasn't putting people at risk by keeping Bruce on the job while Mason did his looking around.

It all made sense. He just didn't like the fact that O'Brien hadn't told Mason that Gwen knew.

He also didn't like that the woman had nothing but praise for his brother. Translated: she wasn't being honest with him. No one was that perfect.

Pushing aside an almost constant desire to call Harper, he moved through his tasks. From meeting Gwen to getting the oil changed in Gram's car, which gave him an excuse to have another look through her house, homing in on her room. And Bruce's. And the home computer, downloading the hard drive to a large-capacity storage disk to peruse later. He couldn't access his brother's personal laptop. He didn't have a warrant, and Gram's permission to search her home wasn't enough. Still, nothing stood out immediately as different or in any way alarming.

If you ignored the filth of his brother's lifestyle during Gram's absence.

He found a locked box in Gram's room. Wooden, about the size of a shoe box, beautifully embellished with a painted ocean scene. He could have picked the lock, but didn't. Instead, he carried the box through the garage and out to her car with him, to move into his SUV later, so he could take it to her, along with the bag of other things she'd asked him to collect. More clothes. A watch. Some earrings. And a round brush she'd forgotten when they'd stopped by her house to pack the night they'd left.

Though he hadn't seen the box before, he

wasn't surprised that Gram had it. She'd always been one for keeping treasures and hoped he could get her to open it and share them with him.

Imagining pictures of him and Bruce when they were kids, of his father, of his grandfather with Gram when they were a young couple, he backed Gram's car down the drive. Suddenly an older gentleman appeared in the rearview mirror, waving at him.

In brown plaid shorts and a short-sleeved white golf shirt, with short gray hair, the man appeared to be somewhere between seventy and eighty. He was pretty spry as he moved toward the car door. Mason put on the brakes.

"I've been—" The man stopped speaking when Mason exited the car, just as the man got close. "Oh."

Staring at Mason, his expression changed from welcoming to guarded. Why his presence brought negative reaction, Mason didn't know. He'd never seen the guy before in his life.

"Can I help you?"

"No." Backing down the drive, the man shook his head, and turned, hurrying to the sidewalk.

"Wait!" Mason called as he chased after the guy. "Who are you? What did you want?"

"No one. Nothing," the guy said over his shoulder, not slowing at all.

"Hey." Mason caught up to him, keeping pace. "You know my grandmother?" he asked. He'd been in Gram's car. The guy must have thought, with the car pulling out of the driveway, that he was Gram.

"Nope." The guy shook his head again. "Wrong house," he said, then turned up the drive four houses down from Gram. Mason had knocked at that door the day before, when he'd been canvassing the neighborhood. No one had answered. "I'm expecting a call from my daughter," the man continued, hurrying to let himself into the house.

He'd had a key, so he could very well have been confused and gone to the wrong place. On the street, staring at the two houses, Mason could see the similarities. Most of the homes on the block were identical in size. All of them featured the typical siding and brick of older California homes.

Still, the man hadn't been heading to the door of the house. His goal had clearly been Gram's car. He'd been flagging her down.

Unless he'd wondered why someone was pulling out of his drive?

He'd seemed completely lucid, but...

Taking one last look at the man's home, he noticed the twitching of a blind in the front window.

And knew that he'd just come across an unexpected piece of his puzzle. The problem was figuring out where the hell it fit.

Did Gram have a neighbor problem? One she hadn't told anyone about? Afraid of what Bruce might do to the guy if he found out the older man had been bugging their grandmother?

Could *he* be the one who'd put those bruises on Gram's face? Broken her arm multiple times? Hard to imagine and yet…the guy was definitely in good enough shape to overpower an elderly woman.

He'd been unpleasantly surprised to see Mason.

And he'd run instead of staying for the casual conversation that would've been more likely in a case of mistaken driveway.

Unless he was worried someone would notice he was missing a beat or two and send him away?

Remembering the story Harper had told him about the resident at the Stand whose family had been threatening to put her in a home, he turned back to Gram's car with a heavy feeling in his gut.

Grace had been pressuring Gram to skydive. Gram had lied to him about Bruce telling her not to go out at night. And she had a neighbor neither she nor Bruce had ever mentioned. A neighbor who'd just lied to him, too.

The puzzle was getting more convoluted by the minute.

He sure hoped something was going to break soon and he could get on with his life.

HARPER WAS BUSY all morning with a new resident check-in—the young woman's abuser, her ex-husband, had shown up at her home early that morning in spite of a restraining order, but had only managed to wrench her shoulder out of its socket and leave a few bruises before the cops showed up, called by a friend in the apartment next-door.

Unfortunately, Bella Anderson's abuser had spotted the police car coming up the street, taken off and was still on the loose. Until he was in custody, the Stand was on high-threat alert—which meant that all entrances and exits, secret though they were, had two guards. Residents were on lockdown inside the grounds, and no visitors were allowed. It also meant that any employees coming or going had to have an armed escort. A desperate abuser might not hesitate to kidnap, hold hostage, hurt or kill an employee in an effort to get to his victim.

While all of this made Harper's job much more intense, the day went on as usual for the residents and children living there. Except for the residents who'd been scheduled to work in the Stand-owned-and-run businesses on the strip bordering their property, who had the day off. There'd been no visitors scheduled. No residents had appointments outside the Stand that day.

Lila handled getting the secondhand store and computer shop staffed.

And then it was time for lunch.

Time to call Mason and let him know she'd be bringing Brianna to Albina in the morning to see Bruce.

Assuming Bella Anderson's ex-husband was in custody. The Santa Raquel police expected that to happen within the hour.

Which was why Harper ate lunch before calling Mason. Might as well make sure she'd be going before raising the alarm.

With the imminent phone call on her mind, she ate alone in her office, thinking about Mason. About the fact that the night he'd slept with her, he hadn't told her his brother had lied about sleeping with Gwen instead of a perp. About the fact that Mason had come looking for her that night, not sent by fate, as she'd always thought, but by Bruce.

She spent a lot of the twenty minutes obsessing about the twenty-four hours after waking in Mason's bed without a phone call from him.

Interspersed with all the memories were moments of fighting with herself. She wanted him. More that day than ever before. Having him in her home had been a worse mistake than she'd ever imagined. She'd woken up over and over in the night, sweating, her body hot for him.

She was still hot. And wet, too. Just thinking about his shoulders lifting those weights. The touch of his fingers on her arm.

Why hadn't Bruce ever made her feel that way?

Feeling as though she should tell her ex-husband about her encounters with Mason, feeling disloyal for not doing so, she put off picking up the phone.

When Bella's ex was in custody she'd call.

Until then, there was no reason to do it.

IT DIDN'T TAKE much time for Mason to know a hell of a lot more about Gram's neighbor. Home and eating a ham sandwich on stale bread, he sat at his computer and signed in to the secure network his government clearance gave him.

Elmer Guthrie was seventy-eight years old. Retired career army man. He lived alone in the home he'd purchased a year ago—four doors down from Gram.

A year. Right about the time that Gram and Grace had had their falling-out.

Grace had never mentioned Elmer. Had she

known about him? It seemed to Mason that she would've said something if there'd been any concern—or even jealousy. Of course, Gram's oldest friend hadn't mentioned skydiving, either.

Was it possible that his grandmother had a new beau? One who she was sneaking around to see? One who was abusing her?

He needed to talk to Bruce, to find out what his brother knew about their neighbor. But he couldn't. Not until he was sure that Bruce hadn't hurt Gram.

Grace had heard Bruce verbally abuse Gram; he knew that Bruce had hauled her off a ladder and dropped her roughly enough into a chair that Gram had been left breathless—according to Grace.

Who hadn't told him about Elmer or skydiving.

He had to get the two women together. With a receipt for Gram's oil change in his pocket, his next step was to hold Gram to her part of the bargain.

Which meant he had to phone Harper to get security clearance for Grace.

Finally. A legitimate reason for the call he'd been yearning to make all morning. And an excuse to head back to Santa Raquel, too.

HARPER WAS SITTING in the surveillance room, watching cameras with Tasha while the officer assigned to that duty was at lunch, when her phone rang. One look at the screen and, heart pounding, she motioned to Tasha that she had to step out and took the call as she headed onto the grounds.

Being cooped up in her office wasn't an option at the moment. She needed air. Space.

He must've found out that she'd agreed to come to town. Had Bruce talked up the visit and he'd heard about it at the station?

Feeling guilty she started right in, "I don't know if I can make it or not. I need confirmation of an arrest here, and was waiting to call you until I'm sure what's going on."

She should've called him. She'd known the second she'd seen his name pop up. He was conducting a legitimate investigation. She'd agreed to cooperate. Hiding Bruce's phone call made her look guilty.

She was a cop. She knew how things worked.

She also loved the sound of Mason's voice. Even when it was saying, "What are you talking about? You know this is Mason, right?"

"Of course I know it's you." Her heart thundered inappropriately in her chest—that, not the phone call, was what made her feel disloyal to her ex.

"Mind explaining, then, what it is you don't know if you can make? Did I sleepwalk through a phone conversation in which we made some sort of plan?"

His tone sounded...teasing. Her entire being flooded with desire.

"No... I thought...never mind. Bruce called me this morning. He wants to see Brianna and now that he's trapped up there on a job all week, wants me to bring her up tomorrow for a picnic lunch on the beach."

"And you told him you would." Not even a hint of teasing now.

"I did. Yes." She was the head of security, a licensed cop, doing her job. "He has a legal right to see her. I determined that it was best to keep him away from Santa Raquel and Miriam."

"What arrest is pending?"

She told him what she could about Bella. Just the basics of having a new resident with an active abuser threat. "Police expect to have him in custody this afternoon."

"And you can't leave until that happens."

"Right."

He didn't sound angry...not exactly.

"Then you were going to call and tell me you'd talked to Bruce?"

He had doubts. She could hear it in his voice.

"I swear to you." She had no doubts herself where that was concerned. "I wouldn't have seen Bruce without letting you know first." Yet, as she heard herself say the words, she felt that prick of guilt again.

Bruce was the man to whom she'd been married. They were raising a child together. That alone denoted a sense of…loyalty.

Ganging up on him with the lover who'd thrilled her more in one night than Bruce ever had was just wrong. *Had* to be wrong. And that was before factoring in their brotherhood.

His silence bothered her. "Wait…if you didn't know about the pending visitation, why were you calling?"

"It's kind of a moot point at the moment," he said. She couldn't tell what he was thinking. Was he upset with her? Did he care that she hadn't called him right away? Put him first?

Why should he care about her or who she put first in her life?

What was wrong with *her* that she was still craving Mason's regard? She had been since the day she'd met him, more than six years before. That family dinner, when Bruce had introduced her to his FBI brother, had been a day she'd never forgotten.

And never remembered without a load of guilt piling up on her.

She'd loved Bruce. But Mason… His presence had overpowered her. It wasn't love or anything relationships were built on. It couldn't have been. She'd just met him. And truly did love Bruce. But that day, and the days that followed, the dreams she'd had—both daydreams and when she was asleep at night…

"Miriam agreed to meet Grace…" She tuned in as he started to explain himself. "I was calling to arrange for security clearance for Grace in the family visiting room."

"We're on a no-visitation lockdown." She repeated what she'd already told him.

"Right."

"It'll be lifted as soon as the arrest is made," she said, hoping, for a whole lot of reasons, that the police were correct in their assessment of a quick capture. "I can run the clearance for you so that as soon as we let in visitors, Grace can see Miriam." She had to contact Grace, which she told him, and to which he agreed. She asked if any of Grace's contact information had changed. She still had her cell number listed on her phone.

And then they were done with business, but no one was hanging up. She wondered what he'd been doing all morning. He already knew what she'd been up to.

"You think Grace will be able to get the truth out of Miriam?" she asked.

"I don't know what I think at the moment, except there's something going on that's split apart two women who've been best friends their whole lives. I'm hoping that being together, looking each other in the eye, might break down some barriers."

"You sound…" *Sad*, she'd almost said. "What did Miriam have to say this morning?"

She'd been wondering on and off all day. Had hoped he'd call. But she hadn't allowed herself to acknowledge any of that. She didn't have to know in order to do her job. Either at the Stand or to help him.

She listened as he told her about Miriam feeling pressured to go skydiving. And shook her head. The woman would climb out a window at night for the freedom to take a walk alone, but claimed to have broken off a seventy-year friendship due to skydiving pressure?

There had to be more. But Mason wasn't telling her about it. Not that she blamed him. She didn't need to know, she told herself again.

She just *wanted* to know.

And where Mason was concerned, her *wanting* was off-limits.

CHAPTER SEVENTEEN

HE HADN'T ASKED if Bruce had said anything to her about Miriam. About his investigation. He hadn't told her about Elmer, either. As soon as Mason hung up, he wanted to call again. But he didn't. Harper wasn't his friend. Or his helpmate. She was a witness.

And the head of security in the facility keeping his grandmother safe.

His task was to keep the designations straight, the boundaries clearly drawn. Living within his boundaries had never presented much of a problem. Even on the night he'd failed, he'd done relatively well. He'd taken a drunk and very alluring Harper back to his place, put her to bed in his room and walked out the door to sleep on the couch. He'd been down for the night when she'd suddenly been there on the couch with him. Giving him everything he'd ever wanted...

Mason could have his pick of beautiful women, and had on multiple occasions. None of those connections, liaisons—whatever you wanted to call them—had ever lasted long.

What cruel twist of fate, then, had decided that the one woman he couldn't have would be the only woman he ever truly wanted?

And then…to know she'd had a child who *could* be his…

He made it through the day, tracing Miriam's steps through credit card receipts—mostly taken from a file he'd gotten from her computer. Talking to anyone with whom she might have been in contact. Repeating the same actions for his brother, as much as he could do so covertly. He made it through a solo dinner of takeout back at his computer.

And he was no closer to seeing the complete picture.

He'd talked to O'Brien about a warrant to speak with Elmer. He didn't want him brought in, though. He needed the old man to be compelled to speak with him at his home. Or some other place that wouldn't draw attention. He'd been told the request might take a day or two.

As much as he wanted the mystery solved, and the man who'd hurt his grandmother charged and away from any access to her, he had to be patient enough to get it done right. Any evidence he collected had to stand up in court.

Gram was safe for a number of days. He could wait a couple.

Funny, though, there was something else

eating at him that wasn't going to wait. You'd think, after five years, another week, another year, wouldn't matter. Not so.

Driven by a feeling that was stronger than all the logic he was throwing at it, he walked down to the beach not far from his home, purchased a beer from a stand and pulled out his phone. Midsummer, the place was populated with couples and partiers, but the sunbathers had all gone home, leaving him a clear, mostly private, path to walk closer to the water.

It was after eight. Her little girl would be in bed.

One thumb-push on his screen and Harper's number was ringing.

"Mason? Is everything okay?" She'd picked up immediately. Made sense, with her job, that she'd keep her phone close by.

"I got your text about the arrest." He'd put off responding earlier.

"Okay, good. So we'll be in Albina tomorrow by eleven. We're meeting Bruce at the south beach, having lunch and then heading back to Santa Raquel."

He took a swig of beer from the plastic cup he'd been given. "Where are you eating?"

"I'm bringing a picnic."

A family picnic on the beach. His gut tightened. "The south beach in July—we'll be surrounded by tons of people the whole time, Brie can play if she wants to, and then we'll get in our car and come home."

Albina's south beach was heavily patrolled, keeping it clean and safe, which was part of the reason it would be so crowded. She'd made the safest possible choice.

"I'll be close, but stay out of sight." He'd debated telling her that he was going to be there. But his presence wasn't negotiable.

"Okay."

He couldn't tell whether she thought his being there was overkill, or necessary. Whether she was glad to know he'd be close. But he was somewhat placated by her lack of argument.

He could only hope that her conciliatory manner would continue into his next topic of conversation.

Sipping his beer, he let the hand holding it drop to his side, the cup next to the pocket of the khaki shorts he'd put on after dinner.

"I should have clearance for Grace sometime tomorrow," she went on. "She's not in any system so it's not as quick as it would be for someone with clearance elsewhere. We have to make reference calls as well as run the normal background check." He nodded, fully versed in various levels of security clearance.

"Thank you." He hadn't called about Grace. She had no cause to know that.

A couple strolled past him, holding hands, their bare feet covered by the tide rolling in. His sandals weren't even wet. Seemed like a nice idea, though, to be walking hand in hand in the tide. With the right woman.

Taking another sip of beer, he toasted the couple who'd already disappeared from sight and said, "I want to have a DNA test done to determine Brianna's paternity."

Her silence told him nothing. He checked his screen to make sure he was still connected.

"I'm sorry to have to do this, but I need to know if she's my daughter," he told her. "I have no intention of upsetting her. I can be introduced into her life as her uncle. For however long…" He hadn't done enough thinking about that part. "I don't have any intention of ripping her away from Bruce. Or him from her…" He wanted that quite clear. "Unless…if he's abusive, he shouldn't be alone with her, whether I'm her father or not."

Her father. He'd said the words aloud.

Crazy how you could live with something buried for so long, and go on as though everything was normal, but once it broke free, there was no stopping it.

She still wasn't speaking. Another glance at

his phone told him she was there. A sip of beer gave him a second of false calm.

"If she's mine, I intend to pay half of her support, retroactively. If you don't want to use it, that's fine, it can go into a trust fund for college. Or whatever. But I have to support her." That one he'd thought about a lot.

He could never pay enough to compensate for what he'd done to his brother that night—another reason he had to pay all the debts he could.

"Bruce has already refused a test."

He stopped as her words came softly over the phone. He'd just told her he had to find out if he was the father of her child and the most she could say was Bruce said no?

"We don't need Bruce." He took a slow step, and then another. People on the beach, the tide, the setting sun all faded into a blurred background. Only her voice mattered. "If we have you, me and her, we'll be able to get a definitive match if she's mine. If we don't, she's probably not. There'll be some markers because Bruce and I are brothers, but not enough to make it conclusive if she isn't mine."

They were in his territory now—puzzle pieces. He might not run forensic tests himself, but he knew how to read the results.

"Okay."

The word was so soft it didn't even sound like her. For a second he wondered if he'd really heard it.

"Did you say okay?"

"You have a right to know."

Damn straight he did. But...

Words slammed him from all sides. Plans. Logistics. Thank-yous. Apologies. Queries. Was she okay? Assurances...he wouldn't ever do anything detrimental to Brianna. Or interfere in Harper's parenting...

Before he could voice any of it, she interrupted him.

"I have to go. We'll talk tomorrow. Good night."

Just that quickly she was gone. Staring at his screen, at the evidence of the disconnected call, Mason stopped in his tracks, his cup of beer splattering against his feet.

He'd made Harper Davidson cry.

CHAPTER EIGHTEEN

It was wrong to feel relieved.

Bruce had refused to allow her to seek Brianna's paternity confirmation. For four years Harper had carried around a need to know—to be certain that she wasn't lying to herself, or her daughter. To be certain that she wasn't being unfair to Mason. And for four years, Bruce had denied her the right to know.

Shaking her head as she watched her ex-husband catch the little girl who'd just thrown herself out of the car and run toward him, she felt crippled with guilt. Bruce adored Brianna. And she adored him, too. You couldn't see them together and not know that.

So what if he didn't call her often enough? She was four. The grin on his face was huge as he pulled his daughter into his arms and hugged her tight. Brianna sat on his hip, staring at him, her expression serious as she put her little hands on either side of his face and said something.

Feeling another sharp jab of unwanted emotion, Harper hurried toward them. Sara, the counselor at the Stand, had had a talk with Brianna that morning, telling her why it was important to keep a secret about anyone who was at The Lemonade Stand. It wasn't about the person. Or about who she might tell her secret to; it was about the very special place The Lemonade Stand was. Brianna had asked if it was like the North Pole and the elves who were there but couldn't tell anyone because people didn't believe in them.

Harper had teared up as Sara smiled and told the little girl that it *was* something like that. She'd explained how people at The Lemonade Stand did very special work, including Brianna when she smiled at the women and children who lived there. She'd said that Miriam was helping, too, but no one, including her dad or her grandparents, could know about it.

"Hey, there." Bruce came toward her with an arm outstretched, and Harper was thankful again that Sara hadn't singled him out when she'd told Brianna not to tell anyone that Miriam was at the Stand, or that she'd seen her great-grandmother—because then she might have to say where.

"Hi," she said, searching his expression for any sign that anything had changed with him. Searching his demeanor was habit. He leaned in, as though he was going to kiss her, and she turned her head so his lips landed on her cheek. Bruce hadn't tried to kiss her since the morning she'd told him she was filing for divorce.

Mason had said he'd be there, watching. She didn't want him seeing Bruce kiss her.

"What was that about?" she asked, as Brianna looked between the two of them. The last thing Harper needed was for her daughter to suddenly start thinking Mommy and Daddy were in love.

"Sorry." Bruce looked and sounded contrite. "It's just so good to see the two of you. A month is too long. And being here, at the beach again…"

He took Brianna to the beach regularly—always while Harper was with her parents.

Which was where she'd be right then if she wasn't somewhat worried that Bruce had hurt his grandmother. She didn't trust him alone with his own daughter.

That reaction brought with it a guilt that half-strangled her.

"I didn't mean to give a false impression," she said now, "but I know your time is limited. I also know how much the two of you love the beach."

She'd needed an excuse to stay with them—which she couldn't have done at his house without revealing that she knew Miriam was gone. And she'd needed their destination to be as public and safe as it could be.

The holster she had on beneath the flowing tie-dyed tank she was wearing wasn't because she feared Bruce and yet...

What the hell was the matter with her?

She was letting Mason's doubts get to her and that wasn't right. Or fair.

But *right* and *fair* didn't stop her from watching every second as Bruce and Brianna, in swimsuits, ran through the sand and played in the waves. At one point Bruce picked up their daughter and carried her out to greet a bigger wave. Sitting in shorts on her blanket in the sand some distance away, Harper tensed, but sat there, staring—and couldn't help smiling when she heard the little girl's squeal and then her laughter as the water crashed over them.

"Again!" Brie yelled, her feet kicking against him. Bruce's laughter traveled in the air as he walked into another incoming swell, maintaining his balance as the water washed over them.

Brianna had told her how Daddy always took her to the wave. Harper now had an image to go with the story. A lovely image. A loving one.

Brianna didn't clutch Bruce's neck out of fear. She sat easily on his hip, trusting him to keep her safe. She'd never shown any fear where her father was concerned.

She just loved him.

FOR ALL THE trepidation she'd felt, Harper found nothing to be bothered about with Bruce that day. He'd always loved her homemade chicken salad and thanked her for remembering as he devoured the two sandwiches she'd brought for him—telling her that, if anything, they were better than ever.

He couldn't talk about his case, but he told her that he was spending some time in a local resort hotel that week and much preferred the beach to the pool, where he'd been hanging out.

His words, of course, drew her attention to his tanned shoulders and the chest that he'd left exposed as he sat down in his wet trunks to eat. She tried to feel even a tiny bit hungry for him. She hadn't slept with a man in four years. And Bruce was, without question, a head turner. She hadn't missed noticing the number of women who'd been watching him play with Brianna.

And figured he'd had his pick at the resort pool. Had probably *picked* at least one of them; that seemed to be the way he got his *in* when he worked.

All of which had nothing to do with her, but might explain why her libido wanted nothing to do with him.

Brianna held his attention after that, and before Harper had expected, the visit was over and she was free to take her daughter and leave.

Miriam hadn't been mentioned, but despite knowing there was something amiss with the older woman, Harper wouldn't mention her. Miriam hated her, and Harper wasn't allowed in her home, so Bruce never mentioned her, either. Miriam was okay, Bruce knew that much. So why would he voluntarily tell Harper that he wasn't allowed to see her? Why risk giving her any cause to doubt him?

"Assuming things go as I expect with the case, I'll be down sometime next week," he told Harper as he strapped Brianna into her car seat in the back.

"Are you coming to our house to see us, Daddy?" Brianna asked, looking up at him with an expectancy far beyond her years.

Bruce turned to Harper, his eyebrow raised. Asking permission to come to her home?

"You're welcome to pick her up," she said. He was Brianna's father and had a right to see where she lived, where she slept.

He nodded, kissed his daughter and told her, "Yes, baby girl, I'm coming to your house so you can show me your room, just like you said."

"Good deal." She nodded, her little feet kicking the back seat.

Bruce looked at Harper, who'd turned around in the driver's seat to watch, partially to be sure that Brianna was strapped in correctly—the cop in her. He smiled, holding her gaze.

"Thanks for today, Harp. It meant…seriously, thanks." His voice dropped, almost as though it was about to break.

She swallowed back her emotion. Nodded. "We'll see you next week, then?" Her hands gripped the steering wheel tightly—a reaction to the sudden swell of need she felt to take her ex-husband in her arms and assure him that she was on his side.

But she wasn't. She wasn't taking sides.

His grin was quick. Sure. All confident, tough-guy cop, Bruce Thomas. "You can count on it," he said. He told Brie he loved her to the moon, gave her one more hug and closed the door, watching as Harper backed out of the parking space.

A glance in her rearview mirror as she exited the lot told her he was still watching. It kind of comforted her, that studied way he kept an eye on them. They were his family. He'd die for them. Divorced or not, there wasn't a doubt in her mind on that score.

MASON HAD A choice to make. He had to decide whether to follow his brother, to make sure Bruce stayed in town or to follow Harper and see that she got safely out of town. Instinctively drawn to protect Harper and her little one, he listened to the stronger part of him—his mind—and stayed on his brother.

Not that he really thought Bruce would hurt his ex-wife. But he'd never expected Bruce to hurt Gram, either.

And maybe he hadn't, Mason reminded himself.

Until he heard that Grace had clearance and he could take her down to visit Gram, his immediate agenda was Elmer Guthrie. He couldn't question the man yet, but he could investigate him…starting with county records and the purchase of his home. He already knew the man had no criminal history, but that didn't mean he hadn't been involved in previous domestic violence incidents. More went unreported than not.

Still, seeing his brother pull into his garage, Mason passed the turn onto the street, and used voice commands to dial Harper.

"I realize you can't say much with your daughter in the car," he said as soon as she picked up. "I just want to check that you're okay."

"Fine!"

"Did he mention Miriam?"

"Nope."

"Does he ever mention her to you?"

"Nope."

"Anything I need to know?"

"No."

"I called a lab in LA. They'll run the DNA test for me. Three-day turnaround. There's a lab in Santa Raquel…" He named it quickly, not pausing to see if she knew it. "If you leave your samples there, a courier will get them to LA the same day."

"I'd like to have Lynn collect them at the Stand." The resident nurse practitioner. Obviously someone Brianna knew, which could make it easier to get a sample from her without raising a million questions.

"That's fine, too. I can send the courier to her."

"I'll have her courier them to LA. Just send me the address."

She was in the car with an incredibly bright and curious four-year-old. There was only so much conversation they could have. Still, her cooperation meant…probably more than it should. "Thank you."

"You have the right to know."

There was so much not being said. He wished he felt more confident that Brianna's presence was the only reason.

"I'll talk to you later, then."

Ending the call, he felt like a damned voyeur in his brother's life. No matter how deeply he might think he wanted things to be different, the truth was, he didn't belong in Harper's life.

But he still had to have that paternity test done.

The sooner the better.

SHE HADN'T GONE into the Stand that day before leaving town, since Friday was her day off that week. What sounded good to Harper was an afternoon at the beach with her little one. Warm sun on her skin, holiday mood, people having fun, water and sand to occupy Brie's enthusiastic energy—no adult conversation needed. Brianna was already wearing her swimsuit under the play dress she'd had her throw on that morning. They had a blanket and leftover drinks in their cooler from the picnic with Bruce.

And in the end, as she'd taken the Santa Raquel exit with nearly two hours of Brianna's incessant stream of sweet chatter ringing in her ears, the picnic with Bruce was the reason Harper opted for the Stand, then, instead of the beach. She'd had enough beach for that day.

She'd also needed to get DNA swabs done before she faced another long, dark night. Her soul felt torn apart. Her duty to be loyal to Bruce, as Brie's father. And the bone-deep need she had to know who Brie's father really was.

When Mason was out of the picture, showing

no interest, offering no hope that he'd acknowledge Brie as his own, there'd been no alterna-
tive but to honor Bruce. Her own feelings meant
little compared to the welfare of her daughter.

But now...

Now what?

Bruce was a great dad. When he was with
Brianna, she had his full, undivided attention.
There was no doubt the child felt loved by him.
Secure in her life. Plus, he always paid his fair
share, on time, every time. Never squabbled
about covering half of any extra expenses that
came up.

Sitting outside Miriam's in her shorts and
flowing shirt, her loaded gun still at her hip,
Harper tried to focus on the sun's calming
warmth as she kept watch. Thoughts trickled
through anyway.

She'd needed the DNA sample. Hadn't wanted
Brianna to ask what it was or why they were
doing it. Couldn't take a chance that the little
girl would have enough interest to store that information—and share it. Lynn had been the obvious answer. She'd treated Brianna for an ear
infection over the holidays and for various other
childhood ailments through the years. She'd
been due for an ear check. Holding a swab in
her mouth at the same time hadn't fazed her.
She'd been more curious about looking through

the lighted microscope that went in her ear, and listening to her own heartbeat through Lynn's stethoscope.

Because Lynn, understanding the situation, had made certain that she'd captured and held the four-year-old's attention. That was how things were at The Lemonade Stand. Everyone worked together, bent over backward to help each other, did what had to be done.

They all knew the sanctity of their sisterhood saved lives.

Drawing on the strength that thought gave her, Harper experienced a guilt-free second. A brief moment without a knot in her stomach. Then she saw movement inside Miriam's bungalow, which she was watching through the living room window. Tasha, Brianna's guard that afternoon, had taken a seat in Harper's view and was smiling at her.

Harper was grateful to know things were okay inside.

Tasha had been on Miriam duty that afternoon, but when Harper decided to return to the Stand—telling Brianna she could swim in the pool there and after her checkup go see her Gram—she'd made a quick schedule change. Rather than calling in an extra guard, she'd taken the outdoor duty herself. Her officers were taxed enough.

Maybe the round-the-clock Miriam watch was overkill. She didn't think so. The second they let up, Miriam would be out of there. But she wasn't going anywhere with someone on guard outside.

If that was what it took to possibly save a life, to save a woman from further abuse, she'd gladly guard her all day every day.

She could imagine Miriam's vitriolic reaction if she knew that Harper had just taken Brie for a paternity test.

And yet, Mason was her grandson, too. It shouldn't make a difference. But she knew it would. During the year Brianna had lived with Bruce after her marriage, the year Mason hadn't been around once, Miriam had never taken his side. Even when Oscar had suggested having Mason over for Christmas dinner, Miriam, with one look at Bruce, had quietly told him she'd rather do their dinner with him separately. She'd made some comment about the timing for him being off due to the job he was on.

Harper hadn't thought much of it at the time—not knowing about the "agreement." But now she wondered... Had Bruce said something to Miriam about Harper and Mason, in spite of his promise that he wouldn't if Mason stayed away from them?

All that time she'd thought Mason really *was*

just working—married to his job—putting the job first. Oscar had seemed to think the same.

She'd known Bruce wouldn't have wanted Mason around her, of course, but she hadn't thought he'd told anyone else that. And there'd been a little part of her that suspected Mason had chosen to stay away because of her.

She'd only been with the family for a year...

But *had* Miriam known? And yet, she'd always been so loving with Harper. Until she'd left Bruce. Miriam wouldn't have been like that, doting on her, if she'd known.

After the divorce, Miriam had suddenly hated her.

What if Bruce had told her then?

Mason's words, saying Bruce always spun things in his favor, to make himself the victim, to gain sympathy and therefore power, came back to her. She wanted to push them away. Keep an open mind.

She'd already betrayed Bruce by sleeping with Mason. And now...after five years of hating what she'd done to the man she'd sworn to be faithful to for the rest of her life, here she was, betraying him again.

She'd taken their daughter for the DNA test he'd expressly refused.

Mason had a right to know—just as she'd told him.

But the truth was, she'd also agreed because Mason had unknowingly given her the opportunity, the means, to do what she'd wanted to do all along. What she'd needed to do.

From the moment she found out she was pregnant, in her heart of hearts she'd wondered if that one incredible night had given her a life-long gift. If maybe, despite her attempts to reassure herself all these years, there *hadn't* been a condom…

It was so unlike her to have sex without protection from disease. She hadn't let Bruce make love to her without one until they'd gotten engaged.

The knot in her stomach became a cramp.

Only the thought of the test showing a negative for Mason eased the cramp. What a relief it would be to know that Bruce really was his daughter's biological father.

What a relief it would be from the debilitating guilt that had been attacking her for far too long.

CHAPTER NINETEEN

MASON SAW THE text from Harper, telling him
their samples had been collected and picked up
by the courier, just as he was pulling into the
parking lot of a coffee shop on the outskirts of
Albina. He'd never been to the place.

Bruce had suggested it.

There was no way he could tell Harper he was
meeting his brother. And yet, it felt…wrong to
do it without telling her. As though the two of
them—he and Harper—were a team.

They weren't.

He was the investigator—albeit on the quiet
and unpaid; she was a witness. And now, Bruce
was a witness, too—as well as a person of interest.

Used to going into interviews without knowing what to expect, he had his professional barriers firmly in place as he approached the shop.
Bruce's car was in the lot, as he'd expected it to
be. His brother always arrived early. He picked
out the meeting place. Kept the advantage—and
control—in any way he could.

The shop was bustling up front and had a patio out back where a guy could make a drug deal without being overheard. No cameras. No electronic devices at all. Just an old, run-down patio with chairs. Didn't face the beach. And you had to go inside to use the john.

Just the sort of place an undercover cop would need to know about. His brother had told him to walk through and meet him outside. He stopped to order coffee, first.

He didn't really want it, but he wanted to order it. Simply because it hadn't been one of Bruce's instructions. He didn't kid himself about that.

Nor did he doubt that his brother would catch the significance.

If they were going to play cat and mouse, if Bruce truly wanted to challenge him, Mason would have to be the cat on this one.

"Hey!" Bruce stood as Mason pushed through the door to the patio five minutes early, coffee in hand. The heat coming through the cardboard cup was pretty intense, but that wasn't the reason he set it down on the first table he came to. He did that because of the hand his brother was reaching out to him.

They shook and Bruce pulled him in for a hug, their hands still between them.

Affection. Man-to-man.

Mason had to admit that the greeting was better than any he'd been prepared for.

"Good to see you," Bruce said, still holding his hand as he drew back, looking Mason in the eye. The affection was there, too, in his brother's gaze.

Soaking him. Sucking him in.

Aware, and yet...not as tense, Mason picked up his cup and followed Bruce to the far table. His brother had said no cameras. Didn't mean there weren't any. Was Bruce playing it up for someone watching?

He used to be able to tell. Reading Bruce had been one of his gifts.

The affection felt completely real.

"I can't tell you how relieved I am," Bruce said as Mason sat.

"How so?" Their conversation was like sitting on the edge of beckoning water, but not falling in.

"Look, we both know as soon as you called telling me Gram's X-rays showed abuse that I had to be the first suspect, and that you had to investigate."

He nodded. No point in not acknowledging it.

"I figure since you were at the house, you'd have some idea of what's been going on... I've done all of my own checking, but you're a better investigator than I am."

True.

Mason sipped at the coffee he still didn't want.

"I knew I didn't do it, but you had to find that out on your own. Same thing any good cop would've done."

Mason nodded again. The back of the shop opened out onto a field of golden wheat-like growth. In the shining sun, it gave the impression of sparkling gold. Probably just weeds. Things weren't always what they seemed.

"Now that we're through with that part, we can take this on together. You said you wanted to talk to me. I'm ready."

No questions about Gram. Shouldn't there have been, if Bruce truly believed they were on the same side? Why not ask where she was? Or how she was?

"First." Bruce maintained conversational control when Mason didn't immediately respond. "How's Gram?"

About time he asked.

"Doing okay," he said, taking another sip of the dark coffee. She didn't know that Harper had just submitted samples for a paternity test.

Neither did his brother.

Mason wasn't sure how Gram would feel about that, but he was positive Bruce would be livid.

He'd thought, when Bruce was growing up,

that there'd come a time when his brother would mature and they'd be equals—friends, even. Trusted brothers fighting crime.

If he was honest with himself he'd admit that he'd still like that.

And yet he saw the implausibility of it. The night he'd slept with Harper had ruined that chance forever. No matter who'd fathered Brianna.

He'd taken Bruce's woman. His fiancée. Admittedly his brother had screwed up royally and Harper had owed him nothing at that point—but Mason had gone after Harper on Bruce's behalf.

"What do you know about Elmer Guthrie?" he asked abruptly.

Bruce shrugged nonchalantly, then raised his brow as he shook his head. "He's an older guy. Moved in down the street a year or two back. Quiet. Retired army."

He was widowed. Had a daughter who'd died of kidney disease three years before. No grandchildren. Was active with the local veterans' administration. And had a decent enough pension to be comfortable for the rest of his life.

All of which could hide another side of the man. The fighting side.

"You ever see him outside? Hear neighbors talk to him? Any run-ins?"

Bruce didn't answer immediately. Mason didn't like that.

"We're talking about Gram's abuse?" his brother asked, gaze speculative.

"We're talking about Elmer Guthrie."

Bruce leaned forward. If he hadn't been Mason's little brother, Mason might have been intimidated by the look in his eyes. "You think he was at the house Monday night when I left for the bar? You think he hurt Gram?"

Even if that was what Mason was thinking, he wasn't ready to tell his brother as much.

"He must have seen me leave," Bruce said next.

"Has he been to the house before?"

Bruce sat back again. Threw a hand in the air. "He and Gram met a while ago. She'd dropped some mail when he was walking past. He stopped and picked it up for her. She had him over for dinner a time or two, said he was all alone in that house of his. That was it, as far as I know."

It was more than either Bruce or Gram had told him before.

Mason's puzzle pieces floated more clearly into view. Not settling yet, but hovering.

"Why would you think he'd seen you leave? Had you given him some kind of indication that he wasn't welcome? That you'd have to be away for him to visit?" He might suck as a brother, but he was good at what he did—zeroing in on the nuances.

"Of course not." Bruce leaned back, his ankle over his knee. "It's the timing. Based on the timing you described, he must have arrived just after I left. And if he had some bone to pick with Gram, which would be indicated by the broken arm and the bruises on her face that you told me about, he'd have waited until he knew she was alone. He's not dumb enough to mess with me."

Bruce was a good cop, too. His theory had merit.

"You have the feeling he'd mess with anyone?" he asked. He was after a character assessment. More than background checks could give him. But it wouldn't be as much as he'd get as soon as he had a warrant to question the guy.

"You never can tell." Bruce's remark was fair. The personal sting Mason felt was likely his own doing.

"Our business makes that clear, doesn't it?" he returned.

Bruce nodded. Mason wished he was in Santa Raquel, at the bar with Harper.

She'd sent in their samples. So had he.

Behind Bruce's back.

Just like the sex they'd had.

"Beyond those few dinners, you're not aware of any association between the two?"

Jutting out his chin, Bruce shook his head.

"How long ago was the last dinner?"

"A month. Maybe two."

"Any special occasion?"

Bruce shook his head again. "It was a Sunday," he said. "I remember because Gram made a roast."

"Which she only does on Sundays," Mason finished, feeling a moment of normalcy.

"Every Sunday," Bruce added, with a grin.

His little brother didn't blame Mason for investigating him. He would've done the same himself. He'd said so.

Mason was tempted to ask Bruce to meet him for a beer later. To test the brother waters again. Five years was a long time. Maybe Miriam's injuries were enough to bring them together. Harper had thought so…that first day…

"You talk to Harper?" Bruce's question came as Mason wrestled with a beer request that wouldn't quite come out.

A loaded question.

"Look, I figured you would. You'd have to if you're any kind of investigator and I know you're one of the best."

"Briefly," he said, his gaze steady. Bruce

was completely correct. Mason had contacted Harper because he'd had no choice.

Bruce's expression held no malice. He didn't ask what Harper had said to him. Didn't seem the least bit worried about it.

And had no cause to be. She'd never, for one second, considered that Bruce might be guilty of abusing Gram.

Neither had she made any move on Mason.

"You talking to her again?" This time his brother's glance was somewhat guarded. Mason would've been concerned if it hadn't been.

And he was prepared. The question was one he'd planned for.

"I will if I need to," he said. "If not, then no."

If something else presented itself, requiring him to bring in a witness a second time, he had the right to do so. The obligation to do so.

"Do you anticipate needing to?"

As a witness to an investigation Bruce was out of line now. And he knew it. But he needed more—and deserved it, too.

"You're her daughter's father and she's loyal to you." The words were difficult for him, but true. "Harper and I have no personal business, nor has there been any indication that either of us would allow there to be." They *wouldn't* allow it. He had no doubt of that. Wanting...now that was a different matter, but Mason had learned years ago that, as the song said, you couldn't always get what you wanted.

In fact, more often than not, you couldn't. From the time Bruce was born, Mason's growing up had consisted of not getting what he wanted. Made him a better person.

A stronger, more reliable, decent man.

"So... Gram's really okay?" Bruce asked him, eye to eye. Brother to brother.

He nodded. Wanted to ask about Grace, but didn't. Not yet. Not until he got the two women together. Saw for himself how they were without Bruce in the picture.

Not until he had some time to process this first meeting.

He'd opened the door with his brother. Grace could wait for another talk.

"You want to do this again, in a day or so?" he asked.

"Sure."

Bruce stood. "Is she...close by? I mean, I'd like to reassure her that I'm here for her. That I miss her and will do everything I can to help you get this guy."

"She knows that."

"I can't believe she's doing well being away from home. She's always been so protective of her space, wanting things done her way."

"She's on vacation."

Bruce seemed to start at that. "You sent her on a cruise or something?"

Yeah, *or something*. Mason nodded. His brother seemed to relax then, dropping all facades. "Thank God," he said, his voice a bit gravelly, his eyes glistening with emotion. "I was afraid the jerk had hurt her worse than you said, that she was in a hospital. I checked locally, but I know how these cases work, and until you cleared me, no one was going to give it to me straight..."

Bruce was almost babbling now. Like the vulnerable kid he'd been inside all those years ago. The kid Mason had sworn to protect.

"She's got a cast on below the elbow," he said now. "Otherwise she's fine and running the show like always."

Bruce smiled as he looked at Mason. "Thank God," he said again.

And that was it. They walked to their cars together, Mason throwing his half-full coffee cup in the trash on the way. Shook hands with another shoulder-to-shoulder hug. Agreed to meet in a day or two, got in their respective vehicles and drove away.

Mason had some calls to return. A new text. Work waiting.

He needed a beer.

CHAPTER TWENTY

GRACE'S CLEARANCE CAME through just after seven Friday evening. Harper had been waiting for an email and had checked while sitting with a bathed and jammied Brianna, who was eating popcorn in front of one of her favorite Disney movies.

Harper was off duty and could have waited until morning. But if Miriam had been any other resident she wouldn't have waited. So she didn't in this case, either.

After today's lunch at the beach, a swim in the pool and helping her grandmother dust, Brianna was falling asleep with her hand in the popcorn bowl. Harper picked up her phone.

Sent her second text of the day to Mason.

He hadn't responded to the first. Maybe he wouldn't respond to the second until she was back at work in the morning. It wasn't as if he and Grace were going to drive to Santa Raquel that night.

Still…he could call her. Plan to drive down in

the morning. He hadn't let her know, which was why she texted, telling him about the clearance.

For the first fifteen minutes afterward, she was on tenterhooks. Watching her phone—and her daughter's drowsy eyelids. After that, she just watched Brianna. As soon as the little girl was truly asleep, she carried her up the stairs, tucked her into bed and kissed her good-night, then turned on the monitor and headed back downstairs. Brianna didn't stir once.

Her mom had told her that she'd slept just as soundly as a kid.

Not anymore.

That was part of being a parent, her mother had also told her. Missing her parents, she called them as she settled back in the living room with the partially eaten bowl of popcorn in her lap, remembering, when they didn't answer, that Friday night was when they played cards at church.

The popcorn wasn't that good. She dumped it in the trash and got some cheese and crackers instead. She poured herself a glass of wine. She decided to turn on the TV and tried to find something to watch.

Five minutes later, she found herself staring at she knew not what. Some show. Maybe a movie. A woman was crying and, although Harper had no idea what had upset her, she could feel her pain.

She'd missed what was going on. She'd been too busy imagining a world where Mason was Brie's father. Part of their lives.

But Bruce wasn't in that world, and he was Brie's father in the ways that counted. No matter what the tests showed, they couldn't cut him out.

Would he cut himself out?

Not if he didn't know.

Would Mason insist on telling him?

Her stomach clenched and she took a sip of wine, assuring herself that Mason *wasn't* Brie's father. Bruce was. The test would prove that conclusively, and the worst pain she and Mason had created that night five years ago would be eased. The doubt would be gone.

She'd have good news for Bruce and he'd forgive her for allowing the test to happen behind his back.

And Mason...

Could she insist that he have a role in Brie's life? That he have the chance to be a real uncle?

Did he want to be?

If he did, would she let him?

She had to, didn't she?

She'd never made an agreement to stay away from Mason. Would never have agreed to that. Which was probably why Bruce hadn't told her about it.

He'd manipulated the situation, just like Mason had said. But could she blame him?

What if Mason *was* Brie's father? Bruce would never forgive her for allowing the test. Some things just weren't excusable. Like sleeping with his brother in the first place.

Not that Bruce had ever thrown it in her face. As he'd promised when he'd begged her to marry him, they'd never mentioned that night again.

If he wasn't Brie's father, did he have to know?

Did Brie?

At some point, maybe, but...

Her phone rang and she scooped it off the table, thinking it would be her mom calling her back. She needed to talk to her. To learn what she thought about Harper agreeing to the paternity test...

Mason. The caller was Mason.

Pleasure rushed through her and then was gone. She wasn't ready to talk to him, afraid of what he might require of her. And what he might not care enough to ask about.

How could you want something and dread it with equal fierceness?

"Hello?" She had to answer. He'd be calling to make arrangements for Grace's visit.

"I was notified that the courier picked up my sample an hour ago." At eight o'clock on Friday night? The clock was ticking. Unless...maybe the lab didn't work weekends. Maybe the three days would start on Monday.

She took another gulp of wine.

"We could hear as early as Sunday, no later than Monday."

No! "You said three days."

"That was the max."

Then he should've said it was max. Harper's agitation was aimed at him, but she knew that wasn't fair. Stress tightened the skin on her face, the muscles in her neck. Excitement bred butterflies in her stomach.

Dread took her voice away.

She was a damned mess and had no idea what to do about it.

She'd get off the phone and go to her private gym.

And think about work.

"Did you talk to Grace?"

"Yes. I'm picking her up at seven. We should be there around nine. Will you let Gram know?"

Did every single thing he needed from her have to be so uncomfortable? So hard?

"Of course." It was her job.

"We also need to talk about what we're going to do if the test comes back positive."

We. What *we're* going to do.

Sitting up straight, Harper looked at the line

separating white from reddened skin at the edge of her shorts. She'd gotten some sun at the beach. And the pool.

We.

"Do I have a choice in the matter?"

"Of course you have a choice." He said the words so matter-of-factly. "You're her mother, Harper. Ultimately all the choices are yours."

For the first time that day, she felt like herself. She recognized her usual sense of control, of being strong and capable.

She hadn't noticed it missing until it had returned, and she was confused by that.

When had it left?

And why?

She reassured herself that she was in control of her own choices, her own life. With full custody of Brianna she was even in control there—until Brianna grew up and took control of her own life.

"If you're her father, you have rights, too," she said softly. And took a breath against the sharp sting of fear left in the wake of those words. Looking around, as though the room was bugged and someone would come bursting in on her for having dared to utter such a blasphemy, she lifted her wineglass with a shaking hand.

She took a sip. Regained control.

"If you aren't, I'd appreciate your letting me

tell him we did the test." Bruce would feel less betrayed if she explained why she'd participated in a test he'd refused—to put his doubts to rest.

"Agreed."

Silence hung on the line. Was he waiting for her to say more? Set more guidelines?

"If you are…" What? She didn't know what. Her body trembled, only she wasn't cold. She pulled Brie's fleece blanket off the arm of the couch anyway and wrapped it around her bare shoulders.

"I won't interfere with your parenting, Harper. But I'll need you to consider a way to work me into her life."

"Bruce is the only father she's known. I can't just take him away from her."

"I wouldn't want that."

Okay. Good. And yet…he *should* want it. If the paternity test was positive, he would already have lost four years of his daughter's life.

"What would you want, then?"

"As I said earlier, I'll insist on financial responsibility—past and future."

"I don't need your money for the four years you missed."

"I have it to spare, and it's something I'd need to do. Put it in a college fund, if nothing else."

He'd mentioned that once before. "Okay."

They'd agreed on two things already. If he

wasn't Brie's dad, she'd tell Bruce. And if he was, he'd be financially involved in their lives.

Feeling a bit better, she said, "Obviously, you'll spend time with her." Retrieving the wine bottle from the kitchen, with the blanket still wrapped around herself, she poured herself another half glass.

"I'd need that, yes."

Thoughts started to sort themselves out. "If the test comes back positive, we need to have a meeting with Sara," she said. "She'll help us figure out how to handle things with Brie." Of course. Why hadn't she thought of that before now?

Because all she'd seen was Bruce.

She wanted to know what Mason was hoping for—if he welcomed the idea of being the father of her child. If their night together meant something special to him, after all…

Would they become some kind of family? The idea of Mason being in regular contact was…

Forbidden territory.

He might regret the night and everything that could have resulted from it. Might be hoping to find out he was off the hook.

It would be easier that way—if he hoped Brianna was Bruce's child.

Calm settled over her as excitement dissipated. And fear dwindled, too.

Her feelings for Mason didn't. Even now, thinking about her child being his, she got those hidden, secret feelings again. The ones she'd had from the first time they'd met. The ones that had driven her that night she'd spent with him.

She'd been vulnerable, unable to deny what she'd felt deep inside.

She hadn't been herself.

"I had a meeting with Bruce today," he said.

Tension took hold again. Just that quickly. Was Bruce angry with her?

"I think it's inappropriate to divulge specifics of the investigation, since charges could be filed, but I thought you should know there's a potential suspect who's not him."

She almost dropped the phone. So Bruce *wasn't* the bad guy she'd been trying to find in her memories? He was the man she knew him to be?

A huge breath escaped her and she lay back. "Did Bruce bring him to your attention?"

Because if he had…couldn't it be more of what Mason had been telling her about him— that he concocted half-truths to make himself the victimized one? To gain a sympathetic response?

"No."

"Wow." What a relief. "Does this mean Miriam can go home soon?"

"Possibly. We have to either get her to press charges, or prove what we suspect, or else she'll be right back where she was."

"So…he lives close by?"

"Possibly."

She could hardly believe it.

"Why wouldn't she have told you about him?"

"That's part of what we have yet to find out."

"'Cause it's hard to imagine her putting up with someone hurting her and just staying quiet about it." Hard to believe anyone would dare lift a hand to her, knowing he'd have to answer to Bruce.

And to Mason. Unless…

"He's not another cop, is he? Retired, maybe?"

"No."

"You think Grace knows about him?"

"Possibly."

Just…wow. Such good news.

Bruce hadn't done it.

She'd known that.

She'd allowed Mason to plant doubts in her mind anyway. To the point of not leaving Bruce alone with Brianna.

Another in the list of ways she'd let Bruce down. Or felt she had.

But thank God Mason hadn't succeeded in turning her completely against him.

Now, if only the paternity test came back negative...

Life could get back to normal.

She wanted that. She really did. Bruce would know for certain that he was Brianna's father. She'd know. He'd forgive her for doing the test behind his back. And would never realize she'd doubted him about Miriam.

All would be well.

So why, when Mason rang off with a casual "see you in the morning," did she feel like crying her eyes out?

CHAPTER TWENTY-ONE

GRACE HAD BROUGHT along a feathery-looking yarn project to work on during the drive. In light green capri pants and a floral short-sleeved T-shirt to match, she sat next to him, fingers flying with her crochet hook, stopping every few seconds to pull on the yarn. She'd said she was making matching scarves for all the women in a choral group she performed with. As he entered the freeway that would lead him straight to Santa Raquel, he wondered what kind of choral outfit would go with hot pink and black, but didn't ask.

He also wondered how many of those little feather droppings he'd have in his car at day's end, but didn't really care. That was what carwash vacuums were for.

He'd rather think about feathers and choral fashions than DNA tests that could come back that afternoon. He had contacts at the lab who were making his test a priority—coming in on a Saturday to handle things for him.

Trying to imagine the mammoth ways his life

would change if he found out he *was* a father put him in a place he didn't want to be. Unsettled. Unknowing. Not in control.

Thinking about having a daughter, Harper's daughter, didn't bear thinking about, either. No matter how much that might complete him in his imaginary life—the life where everything and everyone was ideal, perfect, idyllic—it didn't fit with the real world.

Because of Bruce. He and his brother had met again the night before. Late. Bruce had been out on the job and then called Mason, telling him he had something to show him.

His brother had turned up after midnight at the designated bar, carrying a flash drive. He said he hadn't thought to look at it before, certain that Gram had fallen off her stepladder, just like she'd said. The ladder had been in the kitchen when he returned home. And Gram never lied.

To Bruce it had been an accident, plain and simple. In his opinion, the real problem was keeping Gram safe from herself—and from the effects of aging.

The flash drive had been from a hidden security camera Bruce had installed outside their home. Made sense, with him being a cop—even more sense in case his cover was ever blown. It was the kind he could watch from his phone so he'd know if there was anyone lurking around when he wasn't there to protect Gram.

He'd had a few inside the house, too, for the same reason. So he'd know if Gram ever fell or needed help when he wasn't there.

That had made sense, too. As Bruce had said, accidents could happen at any time and if Gram couldn't get to a phone, who would know?

An alert on his phone could just save her life.

Gram had found the inside cameras and, when she'd objected to them, telling Bruce they were an invasion of her privacy, he'd taken them out. She hadn't been aware of the one outside. When he was off duty, or Miriam wasn't home, Bruce didn't keep the app live with notices because his phone would go into alert mode every time the wind blew. He hadn't bothered to check the app.

Until after his talk with Mason. When, for the first time, he started to believe that Gram really had been abused.

The flash drive showed Elmer Guthrie walking up Gram's drive less than five minutes after Bruce had left that Monday evening. The evening of her "accident." And it showed him leaving again just before Gram's car pulled out of the drive. Presumably on her way to urgent care.

That was enough to get him the warrant to question Elmer at his home. He'd do it as soon as he'd delivered Grace back home.

"You ever hear Gram mention an Elmer Guthrie?" The SUV was on cruise control. GPS said they had an hour and a half until they were at The Lemonade Stand.

"No. Who is he?" Grace's fingers stilled as she studied him and he gave her a brief glance before returning his eyes to the road, shaking his head.

"You'll need to ask her."

Silence fell again. Mason turned on a classical music station, thinking she'd like it, his thoughts once again on his brother. People all had different perspectives, based on how they saw the world, how they perceived events that happened, their belief systems, their upbringings. Maybe Bruce really did see things as he said they were. Maybe his versions of the truth weren't deliberately misleading or manipulative reframing for self-gain.

Could be he was just a bit needy when it came to those he loved, never fully believing they'd love him back, or as much as he loved them. Mason wasn't a shrink, but he knew enough to figure that Bruce's behavior, his reframing of certain truths, could be how he really saw the world.

Mason had listened to enough confessions in interrogation rooms to understand how people's minds could play with them. And now Bruce might have to hear that he wasn't Brianna's father. Mason could only imagine what that kind of blow would do to the guy.

Unless… Bruce didn't *have* to know. Did he?

Except that if Mason was Brianna's father, the child had a right to know. At least when she was old enough for it to matter. At a minimum, Mason was going to be financially responsible for her. That much had already been decided, he reminded himself.

And what about Harper? Did anyone ever consider what *she* needed? What was best for her? She'd never given any indication of how she'd feel if he was the father of her child.

She'd never said a word to suggest that some part of her would be glad. Or that she had any regard for him at all. If you discounted the silent messages passing between them the night they'd been at the bar near her home. And, again, when they'd worked out together.

He had a strong sense that she wanted him.

Was he, like his brother, reframing the world to fit his own self-image? Thinking Harper wanted him because he wanted her? And even if it *was* true…he couldn't start anything with her, make his little brother watch them together.

But God, he wanted her! Worse than he'd ever wanted anything in his life.

So, if minds conjured up their own perceptions, what about the whole Gram thing? Had he been so quick to jump on Bruce as the guilty party because some part of him needed to find fault with his brother, so he wouldn't have to feel bad about wanting his brother's wife?

Ex-wife.

Could it be possible that Mason was far more disloyal than he'd realized?

"You ever ask Gram to go skydiving with you?" The question burst into the silence as Mason, desperate to get his mind under control, focused on the woman at his side, on the reason they were together.

Elmer on a camera was circumstantial evidence. They were going to need more than that to convince the court to take any action against him, any action to protect Gram. Mason knew he was a pretty damned good interrogator, showing his suspects the pieces of the puzzle and how they all fit together, but he couldn't count on the older man to confess what he'd done.

Gram wasn't talking, but even Mason knew that if anyone could get through to Gram, it would be Grace. Her longtime best friend. While Gram was away from whatever influence had turned her against Grace to begin with.

Why Elmer would have cause to do that remained to be seen. Could be as simple as Gram not wanting anyone to know that she'd fallen prey to someone's abuse; from what he'd gleaned that week, shame and self-blame were common reasons a victim didn't speak out. Gram had always prided herself on being a strong, independent woman...

Grace hadn't answered. She was staring at him.

"What?" he asked.

"That last time she and I talked... I told her about a woman who'd gone skydiving for her ninetieth birthday. She accused me of trying to convince her to do things she didn't feel comfortable doing."

Because someone else was trying to convince her to do things she felt uncomfortable doing? Elmer Guthrie, for instance?

"I thought at the time that she was just picking a fight with me, you know, because I'd put too much pressure on her about how Bruce was mistreating her." Grace paused again, her fingers and the puff of yarn still in her lap. "I blame myself," she said softly. "I know Miriam better than anyone. Love her as much as I've ever loved anyone. If she was already being pressured, I should've been the one who was supportive and understanding—not doing the exact same thing to her."

Words telling her not to blame herself on the

tip of his tongue, Mason didn't get a chance to speak before she continued.

"It's just… Miriam and I…we could always say what's on our minds. We're both kind of bossy women, in case you hadn't noticed."

He grinned at that.

"Strong and independent," she went on. "We like things done our way. I just never… I should've known…"

"How *could* you have known? None of us did."

"But… I should've been there for her."

"You're here for her now."

"Does she know I'm coming?" Grace hadn't asked when he'd issued the invitation.

"Yes." He could feel the older woman's gaze on him. "If you want my opinion, and it's only my opinion, I think she really wants to see you. She hardly argued at all when I made the suggestion."

"She didn't argue?"

"Not much. She did have a stipulation, though." He glanced at her, saw her frown.

"What is it? Not that I care. I'd run barefoot on hot tar at this point if it would help her."

"Don't mention skydiving."

"Seriously?" Grace's mouth hung open. "Seriously?" She started in with the yarn and fingers again. "I need to have a talk with that woman."

Exactly what he'd been hoping for.

HARPER WAS WAITING for Mason Saturday morning. They'd planned that he'd drop Grace off in the family visiting room and then come back to her office while the two women had their visit. Miriam's guard would be close by, but she'd been told to give them as much privacy as she could while still doing her job.

After some morning delays at the the Stand, they'd finally settled on a ten o'clock meeting for the ladies. She'd expected him at 10:05. She was in uniform, of course, since she was working, but had put on eyeliner and sprayed her hair so it looked the way her hairdresser had meant it to. Sitting behind her desk, she'd unfastened the top button on her shirt, thinking…she didn't know what…but refastened it immediately.

A cop didn't disgrace the uniform on duty. And she had no reason whatsoever to appear more feminine to Mason.

She'd been okay until the point she'd taken Brianna to day care; she'd kept herself firmly in check, focusing on what mattered most. Brianna's well-being. Her own job. Having a workable relationship with Bruce—for Brianna's well-being. She'd even managed a decent night's sleep, reminding herself every time she woke up that all would be as it was meant to be and then falling back asleep. But standing in the doorway of the day care, wondering if, when she picked up her daughter that evening, Brie would have a different father, she'd come undone.

That had been fifteen minutes of undoneness. It was ten after ten now. Where the hell was he?

He'd indicated he had some things to discuss with her. After her phone call from Bruce that morning, she knew she had something to discuss with him, too.

From what Bruce had said, and Mason's comment the night before had alluded to it, Miriam's case might be wrapped up soon. At least they had a solid perp now. It depended on how quickly Mason could put enough evidence together to do something about it.

It could just be a matter of Grace somehow breaking through to Miriam. Getting her to testify as to who'd hurt her; that would be all it took. Mason could leave and…

He might be the father of her child.

Bruce had sounded so good that morning, telling her Mason had told him he'd questioned her about the case. She could hear the swelling of emotion in his tone as he'd told her his brother had mentioned how loyal she'd been to Bruce, certain that he hadn't hurt Miriam. He'd thanked her.

Told her he loved her.

How much was he going to love her if he

found out that she'd assisted Mason with a paternity test and Mason was Brie's father?

Panic seized her and she stood, needing out with nowhere to go. Mason could be there any minute. She had to get hold of herself. Be the in-control adult woman she knew herself to be.

Disallow the drama that would take control if she was weak enough, or foolish enough, to let it.

Nodding, she raised a hand to her chest, fingers checking her top button just to make sure she'd refastened it. That her collar was straight.

The DNA test was going to prove that Bruce was Brianna's father. Miriam would go home. Mason would go back to his life. Her life and Brianna's would continue as they were, with perhaps a little more genuine warmth between Harper and Bruce.

End of story.

Mason knocked once. Waited for her to admit him. She headed toward the door, to open it. Stopped. That would have her toe to toe with him for a second at least. Their eyes would meet up close and… She returned to the chair behind her desk as she'd originally planned, hiding her shaking hands by keeping them below the desktop and plastering a work-face smile on her lips.

"Come in," she called when she was ready.

He'd been running his fingers through his

hair. Short as it was, she shouldn't have been able to tell, but she remembered, far too clearly, how it had looked that night when she'd run her own fingers along his scalp. Many, many times.

In light-colored pants and a short-sleeved olive green shirt he seemed ready for vacation. Or to go on a date.

No, he was in normal Mason work attire.

"How'd it go?" she asked him as he took a seat, as though Grace and Miriam were the only things on her mind. As they should've been.

"Good, actually," he said. His grin warmed her private places.

She couldn't tell anyone that. Ever.

"There was a long moment when they stood there looking at each other, neither one of them saying anything, and then, just as I was getting ready to take them both by the hand and guide them to the same table, they were walking toward each other and hugging."

He was still grinning.

Mason happy was an unexpected aphrodisiac. Something she'd only seen briefly…that night, of course, in his bed.

The couple of times she'd met him before that night, he'd never seemed happy. She hadn't really considered that before. Another thought to file away.

"So, you think Grace will be able to get through to her?"

"I think they're going to be friends again and that's what Gram needs more than anything right now."

She agreed. But they had to find a way to keep her safe so she could go home again.

And life could return to normal.

She sat there, blinking as the thoughts ran through her mind. When had she ever wanted the status quo as a permanent life?

When had she started to feel *grateful* for it?

"I talked to Bruce this morning." She'd meant to wait until after he'd said whatever he'd come to tell her. Till he'd had his say. She'd meant to see what, or how much, he was going to tell her. She'd barely made it past hello.

"He called," she said, when Mason's eyes narrowed.

He waited without speaking. She tried to read him, but got nothing. Except that she wanted to feel those arms around her again. Those lips against her. Him inside her.

But mostly, just to feel his arms around her right then. Like she was some needy woman who had to be comforted? she asked herself in disgust. Who needed a man to help her feel secure?

She knew that was hogwash. Even on that

long-ago night, being with him hadn't been about being taken care of. Or security.

It had been lust, pure and simple.

Okay, maybe more than lust. And maybe not so pure *or* simple. But the last thing she'd felt was that she needed any kind of protection. She'd wanted him to take care of her, all right. Just as she'd wanted to take care of *him*. In a way that brought both of them satisfaction.

"He told me the two of you are working together now. That he has a tape that showed an older male neighbor visiting Miriam after he'd left that night. The night she ended up in urgent care. I'm assuming that's the second suspect you mentioned?"

Elbows on the arms of his chair, fingers steepled in front of his face, he continued to watch her. And bowed his head once in acknowledgment.

He seemed to be closing himself off, so she pressed him. "Is he right about that?"

"I wasn't going to mention details," he said. "I don't want this investigation to be tarnished in any way."

"I'm not just a witness, I'm a family member," she said. "My young daughter is in that home with Miriam, or was, on a regular basis." She knew she sounded defensive. And maybe she was. Because she wanted Mason to trust her the way Bruce did.

No. No, that wasn't right.

Was it?

It *felt* right.

She wanted Mason to regard her with as much…confidence as Bruce did. Wanted him to know she'd have his back, too.

"I agreed to the paternity test without any argument at all." She hadn't decided to say the words aloud. They just happened.

Dropping his hands to his knees, Mason's entire demeanor changed. The assessing look softened. "I'm not following you. Did you tell Bruce about it? Did he say something I need to know about?"

"No!" Of course she hadn't told Bruce. She was praying that when she did talk to him, it would be with good news. Or that she and Mason would agree not to ever tell him— although she hadn't quite worked out the logistics of that, figuring in Brianna's eventual right to know.

"I didn't tell him," she said. "I just…want you to realize you can trust me. That I play things straight. I didn't think Bruce had hurt Miriam so I told you that, but if I'd thought for one second he had, I'd tell you that, too."

Bruce had been so moved by her loyalty. His

emotion, rather than softening her toward him as it usually did, had cramped her. She hadn't really been loyal. She'd simply told the truth. Or some of it…

The light in Mason's eyes had her looking for his grin again. It didn't appear. But she felt better.

"You asked for a paternity test. Granting it was the right thing to do."

She hoped that was true. That she hadn't just given in because she was in love with him…

Oh. God, help her.

She hadn't just…

She was a straight shooter.

Was she in love with Mason Thomas?

CHAPTER TWENTY-TWO

STARING AT MASON, feeling her world darken and close in on her, Harper couldn't immediately deny the possibility that she was in love with him.

"Yes, the neighbor is a suspect." He chose that second to finally address her initial query regarding Bruce's accuracy about the case. It felt as if hours had passed since then.

"I wouldn't say Bruce and I are working together," he continued while she attempted to get breath into her lungs. And grasp what he was saying. "We're talking. And doing better than we have in years. But this investigation is mine."

Yes, the investigation. The world righted itself.

"I never doubted the case was yours." Mason was as good a cop as they came. Not that Bruce wasn't. But Bruce being a good cop meant subterfuge…

Maybe that was true for Mason, too.

Bruce seemed to think he and his brother were on the same wavelength when it came to work. That he was just like Mason. And had learned everything he knew from his older brother. Was proud of the fact, actually.

"He told me to ask you about Gwen coming to your house after midnight on Tuesday, I think it was." Bruce had said Tuesday. He'd been certain of that.

The night he'd been in the bar with her, when he'd told her about Bruce sleeping with Gwen, not a perp. About him being at a bachelor party, not at work. Mason had driven back to Albina that night and then had Gwen over?

"He said he'd intended to mention it to you himself, but forgot."

Mason's eyes narrowed again. If he'd been anyone else, she might have been intimidated. Or pushed into being aggressive.

"Yet he suddenly remembers when he's on the phone with you?" he asked, his voice filled with more than that question. And yet…not anger or accusation, either.

"I…kind of mentioned her." She'd hoped not to have to admit that part. "He'd…told me he loved me…"

Mason's lids lowered. He glanced away. She'd known she hadn't wanted to tell him.

"He was…talking like maybe we should consider trying again. I asked him about Gwen and had he ever slept with her."

"And he pointed the finger at me?"

Wait. Did that mean that Mason *had* slept with her the other night? After the time they'd spent in the bar together? And talked on the phone as he was driving home, too?

"No." There was no accusation in her voice, either Just sadness. "He admitted the truth to me. Said he figured I'd found out and that was why I really divorced him. The night before Bruce had told me about being unfaithful that last time—and that really was with a perp—Gwen and I had gone out for a beer. Miriam was with Brianna and it was my first night out since giving birth. It was supposed to have been with Bruce but then he'd had to work. He said he assumed she'd told me that night. About the bachelor party."

"Why on earth would she do something like that?"

"She didn't. But he thought she had because we'd been female cops together and she felt guilty. At least that was what he said."

Mason didn't seem to have much of a reaction. Just sat there looking interested in her conversation.

"Did Gwen ever contact you?" he asked.

"No. Not about that. The first I'd heard of Gwen's...involvement was when you told me."

"But you believe he only slept with her once?"

"What would be the point of lying about it now? Why would he bother? We're divorced." She thought over her conversation with Bruce. "I didn't even ask. He was just telling me why he thought she'd told me."

"Do you care? Whether he's been sleeping with her since?"

"Has he?"

He shrugged. "I have no idea." He watched her, as though waiting.

Did she care? How was that pertinent to Miriam or the paternity question?

"I care that he slept with her the night of his bachelor party." Which didn't answer his question.

He didn't push.

But she had to. "So…what about her being at your place the other night." What business was it of hers? Even if she had feelings for him, they weren't anything she could act on.

His eventual nod shut down a good deal of the emotion that had been swarming inside her.

He'd been with Gwen this week, and he hadn't so much as mentioned it—knowing he'd just told her that her ex-husband had been unfaithful to her with the woman.

And yet…why shouldn't Mason be with her? It wasn't like Harper had any kind of intimate relationship with him. Or ever would.

He had no responsibility for the feelings she had toward him. Feelings she hadn't even shared with him. She'd barely admitted them to herself.

"She showed up drunk and angry, came at me for going after Bruce, and then puked in my bathroom, after which I drove her home."

Oh. Emotion surged again. A load of it. The kind that made you think of flowers blooming, their scent filling the air, and soft petals scattered over naked skin...

Thankfully her brain kicked into gear. "Did Bruce tell her you were going after *her*? As part of the investigation?"

"She claims not. I met with her Thursday morning. She was sober, but no less judgmental. She wouldn't tell me how she'd found out. For all I know O'Brien said something to her, thinking she'd roll on Bruce if there was any truth to the claims about Miriam. She told me she hadn't spoken with Bruce since before that happened. I couldn't find any proof that she had."

"I'm sure he's been at the bar, where all the Albina cops hang out."

"I wasn't going to go in there asking around. We're trying to keep the investigation from touching Bruce's career."

"Thank God, now that we know he didn't do it."

Mason didn't respond. But he watched her

with an expression that looked like he wanted to tell her more. Leaving her crazy with the need to know.

And sane enough to move past both.

"Did you ask him about her?" Harper asked.

"No. I asked him what I needed to with regard to Gram. How Gwen found out isn't relevant to that."

"Unless Bruce was trying to insert himself into the investigation through Gwen."

"Why would he do that if he's innocent? And," he added, "how did Bruce know Gwen had been at my house?"

"She told him." He'd said as much. "At the bar Thursday night, after she met with you. Said she wanted him to know in case he heard about it."

"Did she say anything else?"

"He said no. But he thought it was odd that she felt she had to tell him about it."

"Or he wanted you to know she'd been at my house late at night."

"Why would he do that?"

"Bruce might not be an elder abuser, but Bruce is still Bruce," he said. "I'm beginning to think he doesn't realize he reframes things to manipulate people into his camp. I'll even go so far as to say it's possible he means no harm— that it's only to get, or keep himself, in people's good books—but he does it."

She couldn't argue with that. "He did mention her after I told him I knew he'd slept with her." Which was her response to Bruce's suggesting they think about trying again.

"You'd consider getting back with him?"

"Hell, no!" She pressed her lips together when she heard the adamant tone of the response that slipped out. And then, looking at him, said, "I can't. Not feeling the way I do for—" She stopped herself again, still looking at him.

His expression didn't change from respectful interest. She wanted that one night back. Even if she only got it for one more night. She needed to know she hadn't imagined the complete and utter joy she'd found with him. Not just the sex, but the entire night.

"My reasons for divorcing Bruce were valid. They still are." She had to break the silence. "I don't trust him to stay faithful. His undercover persona blurs too many lines."

He was still watching her.

"I'm the type of woman who needs complete monogamy in a relationship." Just in case he didn't know that. How could he? She'd given him a one-nighter and then married his brother the next week.

"I've got a warrant to question Elmer Guthrie, the neighbor, when I get back to town this afternoon. That's for your ears only."

She nodded. Thankful he'd rescued them from the dangerous and stupid path she'd veered onto.

"I'll keep you posted on the rest of the investigation from here on out," he added. "You're a witness, but you're also a cop. Since Bruce opened that door, I don't see any harm."

She smiled. A damned foolish thing to do in a professional situation. His letting her "in" *was* professional, not personal. Not worthy of a smile. She felt she should explain, but couldn't come up with anything that wouldn't be equally imbecilic.

"Grace had never heard of Elmer." He didn't seem in any hurry to leave—not that he really had anyplace to be until Grace was ready to go home.

"Bruce said she'd had him to the house for dinner a time or two."

"Yeah, that's what he told me. Tax records show that Elmer bought his place right about the time Miriam broke off her friendship with Grace."

His puzzle pieces were all falling into place. He had to be happy about that.

"I'd like to talk about how we're going to handle things where Bruce is concerned if the paternity test comes back positive."

Her heart pounded. There it was again. That

surge of emotion that seemed to clog up her entire chest—leaving no room for air.

For a woman not prone to drama, she sure seemed to be wallowing in it all of a sudden.

"It's going to be a tough one," she said, cringing at the thought of that conversation. "He doesn't deserve it. He's Brianna's dad…" She couldn't make that one right.

Or come to terms with the idea that her action—and Mason's—could have such painful repercussions for someone else. How did you live with something like that and still like yourself? She studied the top of her desk, the calendar, inbox, stack of files. Her cell phone lying there.

"I was going to suggest we not say anything for now."

Raising her head, she stared at him, wanting to grab the lifeline he'd just offered. Could it be that simple? All of this could just go away? "Brianna's too young to understand…" He'd started to speak again. "We should give ourselves time to adjust, to figure out, as her parents, how we're going to handle the situation. We can get finances set up for her, that kind of thing."

"Bruce pays child support and half of any extra expenses."

"That's fine. Although he'd probably have grounds to sue you later for any monies you take from him after you find out."

"I can open a special account for his money. Not use any of it."

Were they really making plans as though his being Brie's father was a real possibility?

"So, we're agreed? If the test is positive, it stays between you and me for now?"

She nodded. Scared because she liked the idea of her and Mason being partners in something. Having no idea what she was getting into with him. No matter what the test said.

Then, without giving herself a chance to think, she stood up and said, "We're here at the Stand. You're a cop. Here on official business. Kids are used to police officers coming around…"

She was babbling. He was staring.

"You want me to go meet her? As a cop visiting the Stand?"

Brianna wouldn't think anything of a police officer visiting the day care. If she talked about it, no one else would think anything of it, either.

Crippled by guilt, and driven by emotions welling up from deep inside her, she couldn't take the words back. He had a right to know his own flesh and blood, even if she was his niece, not his daughter.

CHAPTER TWENTY-THREE

WHAT DAMNED FOOL thing did he think he was doing? Walking beside a uniformed Harper, fighting fantasies of her wearing the uniform for him—with nothing on underneath—Mason knew he had no business going where he was going.

Even if she was his.

Brianna.

He liked the name. He'd seen pictures of the little girl on Gram's refrigerator—and could see that she had Thomas blood in her. She was blonde like her mother, had Harper's blue eyes, but the nose and chin were all them. It was something that always set them apart. And, in his opinion, looked great on a girl.

Until Brianna came along, Thomas men had only produced male offspring.

There was so much he wanted to say as he kept stride with Harper along the sidewalk that led from her office section around to the building that housed the day care. But he suspected that if he opened his mouth he'd say too much.

"The building actually connects from inside," she said, breaking the silence between them. Their hands bumped as they took a step out of synch and she jerked back, stepping away from him. The feel of her touch lingered. Calmed the doubts raging through him for a long moment.

"But this way is shorter and I always take the outdoor route any chance I get," she continued. He wanted to stop her. Didn't.

And then they were about to enter a door that would take them to Brianna's classroom door. He could tell because Harper was still babbling on about buildings and such.

It was so unlike Harper, he touched her shoulder and came to a halt. She looked up at him, and it was like they'd gotten naked right there on the sidewalk for all the world to see.

"Are you sure about doing this?" he asked. "I understand if you're not. I'm not going to push, either way."

"Do you want to see her?"

More than he wanted just about anything. But…it might kill him, too. Because he'd missed so much.

"I have a clearer understanding of what it means to open Pandora's box," he said, and wasn't surprised when she nodded with understanding.

"It's up to you," she said.

"Of course I want to see her! I've wanted to see her since the minute she was born. Even if she's not my daughter, she's my niece. She's a Thomas. Family."

He'd put it out there—the words that he'd denied himself every single time he'd walked into Gram's house and seen those pictures on the fridge. Every time he'd talked to her after a weekend visit. Bruce was family, too. Not talking to him for all those years had been wrong.

And yet, by his own action, he'd left himself no choice. He'd put Bruce in a corner. Forced his brother to protect himself.

Harper touched his arm. She smiled at him, and he smiled back.

"Let's do this," he said, looking straight ahead as she led the way inside.

Brianna's door was to the right. Harper peered through the small viewing window at the top, and then, without giving him a chance to change his mind, to change anything, she opened the door and walked in, leaving him to follow her as she and the teacher met halfway across the room. "This is Mason and he's an officer," she said, loudly enough for the kids to hear. They'd all glanced over, but as soon as they heard Harper they went back to what they were doing.

Clearly it was as she'd said; the kids at the

Stand were used to officer visits—or at least, familiar enough with them that his presence wasn't fazing them.

Only one of them got up. A little blonde girl in light green shorts, a white-and-green matching T-shirt with butterflies on it and tiny white sandals, who'd been sitting at a small plastic table with a piece of paper in front of her and a crayon in her hand. She set the crayon down and was heading toward them.

"He's here to speak with one of our residents and checking out the classrooms," Harper was saying.

The teacher—Miss Maisy, her tag read—nodded and, as a boy came up to her, tugging at her shorts and said he had to "go," led him away.

"Hi, Mommy."

Mason was hardly breathing. The girl, a little sprite, had reached them, her face serious, her nose scrunched up as she looked at him. And then back at her mother. It was almost as though she knew and he had a crazy thought that kids could recognize their parents, even if they'd never met them before. And then she said, "How come he isn't wearing a uniform?" Such a small voice for such a big question.

No way she was his kid. She was just too... perfect.

He knelt beside her. "I know all the officers

here wear their uniforms all the time, but I'm not employed by this place, so I left mine at home," he told her.

"Are you on a special job?" Her voice hooked him, her gaze hooked him, and he knew she wasn't ever going to let him go.

No matter what the paternity test revealed.

HARPER HAD TO pretend she didn't know them. It was the only way for her to get through those seconds as she watched her precious little girl so adeptly handling a situation her mother couldn't seem to manage. If she opened her mouth, she was going to cry. So she took a mental step back, like she did when faced with a horrendous act in her job. She put barriers around her emotions and reminded herself that she was working.

"I am on a very special job." Mason's tone wasn't condescending, yet it held…a note that was different, unlike any she'd ever heard from him as he answered Brie's question.

"My daddy has special police jobs, too, where he sometimes wears jeans to work," she said and then held out her hand to him. "It was nice to meet you, Officer."

Mason's hand engulfed that little palm, but he shook it softly and said, "It's been so nice to meet you, too."

"My name's Brianna," she informed him in a serious voice, nodding once, just as Mason had done earlier in Harper's office, although she figured only she would pick up on something like that.

"That's a very pretty name," Mason said, his expression equally solemn.

"I'm going to finish my picture now," she said. "We have to finish before it's music time."

"Then you'd better get back to it." Mason stood, his gaze never leaving the little girl.

"Bye, Mommy, I love you." Brianna gave her a hug around the knees before heading back to her chair. Harper wanted to hold on to her and never let go.

MASON HAD FELT his phone vibrate a text when he was talking to Brianna. He pulled the phone out of his pocket the second the littlest Thomas turned her back, needing to focus on work if he was going to get out the door and back to the life waiting for him.

He didn't kid himself. Whatever results came from the DNA lab, whenever they came, his life would go on unchanged, as far as anyone would ever see. He and Harper had agreed. No matter what the test showed, he wasn't going to play a key role in Brianna's life.

He wasn't going to do that to his brother.

Or to the little girl who adored her daddy.

All these years he'd been waiting for Bruce to grow up, to become the man he'd always known he could be, and his younger brother had finally gone and done it. In some ways... By all accounts he was a great father. Brianna had shown confidence, pride and security when she'd mentioned him. Her tone. The look on her face.

He'd thought, when he insisted on the paternity test, that he'd need to protect the child from Bruce, from his manipulative behavior.

He'd been wrong.

Thank God, he'd been wrong.

He'd touched his screen, was typing in his password, when Harper caught up to him in the hall just outside the classroom door.

"You okay?"

"Fine," he said, typing the password a second time.

"Mason." They weren't even out of the building yet, but she stopped him with a hand on his arm. "It's okay to feel things," she told him.

"She's a great kid," he responded, giving his voice enough strength to convince her that he really was fine. "I'd like to be a regular part of her life...assuming Bruce is okay with that."

It had to be up to Bruce.

"We'll work it out somehow," she said. "You're her uncle—"

She broke off and they stared at each other. "No matter what, you're related to her, part of her family. I'll tell Bruce that since you and he are talking, it's time for Brianna to get to know her uncle. If he wants that to happen on his schedule, in his presence, that's okay, but at least you'll see her."

Every time he tried to shut the door on things he couldn't have, she opened it up again. Did she know how much she was messing with him?

Or how grateful he was to her?

Nodding his thanks, he started to walk again. And to type in his password for the third time. Plenty of people had his number and would text rather than call. All people associated with work.

He got into his phone. Saw the time. "I'm due to get Grace in another ten minutes. I'll head up there now," he said, leaving Harper to get on with her day.

Too much time with her and he was going to do something he'd regret. Like take her in his arms and kiss her in a way that showed her there'd never be another woman for him.

"I'll walk up with you," she was saying, beside him on the sidewalk. He opened his text app.

The lab had texted. Probably either telling him the results would be in later that afternoon, or that they might not have them until Monday. Wallace, the tech who'd said he'd put Mason's job first, had told him he'd pass on the results as soon as possible. He wasn't going to make him wait any longer than necessary.

Mason had known the man a long time. They'd worked together on several cases—one involving a psycho who'd turned out to be a serial killer of young women. And Mason had told him what the current test was for. *Who* it was for.

He clicked to find out when he'd know.

Read the message.

Hand shaking, he almost dropped his phone.

"Mason?" Harper was looking at him. He'd stopped walking, staring at his phone. He could see it all happening as though watching himself from outside. Could hear Harper's voice.

There were residents in the distance. He saw two of them walking together, while another, on a different path, was walking alone.

Harper touched his hand—the one holding the phone. Her hand was soft. Warm.

"Mason, what is it?" He would have showed her the phone, but didn't want to dislodge her hand. He looked at her, not moving at all. Saw her as he'd never seen her before—connected to him.

Part of him.

The only woman he'd ever really wanted.

The one woman he could never have. Because his brother had loved her first. And loved her still.

"I just became a father," he said.

SHE WAS AT WORK. With victim residents relying on her to keep them safe. As Harper's reality receded, she focused on the hard sidewalk beneath her feet. On the job. The women moving around the shelter. On the warmth of the sun on her skin.

She started to walk. When she felt Mason move beside her, she stopped. Turning, she looked up at him and couldn't prevent the pressure of tears in her eyes.

There was so much to say, none of which she felt she *could* say.

He pulled her into an alcove, and then another, the outdoor entry to a room used for music lessons during the week. They couldn't be seen. Or heard. And she still couldn't speak.

She could only continue to look at him, pouring her heart into that gaze. Keeping her needs to herself, as she thought about him.

"Congratulations," she told him, not sure if he was glad or not. Not sure if the word was appropriate or not. She was congratulating a man who'd just found out he'd lost the first four years of his firstborn's life.

He nodded. "It's…surreal." He seemed…almost lost, and it occurred to her that they were both in shock.

"How do you feel about this?" If she focused on him, she felt stronger.

"You want the truth?"

"Of course."

"I'm thrilled to death. That little sprite…she's mine. Mine and yours."

Everything changed then. Got personal. She nodded.

"When I think of Bruce and the years I've lost and the future I'm going to lose… But for the moment…"

She knew what he meant. What lay ahead of them, keeping their secret, going on as though nothing had changed, was going to be impossible. Already guilt was filtering through the initial state of shock.

"We'll set up regular visitations," she said now. "She'll get to know you, to spend time with you. You can teach her things and come over for dinner. I'll call you every day with school updates…"

"And what if Bruce catches wind of it and thinks we're starting something between the two of us?"

He was right, of course. "So we'll make it more sporadic," she said. She owed a loyalty to

Bruce. But she owed Mason, too. He was the father of her child. "No one will know if we talk every night, if you call for updates."

His intense stare made her reconsider the world she was creating. If they talked every night, they'd be playing with fire. And Bruce was the one who'd get burned.

Again. He'd hurt her, but he'd never cut her as deeply as this would cut him.

What about Mason? She studied him, the father of her child, and needed to wrap him in her arms and hold on for life.

"We should get back," she said instead. "It's time for you to pick up Grace."

He kept looking at her, searing her with emotion.

"Are you okay?" he asked, standing his ground.

She nodded.

"How do you feel? Are you disappointed?"

"No." Tears filled her eyes then, as shame swept through her. "I was hoping it was you."

He seemed to settle into a calmer state, and motioned for her to lead the way back to the main building.

They weren't lovers. Would never be a couple with Bruce, their feelings for him and Bruce's love for Harper, standing between them. And yet she felt as though they'd just gotten married.

CHAPTER TWENTY-FOUR

APOLOGIZING, CITING WORK as his reason for barely taking time to say goodbye to Gram, Mason accompanied Grace out to his SUV. He vowed to get back to Santa Raquel as soon as possible and make it up to her. Gram had been there for him all his life. She was floundering and it was his duty to be there for her now.

First, he had to deal with Elmer Guthrie.

And get himself back in line.

He was a father. And couldn't tell anyone he cared about—particularly not Gram. She'd never mentioned the night he spent with Harper; it was possible his brother had kept his word and never told her about it. From what he understood, Bruce had simply explained that the brothers had had a falling-out and that it was between the two of them.

Gram would definitely not approve of what Mason had done. Infidelity was one thing, and bad enough. Sleeping with your brother's fiancée was something else entirely. Especially since he'd been on a mission for Bruce—sent to comfort Harper, to make sure she was okay, until she calmed down and Bruce could talk to her.

Made from the same cloth as his grandmother, Mason didn't approve of what he'd done, either.

Thankfully Grace talked, and did whatever she was doing with her yarn, most of the way home. She and Gram had a great visit, she said, and they'd caught up on so much. Gram hadn't offered any insights that could help Mason's investigation and Grace hadn't pushed. She hadn't wanted to lose Gram a second time. She'd apologized, on first getting in the car, for not learning anything new regarding Gram's injuries.

"I really do think she fell off a stepladder," Grace told him again as they approached Albina. "She looked me straight in the eye when I asked her about it. I don't know, maybe I *should* have pushed harder, but that's what caused our problem to begin with. I just kept hoping she'd tell me something, but… I didn't ask her about that man you mentioned, Elmer Somebody. I figured if she didn't bring it up, I shouldn't, either."

The older woman's wrinkled forehead was furrowed as Mason glanced at her.

"You think that man hurt her? And not Bruce? I feel awful blaming him if he really didn't do anything, but I know what I heard that one day on the phone, and I just put that together with everything else and drew my own conclusion. No wonder she was so upset with me for maligning him."

"You weren't the only one who suspected him," Mason pointed out. There'd been valid reason to suspect his brother. That reminder was one he needed.

"So you think this other guy did it? I mean, like I said, I think she really fell off the stepladder, but you said the breaks in her arm weren't consistent with that...and the bruises on her face... So it must be this guy."

"It's possible."

"I should've asked her about him. I probably didn't do enough..."

"You did fine," Mason assured her. "Great. It's my job to take care of the criminal situation. She needs you just to be her friend. If she tells you something, then by all means, I hope you'll help us by sharing it, but if she doesn't, that's okay, too."

He wasn't as desperate for Gram's confession anymore. He expected to get one from the abuser himself that afternoon. Much better than Gram having to testify.

They'd quietly take care of Guthrie, make certain he never had the chance to hurt Gram again, and Gram could move home and resume her old life.

"I asked her to come back to the choral group when she gets home," Grace said.

"Did she say she would?"

Grace shook her head. "She said she didn't want to tire herself out. That she had a lot to take care of at home."

He glanced her way. Saw her frown. He wished Gram's answer had been different, but thought it might take time to get her confidence back.

"I wonder if maybe I pushed her too hard there. We're in the second half of our seventies, heading toward eighty. I do my housekeeping, but not like I used to. I don't have anyone else to clean up after or cook for, and I still tire more easily than I used to. Stands to reason that keeping house for someone else, doing all the cooking... She's probably too tired to handle a full social schedule, too."

He didn't like the sound of that any better. He thought of the dirty dishes in the kitchen of Gram's house when he'd gone there to investigate. Bruce's things strewn all over.

He thought of his daughter in that house, thinking Bruce was her father.

"Then I guess it's time my brother learned how to do some of his own housework," he said, focusing on keeping his voice even. "Not enough to make her feel less useful, but enough to give her time to spend time on other endeavors, as well."

Grace's expression cleared. She nodded.

Having a plan, Mason felt better.

IT WAS LATE afternoon when Tasha, who'd been assigned to Miriam for the afternoon shift, summoned Harper, saying Miriam wanted to see her.

Brianna was at the pool with a couple of residents and their kids for another hour. Thinking this was a day for miracles, hoping that Grace's visit had changed something for Miriam, enabling her to testify regarding her injuries, she left the reports on her desk and hurried across the resort to Miriam's bungalow.

Tasha smiled at her as she went inside. "She's alone," was all she said.

Expecting Miriam to be there to greet her, Harper glanced around the living room and then through what she could see of the bungalow. "Miriam?"

Dressed in blue capris and a matching short-sleeved top, with white sandals, Miriam looked her usual classy, put-together self as she came out of the kitchen, drying her hands on the burgundy towel she held.

"I'd like a word with you," she said, motioning Harper toward a chair at the dining room table—out of sight of the front window, through which Tasha could see them.

Understanding Miriam's need for privacy, she joined her, taking a seat. Looked at Miriam's cast, and then saw the anger in the other woman's eyes.

Had Mason told her about Brianna? That was unthinkable. He wouldn't have.

All the way over here, she'd been imagining her phone call to him, letting him know about Miriam's breakthrough.

"What's wrong?" she asked.

"I want you to stay away from Mason." Miriam's tone didn't carry the same anger Harper had read in her expression. It might have been there, but was veiled.

"I don't…"

"Grace told me, when he was late coming back for her, that he said he had a meeting with you while she was with me. I thought he was waiting outside, or running an errand, or maybe having breakfast…"

With no idea where this was going and Brianna's paternity heavy on her conscience, Harper didn't respond.

"Bruce will be hurt all over again… Mason seeing you… I want you to stop."

It was like a curtain of black gauze came down over Harper, a barrier, and yet offering no protection. The pain Miriam was inflicting came from within Harper.

"He's investigating a case of abuse against you." She chose her words carefully. "I'm the officer in charge of your protection."

"Don't try that one on me…" Miriam stopped and visibly gathered herself as her anger started to appear.

"Bruce has been in touch with me, too," Harper added, to reassure her. "He called to let me know that he and Mason are working together to bring you home."

"The boys are talking? Working together?" The light that suddenly appeared in Miriam's eyes was a beautiful thing. Harper had loved Miriam deeply during her time in the family. There was no doubt in her mind that Miriam's heart was good, that her entire life was dedicated to her family.

She nodded, as Miriam looked to her for confirmation, but didn't say any more. The details of the case weren't hers to divulge.

Disappointed that she hadn't been called for a big revelation, she was nonetheless relieved that she'd been able to allay Miriam's fears and started to rise, to get back to the work that was going to keep her sane over the coming weeks.

Mason was Brianna's father…

"That's even more of a reason. I'm begging

you." Miriam spoke again, and Harper settled back in her seat. "Leave Mason alone. I…" Miriam's hand on Harper's was weaker than she remembered. And a huge surprise. "Please, Harper, you're a good mother to that sweet little girl, a good cop. Just…please…leave Mason alone. If you want to be part of our family, I will welcome you, but you belong with Bruce. He adores you."

After her time with Mason in the alcove that morning, she was pretty sure *he* adored her, too. And knew she adored him. So what *about* him? Did he simply not matter because Bruce, who'd been unfaithful to her on many occasions, had met her first?

She'd slept with Mason before things had been fully resolved between her and Bruce. After she'd formally broken their engagement. And then she'd married Bruce anyway.

She'd made that choice.

"He told me about you and Mason." Miriam's tone was soft, but there was no disguising the anger brimming in it. "After you left… he told me."

Harper had no words for that.

"I can understand how much it hurt you that he slept with that perp, but it's acceptable, from a legal standpoint, for an undercover to have sex while undercover if he must do so to preserve his cover as long as it's not entrapment, as in a prostitution case. While doing so as a married man carries other ethical concerns, at least he came right home and told you. But you—you who'd slept with his brother—couldn't forgive him."

Bruce had told Miriam about her and Mason? *Deflecting the blame from himself.*

It was like Mason had said. Bruce used his own version of the truth, his own perspective, to keep himself in people's favor. He hadn't told Miriam about sleeping with Gwen, though.

"He said you'd always wanted Mason…" Oh, God. It was true. She hadn't realized Bruce had known. She hadn't even admitted the truth to herself until the past week.

Not with full consciousness.

"He told me how it happened, that you got drunk with Mason one night, and Mason took you to his place to sleep it off. How he gave you his room and took the couch. Then, when he was asleep, you went to him in the living room and threw yourself at him. When he didn't call you the next day, you still wanted to marry Bruce. But it wasn't like you thought it was going to be, was it? Being with Bruce wasn't a way to stay close to Mason. To see him, when he shunned you. He never came around. You being there kept him from his brother, from his family, out of loyalty to Bruce because of what he'd done."

Other than her motives, it was all true. Or at least a pretty close version of the truth. Harper felt sick.

Miriam didn't even know the worst of it.

"Then when Bruce makes a mistake with a stranger who meant nothing to him, you leave him high and dry, so you can pursue Mason. But until now, Mason had nothing to do with you. He's a good man. A Thomas."

She'd never, ever pursued Mason. Unless you counted moving from his bedroom to his living room that night. *That* she'd done.

But she'd never gone after him. Never contacted him. Not that night. Not before it, and not after.

She could see how Miriam might think she had, though. With the facts being presented to her as they'd been.

How could she not have realized that Bruce had seen what she hadn't? That her heart had always belonged to Mason?

How awful that he'd known it.

And he'd loved her so much, he'd married her anyway.

"Now, with all of this, you've got your chance. Mason is here, talking to you. I'm begging you, Harper, please walk away. Leave him alone."

She couldn't. Not completely. He was the father of her child.

She could tell Miriam about Gwen. About the other times Bruce had found it necessary to sleep with a perp. How he used sex even when it wasn't completely necessary. But that would only make Miriam defensive and they needed her to tell them who'd been hurting her. If she didn't press charges, it would be much more difficult to protect her.

Needing to find a way to reassure Miriam that neither she nor Mason had any intention of pursuing so much as a close friendship out of obligation to Bruce, Harper was searching for the right words when her phone rang.

"It's Bruce," she said, glancing at the screen, and took the call.

"Hey, babe, I'm here with Mason." *Babe?* He hadn't called her that in years until this past week. Not even when he'd been trying to get her to agree to think about giving them a second chance.

That felt like a lifetime ago. Before she'd known Mason was the father of her child.

"We need you to bring Miriam to meet us..." He named a place, a national park, halfway between Santa Raquel and Albina. "We're hoping, with the two of us together, and apart from anyplace that has any emotional hold on her, she'll tell us the truth about what's been going on."

At first she wondered if he was drunk. Glancing at Miriam, who was clearly interested in finding out what Bruce was saying, she said, "Okay, when?" The last time Bruce had asked to meet with her, Mason had told her to do it.

But taking Miriam out of the shelter? She had to speak with Mason. And couldn't very well challenge Bruce's statement that he and Mason were together. Not in front of Miriam, who knew Bruce was on the phone and who'd just warned her away from Mason.

"We were thinking tomorrow morning?"

Smiling for Miriam's sake, she agreed to a time the next morning and rang off.

To Miriam she said, "He's got some free time tomorrow and wants me to meet him."

"And you agreed." Miriam smiled, too, patting her hand. "You're a good girl, Harper," she said. "Just...stay away from Mason."

A warning tone had crept into those last words and Harper found it hard to believe that anyone was getting away with abusing this woman.

CHAPTER TWENTY-FIVE

IT HAD BEEN the right thing to do, letting Bruce make the call to Harper. Considering the circumstances. That didn't mean it had been easy.

He was relieved when, five minutes later, he saw her name show up on his caller ID. He'd just left his brother in the bar where the two had met after his session with Elmer Guthrie. On his way home, he pulled off at the next beach entrance to talk to her, sitting in his car facing the road.

"Are you with Bruce?"

"Not anymore."

"But you were with him when he just called me?"

This was wrong. All wrong. He and Harper needing to talk to each other. *Knowing* it was wrong...

But neither of them could give up their ethics to be together. That would surely doom any relationship they might be able to create. If she even wanted to try.

"I was with him, yes."

"You told him Miriam's with me at the Stand?"

"Yes. He figured you were involved, apart from my having questioned you, based on what you do for a living. But he thought you'd probably referred her to another place, considering her, uh, ban on your presence."

He remembered how he'd worried that his brother had made a trip to Santa Raquel earlier in the week, his first to see his…to see Brianna, because he'd suspected Gram was at the Stand. Another false assumption.

"So you really want me to bring Miriam to a state park in the morning?"

"It was Bruce's idea, but I think it's a good one. Elmer swears he never touched her. He said he stopped over Monday night to get a cup of milk. He'd started his dinner and then realized he was out of milk. Said he was only at the house for five minutes. The flash drive says ten."

"Did it show him leaving with a cup of milk?"

"Of course not. But his left side is hidden from view."

"So it's possible."

"Technically, yes."

"Lying about five minutes won't convict him of a damned thing."

"He was uncomfortable, Harper. I'm certain he was hiding something. But nothing I said or did swayed him even a little from his story. The only way we're going to take care of this is to get Gram to tell us what happened. Bruce thinks that with the two of us together, we have a shot, and I agree with him completely. But we can't do it at her place. Elmer's hold on her will be stronger there. And we can't do it at the Stand, either, since she's there because of what happened. Obviously she doesn't feel safe enough there to tell us the truth. She didn't even tell Grace anything this morning. In a sense, we're ganging up on her with this plan, but it really is our best shot. We sure as hell can't bring her home and let it happen again. And she's not going to stay at the Stand forever."

Gram had given him limited time. They not only needed to know what had happened, but they needed time to get official testimony and then an arrest warrant. Which could take an hour or a few days.

"Why do you think she'll even agree to get in a car with me?"

"Again, Bruce pointed out that you're an obvious choice, given your job, but since you're being family, too, she'll be more apt to tell us the truth if there isn't a stranger present. Third, we both want her with a cop."

He wasn't sure what Harper's pause signified. What she was thinking. They did most of their talking with looks, not words.

He also didn't like his brother being so confident with Harper present, as though he knew that Harper would agree with whatever spin Bruce put on things.

He'd deal with that later. He was making it through the day dealing with one thing at a time.

First priority was Gram's safety. Getting the case done.

Then he'd face the life he'd built.

"You're all about Bruce all of a sudden." Whatever he would've guessed was on her mind, that hadn't been it.

"I'm trying to get Gram home safely and as expediently as possible."

"This whole conversation…it's been Bruce says, Bruce thinks, Bruce's idea…"

She had a problem with Bruce now? *She* was the one who'd been so certain he was a great guy, a great dad, would never hurt anyone.

Mason pulled himself up short, thankfully with his mouth shut. He'd never felt so out of control. So…

He didn't know what.

He was a father who couldn't claim his child.

A man in love who'd never hold his woman.

A guy who'd betrayed his own brother.

He needed a case that didn't involve someone he knew. A challenging one that would result in saved lives when he succeeded. Work had always been where he'd found fulfilment. Peace.

"I'm doing all I can to give Bruce his due," he said now. Harper deserved as much of the truth as he could provide. "You have any idea how it feels—" He stopped himself. Of course she did. "I accused him of abusing our grandmother. He's being really decent about what I said and did. Getting her out of the home and investigating him *was* the right thing. He'd have done the same with me if the situation had been reversed. But I really believed he'd done it. I'm doing what I can now to show him the respect I wasn't able to give him earlier in the week. He's a good cop. Has the highest closed-case ratio on the force."

"I know. And... I understand. I just..."

"What?" Something was bothering her, which bothered him.

Looking over his shoulder, as though his brother would be standing there outside the car, Mason knew he had to get a grip.

It wasn't every day a guy found out he was a father. He wasn't handling it well.

"She asked to see me this afternoon. I just left her."

Sitting upright, Mason tuned in, recognizing himself for the first time all day. "What did she tell you?"

If there was any way they could avoid the somewhat manipulative meeting the next morning, he'd welcome it.

"That Bruce told her I'd seduced you. She doesn't blame you, but it's why she turned on me. He told her that when he was telling her why I left."

"To make it look like you'd done something worse than he had." Bruce was Bruce.

"Yeah."

"I'm sorry."

"I'm not all that eager to see him at the moment."

He didn't blame her. He'd had a lifetime of living with Bruce's insecure shadow side, and an incident like that still turned his stomach. That was partially why he'd been so ready to see his brother as the bad guy at the beginning of the week.

"I'm sure he figured it wouldn't make any difference to you," he told Harper now. "You were already gone."

"I know. I just..."

Again she didn't finish. Filled with a frustration that had been building all week—caused, in part, by his inability to have a completely open conversation with her—Mason knew he had to let it go. At least for the moment. For the day. Or the week.

"You think you can convince her to come with you in the morning?"

"To see the two of you? I'm fairly certain I can. But… I didn't say anything about it and don't intend to mention it to her until morning."

He agreed with her decision. Told her so.

He wanted to tell her much more. To ask how she was doing. How she felt. If she'd spent the day, as he had, thinking about the newfound connection between them. He wanted to know if she'd been with Brianna since they'd seen her together earlier.

He wanted to hear every single word the little girl said. To know every minute that he'd missed of her life.

To ask about her delivery. What kind of labor Harper had. If she'd been alone.

And how old Brianna had been when she'd said her first word.

What it was.

He wanted to know his daughter's favorite color. What foods she hated.

He wanted to know everything about both of them.

He told Harper good-night instead.

HARPER HAD THOUGHT she'd already lived through the worst times of her life. Put the mistakes behind her and was on the right course, living a decent life. Sunday morning proved her wrong. Delivering up an abused older woman to grandsons Harper knew were going to pressure her hadn't been a grand or decent moment.

She knew the decision was the right one—better that Miriam be coerced by those who loved her and were trying to protect her, than abused and perhaps eventually killed by the man who'd broken her arm more than once. But she felt like crap.

Other than mentioning, more than once, that she should've brought her stuff so she could just go on home, Miriam hadn't spoken to Harper during that hour-long drive—not even to ask about Brianna, who was at the Stand. Harper had been due on staff that day and she'd had to call in another officer for the time she'd be gone—hopefully no more than three hours.

All of that had been...unpleasant, but standing there by a tree, while the three of them sat at a secluded picnic table yards from where they'd parked their vehicles, Harper had never felt so trapped. She'd wronged Bruce in so many ways. And Mason, by coming on to him as she had that one night. She'd wronged Miriam by wronging her grandsons. And yet she couldn't get away from the situation. For the rest of her life.

One of those men was the father of her child.

The other thought he was. Miriam was grand-mother to both of them. Great-grandmother to Harper's daughter.

It was like every bad moment in the past—from the first time Bruce had told her he'd been unfaithful to her to that final time when she'd told him she was divorcing him, when she'd taken Brianna and left. They were all right there, larger than ever, happening all over again.

And...

"We know about Elmer, Gram." Bruce took the lead as soon as they'd all hugged and sat down. He'd also chosen to sit next to his grand-mother, leaving Mason to take the seat across from them.

Harper had tried to stay in the car, but Bruce had insisted she join them. He'd wanted her to sit with them, too, beside him on the bench. She'd drawn the line there.

She wasn't family. Only Brianna was. Harper's place was on the outside looking in.

Miriam glanced between the two of them, straight-faced, but Harper noticed that she'd started to pick at the edge of the cast in her lap. She'd worn capris again, royal blue, with a red, white and blue top and red sandals.

She'd dressed for a day out with her boys.

"Elmer Guthrie? Of course you know. He's been over for dinner a few times," she said, her tone as commanding as always. And then, looking between the two of them again, she said, "What is this? Some kind of inquisition? You're going to try to put me away, aren't you?"

She turned on the bench, frowning at Harper who was leaning against a tree off to the side. "You knew about this? And you brought me here?"

Harper stepped forward, feeling somewhat protected by the uniform she wore. She was a professional who was used to dealing with distraught women. "I know nothing of any plan to put you anywhere but back at home, living your life as you choose to live it," she said with the strength of conviction. Happy to actually be able to speak her mind.

The look of confusion that crossed Miriam's face struck her hard. Something wasn't right. The strength with which Miriam defended Bruce, insisted that she'd fallen off a ladder, talked about Elmer coming for dinner without any sign of hesitation or discomfort, climbed out a window specifically to assert her independence...

Who did that unless she felt her independence had been threatened by more than a voluntary two-week stay in a safe resort? No matter what Mason said, Miriam had known she didn't have to stay at the Stand. The final choice had been hers. Lila wouldn't have allowed it any other way.

And yet...that confusion...the abuse that she wouldn't admit to—someone had clearly made her doubt herself. "We know Elmer was over the night you got hurt, Gram," Mason said, his tone less condescending than Bruce's, yet more compelling, as well.

Had Miriam fallen in love with the older man? Had he told her that if she let anyone know he'd hurt her, he'd make it look like she was crazy? Or that she couldn't take care of herself anymore? Had Guthrie put that fear in her?

It was how abuse worked. She'd seen it more times than she could count—the way an abuser insidiously infiltrated the brain, successful because that abuser was a trusted person with intimate access to one's heart and mind...

"He was over to borrow a cup of milk," Miriam said now, leaning toward Mason. "Why are we talking about Elmer? What does his milk have to do with anything?"

With gentle fingers Mason reached over and touched her chin. What was left of the bruising was hidden beneath her makeup, but Harper wouldn't ever forget how Miriam had looked when they'd first brought her in.

She knew Mason wouldn't, either.

"Someone grabbed your chin that night, Gram,"

he said softly. "It's not your fault—no reflection on you whatsoever—but we can't let you go back home until we know who did this. Until we can be certain it won't happen again."

"You said you were going to figure it out," she challenged him, a vision of her former self. "You've had a week, and that's all you've come up with? A neighbor borrowing a cup of milk?"

Mason continued to watch her, his face showing only love and concern. Harper's view of Bruce was partially blocked by Miriam, so she couldn't tell what he was thinking. She watched Mason instead.

"For the hundredth time, I'm telling you I fell off a stepladder!" Miriam insisted. "I figured you'd get there on your own."

"We know Elmer did this to you, Gram." Bruce spoke again, his tone lacking Mason's compassion, replacing it with that condescending tone he had when he was having difficulty getting his point across. Still, she could hear the love he had for his grandmother. "He's been visiting you when I'm at work…"

Another flash of confusion crossed Miriam's face, to be replaced with a glance at Mason. "You don't seriously think Elmer did this to me, do you?" Her quiet tone commanded attention.

Mason's slow nod stabbed Harper. She hurt for him. For Miriam. And for…

"We know he did it, Gram." Bruce took over. "Mason already got a warrant for him."

Harper cringed. *Got a warrant.* It was true, but only for questioning. Such strong talk, which was his usual manner, but at the moment, in this situation, way out of line. She wished he'd leave the next few minutes to Mason.

"You got a... He's under arrest?"

"No." Mason shook his head. "The warrant was for questioning." Mason sent Bruce a look, one Harper interpreted as suggesting he take it down a notch. "I talked to him yesterday afternoon."

"You seriously think he did this," she said again. "You're going to arrest him?"

Mason didn't deny it. How could he? Harper knew he had every intention of following through as soon as they got Miriam to press charges.

"You're going to arrest him?" she asked again, her tone gaining so much strength Harper took another step forward, inexplicably drawn toward her.

"Gram..." Bruce reached for her...and Harper froze. Just froze in her tracks. Those arms... thrust toward... She wasn't there. She was somewhere else. Another time...

Before Bruce could calm Miriam, she was

standing at the side of the table, facing him. "You're going to arrest Elmer? On what grounds?"

Harper saw it like a movie on TV. Separate from what was going on in her real life.

Mason was beside Miriam now, an arm around her. "Gram, we just want to talk. Please, sit down and we'll get through this. Together."

Gazing up at Mason seemed to calm her for a minute, while Harper stood there, completely separate from Miriam's situation, horror filling her to the core.

CHAPTER TWENTY-SIX

MIRIAM WAS SHAKING her head. Harper forced herself to focus on the older woman. Just as her mother had taught her. When emotion seemed overwhelming, you thought of others. Tended to others.

"Elmer and I are in love," Miriam announced. "Yes, he came over that night. He comes over a lot of nights when Bruce is gone and he...usually stays longer. We sit and watch TV together. I understand why Bruce doesn't approve. I *am* old. I've already got my family and my life. I also have twice as much money as Elmer does, and he might be after that. I don't even care. Bruce was the one who cared. Always worrying that you'd think he was after any assets I had. That you'd really send me away..."

Harper needed to sit down. Mason's glance at his grandmother held pure shock.

"I'd send you away? What are you talking about?"

"Him." She pointed at Bruce. "He said you were concerned about me getting older. That you'd said some things. That I had to do what he said so you'd let the two of us live together in peace."

What? Harper wasn't sure she was following it all. Her gaze stayed on Mason—it was the only way she seemed to be holding herself together. There. In the present moment.

When Bruce had reached for Miriam...the past had slammed back on her. She couldn't find her way...

"Why did you get so defensive with Grace?" Mason's tone was loving as he faced his grandmother. At least Harper thought it was. "Why not tell her about it? She'd never even heard of Elmer."

The way Miriam stared at the ground hit Harper hard. She felt as though she was living inside the older woman. "Because I know that Bruce is right," she said. "I'm seventy-five years old and here I am, thinking I'm falling in love? What do I know? How can I know for sure that I'm not losing my mind? Grace was already telling me I wasn't seeing things clearly, telling me Bruce was turning me into an old woman before my time, robbing me of the life I had left and that I couldn't see it. And... I've never felt anything like I feel for Elmer. Love's always been practical and calm for me. Like a gentle flower that blooms forever. With Elmer it's more like a burning fire." She shuffled her feet. Lifted her cast, then lowered it, and looked up to the sky. "At seventy-five I'm finally feeling a burning fire?" She shook her head. "I tried to stop seeing him, but I knew he was just down the street, that he was alone, and I missed him so much…"

She broke off and Harper, feeling that moment of insecurity acutely now, wanted to take Miriam's hand, regardless of whether or not she'd be pushed away.

Before she could move, Miriam faced Mason. "Monday night, Elmer saw Bruce's car leave and came over. When he saw my face, my arm, he insisted on taking me to the hospital right away. The only way I could get him to drop the idea was to agree to drive myself. I couldn't let him take me for just this reason. I knew everyone would blame him. Bruce would blame him, and Elmer's an easy target. He's a guy down the street with no one to defend him. He's not a cop. Not the grandson I adore and who adores me."

She started to cry then. Not racking sobs. Just tears filling her eyes and spilling over to run down aged cheeks.

Bruce stood, joining Mason beside Miriam. "Come on, Gram, let's sit back down," he said. Following his brother's lead, he reached behind her, putting a hand between her shoulder blades.

Harper cringed at that touch, and very slowly

Miriam turned toward her. She must have made a sound. The older woman met her gaze, seeming to find something there, and then turned to Bruce.

"Maybe I'm so old I should live very carefully for the rest of my days, preserving what time I have left," she said, enunciating her words slowly. "You say I should take precautions so I don't inadvertently cause my own death. I'm sure you're right that I'm too old to start over. You're completely right that I get tired more easily now than I did even five years ago. I fully believe you when you tell me that if I won't take what you've determined are those necessary precautions, Mason will put me in a home where they'll watch over me and make sure I'm safe. And if that happens now, then so be it…"

"What!" Mason's bellow, his look of horror, had Harper as transfixed as Miriam's words did.

The woman didn't seem to notice either of them. She actually poked a finger in Bruce's chest. "But if you think, for one second, that I'm going to let you do anything…*anything*…nasty to that dear, sweet man, then you've grossly misjudged this tired-out, weak old woman."

Harper had to do something. She knew she did. But her feet were planted to the ground where she stood, and she could feel her heart thundering in her chest.

Miriam glanced at Mason. "*He* broke my arm," she said, pointing at Bruce. "He didn't mean to. I'd climbed up on the stepladder again when he was right there and I could've asked for help and he was just trying to get me down without me hurting myself."

Everyone stared. At Miriam, at Bruce, at each other. Like fools the four of them stood there, looking from one to another.

"I—" Bruce started, and Miriam stomped her foot.

"I won't hear it, Bruce," she said. "I fell off that ladder. I told everyone. I didn't mention that it happened when you grabbed my arm, because I know that you were only trying to get me down safely, that you didn't mean to hurt me. I know if I was younger, your grip wouldn't have broken my arm. I even called Gwen, crawled out of my bedroom window at the Stand to get to a phone without anyone finding out, so she'd go to Mason and get him to stop thinking you did anything wrong. I knew what they'd say if they ever found out it was you. I'd have gone to my grave with the truth, but for you to stand there and blame Elmer…"

So much to process. Harper could barely take it in. Couldn't move.

"I would never hurt you, Gram." Bruce's voice broke. He turned to Mason. "I swear to

God, I'd never hurt her, you know that." His gaze turned to Harper next, still a couple of yards away from them.

"She's old." He returned his attention to Mason. "Her bones are frail. You try to help her and she breaks. I…I'd lose my entire life, my career, all the people I help, the lives I save… So many people would be put at risk, and you just weren't going to let it go. You had to have someone to blame. I don't grab her hard." He looked at Harper again. "Just enough to keep her from falling. She won't listen." He said the last part to Mason. "If she'd *listen* I wouldn't have to hold her chin to get her attention. She's on that blood thinner, you know, and if you just touch her she bruises."

He turned back to Miriam. "You leave the room when I try to talk to you. If you'd stay put and listen, I wouldn't grab you, to hold you back. I've told you that. We've talked about it so many times. But you still walk out. I couldn't let you walk out when you were upset. You might hurt yourself…"

Bruce came by it honestly. The thought struck Harper out of the blue. Walking out was what he did when he got upset.

"You know how much I love you, Gram. When Harper left, you were all I had. You were there for me and for my daughter. You know that. I'd die for you." He had tears in his eyes.

He looked at Mason again. "I can't lose her, man. When I lost Harper, it practically killed me. You remember that."

Then his gaze turned to her. "This week... please don't let this change anything, babe. You and I...we're finally finding our way back. The picnic at the beach... We can be a family again, Harper. A real family. I'm begging you..."

He said more. She didn't hear him. Didn't hear anything but the sound of her own blood rushing. She was back in the past, hearing him beg.

And...

She took a breath so deep, it hurt clear to the bottom of her lungs. "He grabbed me, too." She admitted something she'd pushed so deeply inside that she'd forgotten. Because, as a cop, she would never be a victim. Hadn't ever allowed the vision of herself to formulate. She'd gotten out instead. Downplayed. Justified the one second in a lifetime as a normal reaction of a man watching his wife walk out on him. Until she'd seen Bruce reach for Miriam's arm at the table. She'd been trembling with the truth ever since. "That last morning, when I was leaving. I had my three-month-old baby in my arms and he grabbed me so hard I almost dropped her. He had his hand under her. He'd have caught her. But the next day...my arm was bruised."

She looked at Bruce then, aware of Mason's presence in the background of her life, but knowing she had to do this on her own. "There will never be an *us*," she told him. "I see now that there never really was."

She might not have consciously remembered that last act. He hadn't meant to hurt her. Hadn't come at her with violence, but merely with a desperate need to keep her from walking out on him. He'd let her go the second she'd told him to. But she'd never lost the feeling that she couldn't go back—under any circumstances. She'd convinced herself it was the cheating. The lack of trust. She'd made her decision to divorce him because of those things.

"I had a hand under Brie that day, Harper. I would never have let her fall."

He was right. She'd already admitted as much. "It doesn't change the facts. You grabbed me with force. You lied to me throughout our whole marriage. Yesterday when you told me about Gwen going to Mason's house, that was just to put doubt in my mind about Mason. You told Gram I'd always been after him, when, in truth, you'd *sent* him after me that night. And you failed to mention that I'd given you back your ring because of your infidelity. When I ended our marriage because you were unfaithful, you made it sound like it was the first time you'd been with someone else. It *wasn't* the first time. I feel pretty certain it wasn't just the third or fourth time, either." She remembered his lies about Gwen and the bachelor party, but everything was coming at her too fast. "A few minutes ago, when you were talking to Gram, you were talking about how you were just trying to keep her from getting hurt, but you knew her bones were fragile and you grabbed her anyway. It's about control with you, Bruce. You have to be in control all the time. That's what it's always been about. That night I spent with Mason... You'd lost control. The only way for you to get it back was to get me to marry you. You had to make sure he never had a chance to take me from you again, didn't you? You kept him away by making him feel guilty about the night we'd spent together. And then you played on my guilt. All these years..."

The words, when they started coming, wouldn't stop. "There's always an excuse with you. An explanation. A justification. It's always someone else's fault."

Bruce raised a hand, and she thought he was going to hit her. She put her arms up to protect herself, but the blow didn't come.

Instead, he strode away, swiftly, got in his car and squealed out of the parking lot.

Someone had to call the police. Put a 9-1-1 out on him. She looked at Miriam.

Mason pulled out his phone.

HE'D BEEN LEFT without a ride. Letting Bruce drive them to the park had gone against every instinct Mason had, but he'd been so focused on making up to his brother for the fact that he'd stolen away his only child, he hadn't been on his game.

He'd nearly put both of the women he revered in danger.

Miriam's abuser *was* Bruce.

Mason had been so certain earlier in the week and yet, now that he'd had confirmation, he could hardly believe it.

Not only had his brother been regularly abusing their grandmother, he was more mentally unhinged than even Mason had suspected.

He had to surmise that the only reason Bruce had made it on the force for so long was that he'd spent most of his working hours pretending to be something he wasn't—with no direct supervision. He'd successfully closed cases that won convictions without actionable complaints. That was all the department knew.

Riding in the back seat of Harper's SUV, he

felt like something of a criminal himself. The one thing which he'd prided himself on had been his ability to put the puzzle together. But when it had mattered the most, he'd blown it.

He'd known his brother was a manipulator. A controller. And yet he'd left Gram there with him. Had left Harper with him before that.

Harper was getting Gram back to the Stand, where she'd be safe. Until Bruce was in custody, they were all at risk. Once they arrived, Mason was going to order a rental car. There was no way he was leaving any of the three females in his life until his brother was behind bars. Gram, Harper and Brianna weren't going to be out of his sight if he could help it.

"You can't back down on pressing charges, Gram," he said from the seat behind her. "No matter how much you love him. No matter what kind of guilt attacks your heart."

"I know." Miriam reached over to Harper with her good hand. "We're going to do it together, aren't we?"

It was the first time that it had been mentioned, that Harper would be part of bringing down the man Brianna believed to be her father.

Whether Harper had recognized it before or not, it was clear that she'd been a victim of Bruce's manipulation. Even her leaving him hadn't prevented him from keeping a measure of control over her.

Harper glanced at Miriam, and then quickly back at the road. He'd noticed she'd been avoiding her rearview mirror since he'd slid into her car.

"Yes, we are," she said now.

He had a feeling that the decision to help prosecute her ex-husband, even if it was only with testimony to add further weight to Miriam's, had just been reached.

And that she had other decisions to make, as well.

Did he dare hope he might figure among them?

Did he deserve to?

It seemed obvious that Bruce's initial breaking point had come when Harper had slept with Mason that night. His brother had responded by begging her to marry him. And what she'd said that day made sense. He'd done it as a way of making certain that Mason couldn't have her. Couldn't be with her.

Bruce always had to maintain control.

As Mason thought about it, he realized that everything Bruce had done in his entire life had been geared to that end. From how people looked at him, what they thought of him, how they treated him—he'd needed to control it all. Maybe because of his insecurity?

Maybe he'd truly loved them and the vulnerability that had caused had been too much for him.

Where that left any of them, he had no idea.

One thing he knew for sure, though. He had to let Harper figure that out for herself. She had to figure out her past—and her future.

She'd already lost too much of her life to a man's manipulation.

Mason had been pretty adamant about Harper and Brianna's staying at the Stand overnight until Bruce was in custody. Police officers were on-site to take Miriam's and Harper's statements, and an official warrant was issued for Bruce's arrest. No one knew if that would go easy, or if, knowing he'd lost all control of his life, he'd be on the run.

Domestic violence charges would get him some jail time. But they weren't going to put him away for long.

They could end his career, though. And Harper couldn't even imagine what that would do to him. Or what he might do because of it.

To better ensure her daughter's safety, Harper agreed to stay at the Stand on Sunday night. Lila offered her and Brianna her own personal suite, used whenever she had reason to be at the Stand overnight.

Just off the managing director's office, the suite, decorated in Victorian style with lace and roses, included a little kitchen and sitting room as well as the bedroom.

Mason had driven his rental car over to her apartment to pick up a list of things for her and Brianna. Bruce had never been to the apartment, but he knew the address. As she tucked Brianna into bed that night, the little girl was a bit hyper due to her excitement at having a sleepover and being able to play with her friends after supper. Harper sucked in her breath over another stab of debilitating doubt, accompanied by a physical pain that sliced through her.

Bruce had grabbed her with such force, she could have dropped their child. He might have caught her. He might not. The fact that there'd been that much violent anger in him…

How could she have forgotten that?

Was she nuts?

Miriam had gone into a session with Sara, who'd been called in, as soon as they'd returned to the Stand that afternoon. Lila had suggested Harper have a session, too, if she needed one, but she'd said she was fine. She'd gotten away from Bruce. Wasn't afraid of him even then.

No, what she was afraid of was not being in

control of her own mind. Bruce had spent so much time convincing her that he adored her, that he'd never hurt them...she'd somehow dismissed the time his fear of losing control had gotten the better of him—the morning she'd taken away all his control of her by leaving.

He'd shown her, and she hadn't seen. She'd felt bad for him—knowing how much he loved her. Knowing how much she'd hurt him. Not once, but twice.

And now...as of that morning...a third time. He'd kept her on the hook by manipulating her heart, taking advantage of her ability to feel compassion, commanding constant sympathy from her as if she was a damned emotional puppet.

How did she trust her own heart when she knew it could be so easily manipulated? How did she know if what she was feeling was real, or orchestrated by someone else?

She'd called her parents shortly after she'd returned to the Stand, telling them what had happened. O'Brien and all the Albina police had been notified and were on alert. They'd be putting extra patrols on her parents' home. Her father had loaded his shotgun, too, he'd told her.

She'd smiled then, remembering how he'd used that old thing to teach her to shoot—strictly target practice. Remembering their conversation as she closed the bedroom door behind an already-drowsy Brianna, she felt an acute longing to be back home—with her parents—tucked securely into the twin bed she'd had as a child. Wanted to work the fields with them, where you could believe what you saw, where everything followed the rules. Weeds were weeds. They were hardy and determined, and you could dig them up. They'd be back. You'd always be fighting them. But you could always dig them up. You just had to stay diligent.

Her parents had taught her that lesson before she'd started kindergarten, before she'd ever ventured out into the world.

She'd been prepared. Had the inner resources, the proper tools, to make it in life.

She'd been so strong. Physically, but mentally and emotionally, too. So aware. She'd left Bruce when she'd seen that the relationship wasn't going to be healthy because of his lack of trustworthiness. She'd divorced him.

But she hadn't gotten rid of him.

She'd just never seen that Bruce was a weed.

And had no idea how to live with the damage his roots had done.

CHAPTER TWENTY-SEVEN

Three Months Later

MASON STOOD AT the side of the grave, in a three-piece suit and tie, his gaze on the closed casket raised above the hole in the ground. Next to him, close enough that her arm touched his, was Miriam, her hand in Elmer Guthrie's. They'd had a quiet wedding at the Albina courthouse the month before, and were living in Miriam's house.

In three short months Mason had grown truly fond of the man.

On his other side, not as close as Miriam, Brianna stood holding hands with her mother. In full dress uniform, Harper bent to say something to her daughter, then straightened, her gaze ahead. Behind them, more than a hundred cops stood, fully dressed, their hands crossed and resting in front of them.

Music played, a flutist behind them, while directly across from him, on the other side of the casket, stood a thirty-year-old blonde woman with three children, huddled together and crying. A host of other family members of hers, many of them known to the Albina police as key players in a drug-trafficking business, stood behind the woman, dressed in suits and ties, their hands crossed and resting in front of them.

Oh, brother, what have you done?

Mason's chin twitched, and he could feel the emotion building up inside him, threatening to break free. He'd loved the guy. From the second his parents had brought him home, he'd loved him. And loved him, still.

More than a hundred people were standing around that grave because every one of them had cared about and respected the man.

Bruce had had what he'd always wanted—the love of everyone with whom he came into contact—and it hadn't been enough.

He looked across at Emily, Bruce's secret wife, and the three children, one older than Brianna, two younger—the family he'd lived with on and off since before he'd married Harper. He still couldn't understand what his brother had been.

What he'd done.

Falling in love with a perp, the one he'd really been sleeping with before he married Harper, knowing his family would never accept him living that life, he'd fooled them all. His marriage to Harper had been a cover for his real love. Both times he'd admitted infidelity to her, it had been because he feared he'd been caught out. After the divorce, he'd needed to keep her on the hook so people wouldn't suspect he really had a thing for a woman in his make-believe life. The nights he'd spent away from home as an undercover cop, he'd spent with Emily. The ones he'd spent with Harper, and later in Gram's house—Emily had thought he'd been on the road, taking care of family business. Drug business. He'd been able to keep up the pretense, even with her father and brothers, because he'd lived his cover—as a man who had contacts and could let them know what the feds were doing so they could run their business without fear of getting caught.

And he'd played the department, too. Bringing in bad guys—always enemies of "the family."

He'd been a dirty cop. A man who'd loved his real life, a life that everyone thought was just the cover. But a man who'd also deeply loved the family he'd been born into.

The family he couldn't bear to disappoint.

Emily was why he'd been desperate to marry Harper, even after she'd slept with Mason. Gwen had begun to suspect that he was in too deep with his cover girlfriend, and he'd had to get her off track. It was also why he'd slept with her the night of his bachelor party. To convince her that sex was a moment in time with him—whether with Emily or with her. Sex with Emily meant no more to him than sex with Gwen.

Emily was where he'd run whenever he got mad and walked out. Emily was where he ran that day he'd left Mason, Gram and Harper in the state park.

He'd taken her and the kids on an impromptu vacation to Europe. And when he returned, when he'd known that Mason, the FBI and the Albina police were closing in on him, he'd finally told his first wife, the love of his life, Emily, the truth.

By all accounts she'd stood beside him. The fact that he'd ended up dead in his car the next week could have been attributed to her—she'd certainly had motive—except that Mason had found no evidence whatsoever to prove that she'd had anything to do with his death.

Perhaps a member of her family had something to do with the close-up gunshot to his head. He'd been playing them for years. Maybe a cop had taken him out. Perhaps it was self-inflicted, as it had been made to appear. Perhaps no one would ever know.

"Why are those people so sad if Daddy's in

heaven with God?" Brianna's sweet voice was more than a whisper, but not glaringly loud.

Mason heard the question with pain in his heart. Saw, out of the corner of his eye, as Harper bent down to speak with her.

She'd been true to her word. Over the past three months he'd spent a lot of time with Brianna between jobs. Taking her out for dinner, just the two of them. Playing on the beach. He was getting to know his daughter and had never been more thankful for anything in his life.

Or known such truly happy moments.

He was Uncle Mason to her. But there was no doubt in his mind that she loved him.

He'd seen Harper, too, from a distance. Even when, like now, she was standing so close. They'd spoken. But only about Brianna.

Even after everything Bruce had done to him, to Harper, to both of them, he stood between them.

Just as his casket stood between the two sides of his life.

Bruce had walked a line between good and evil. Law and crime. One foot on each side.

He'd played them all. His families, his colleagues, his friends.

And there they all stood, crying real tears, because he was gone.

THE NIGHT THEY buried Bruce, Harper was restless. She'd put Brianna down in her old room, left just as it had always been, at her parents' house. Brie had been spending every other Saturday night there since she was born and went to sleep with surprising ease.

"You want to talk?" Mom asked as Harper sighed, put down the book she'd been staring at and got up for a bottle of water. Her father turned down the sound on the news program he'd been watching.

"I think I'll go for a walk," she said, needing to be out with plants that, although they were infested by weeds every single year, still managed to thrive. To produce succulent fruit and vegetables that gave healthy life to the people who ate them. "Will you listen for Brie?"

"Of course," her parents answered in unison. And then her mother added, "Keep your phone on." Harper almost smiled when she heard her father telling her mother that Harper was perfectly capable of keeping herself safe. That they'd taught her well.

He'd probably gone on to remind her mom that Harper spent her life keeping others safe. That she was the one who dug up the weeds. Just as Harper had heard him do many times before.

She didn't feel like that woman, and yet…tonight, she didn't feel infested anymore, either.

Her weed hadn't been dug up. He'd been buried so deeply in the ground, he'd never see the light of day again. Or breathe fresh air.

She felt his presence, though. Which was why she'd needed to go to the fields. She didn't stray far, stayed close enough to the house that the security lights her father had installed kept her on track. For three months, she'd been trying to shake what was left of Bruce's infestation in her mind. In her heart. And yet...

The cucumbers were doing well. They were her favorite vegetable, and her parents had a banner crop that year. Weeds didn't stop them from growing. They took nourishment away, but didn't kill them.

Bruce hadn't killed her, either. She was there. Alive. Living her life. Other than Brianna's visits with Mason, which weren't unlike her visits with her own father, Harper's life had returned to the status quo with which she'd always been happy.

Status quo.

There it was again. When had she decided to settle for that? To be okay with just okay?

Mason seemed fine with it. He'd never asked her for more. Had done everything he'd said he was going to do. Paid child support. In fact, he'd paid four years of back support. He was faithful about the time he spent with his daughter.

And he asked nothing of Harper. Didn't try to make suggestions where Brianna's parenting was concerned. Or try anything else, either.

Bruce was gone and yet…he still lay there between them. A weed that hadn't ever been picked. A weed that would always be part of their ground. The previous week, when Harper had submitted the forms to have Bruce's name taken off Brianna's birth certificate and have Mason's added, he'd been grateful. She'd hoped for a hug. Or a look—one of those that said they were connected forever.

He'd thanked her for sharing Brianna with him, instead, calling the little girl back to the door so he could hug her goodbye.

Did he need someone to hug that night? He'd said, after the funeral reception at Miriam's, that he was going home to do some follow-up reports on a case in North Carolina he'd closed the previous week.

She couldn't picture him there, home alone, doing paperwork, on the night his brother was buried.

Walking along a second row of cucumbers, noticing the numbers and sizes of vegetables on the vines, she thought about the night Bruce had sent Mason to find her. The way Mason had done exactly as his brother had asked, in spite of the fact that Bruce had been unfaithful the night before.

Mason had been a victim of Bruce's, too. Whether he knew it or not.

Was that why he hadn't contacted Harper after they'd spent the night together?

Why he'd let five years of silence fall between them? Because Bruce had manipulated him into thinking it was what Harper wanted.

Shaking but not cold, Harper wrapped her arms around herself. Turned to walk back up the same row, seeing the house in the distance. Her vehicle out front.

Bruce was buried. Gone.

Unless she and Mason let him continue to manipulate them.

The only way he could still come between Harper and Mason was if they let him.

Heart pounding, she sped up, at a full run by the time she got to the back door. Inside, she grabbed her purse. "I'm going out for a while," she told her parents. "I'll have my cell on."

They nodded. Her mother looked worried, told her to be careful, and her dad turned up the volume on the TV.

SHE'D BEEN PLANNING to drive to his house, but parked before she got to the road that would lead her there. He wouldn't be home. But she had a pretty good idea where he'd be.

Where she would've gone if she hadn't had Brianna to care for, feed and put to bed.

In jeans and a long-sleeved shirt, she wasn't really dressed for October on a northern California beach, but not even her tennis shoes in the sand slowed her down.

She hadn't brought a light with her, but she knew where she was going, had the moon to guide her, her cell phone in her back pocket and her gun to keep her safe.

No one else was out that night, and for a second she stood still, breathing in the ocean air, feeling the cool breeze on hot cheeks, listening to the sound of a gentle tide. If she was right, he'd be about a quarter mile up the beach to the right. There was an embankment there, one that would shield you from most of the cold, provide a support for your back and keep you somewhat sheltered from peering eyes.

She knew because it was the same place she'd chosen the night her life had fallen apart. For the first time.

Four years earlier had been the second time.

Three months ago had been the third.

She wasn't going to let it happen a fourth.

She saw him while she was still several yards away, and had a feeling, from the turn of his head, that he'd seen her first. He wasn't standing, but he hadn't tried to leave, either.

"Hey." She walked up. Stood there looking at him still in his dress clothes, shiny black shoes and all, sitting in the sand. He'd lost the tie. His shirt was undone a couple of buttons, as though he'd been too hot.

"Mind if I sit down?" she asked.

He motioned at the sand.

"You did everything you could do for him," she said, not bothering with small talk. There was nothing small about this moment.

Chin jutting out, he nodded, facing the ocean. The moonlight left a streak of light across the bridge of his nose. The rest of his face was in shadow.

"He was a master, Mason. He had the ability to do great things. But he was also human. And weak. And his weak side pulled him down as much as his good side lifted him up."

She'd spent some time with Sara over the past couple of months, mostly just to talk. To check her own mind. To be certain, absolutely certain, that she wasn't fooling herself.

He was looking at her now, and she felt encouraged.

She was pretty sure she knew some of what he was feeling—some of the same struggles she'd faced. She'd been a little ahead of him, maybe, in that she'd been strong enough to pull away, at least in part, four years before Bruce's final reckoning.

"He was gifted with the ability to motivate people, to get them to do as he needed them to do. We couldn't fight that," she said. "Just like we wouldn't be able to play the piano like Mozart. Or be immune to the beauty of his music." She'd come up with that analogy on her own, but had run it by Sara.

Wanting to reach for Mason's hand, she settled for holding his gaze. He was looking at her again. Tears sprang to her eyes. "He was a master manipulator who preyed on, or fed off, what was good and pure in people. Their open hearts. Their trust. Their compassion. And he was so successful because he truly cared about the people he manipulated. He truly needed our love. The only way we could have guarded against that would have been not to care. Not to love. Not to trust. And I'm not just talking about him, but everyone. Because we couldn't have known that he had a rotten spot at his core. He had the uncanny ability to make the people around him blind to that. We don't want to be deaf to music like Mozart's," she finished, giving him the decision she'd made for her own life.

Wondering if it would work for him, too.

"I saw the rotten core," he told her. "And I

did nothing." His voice was soft in the night. It sounded dry, as if he'd been sitting there for hours.

"You did everything, Mason. You saw the bad, but you also saw the good. And hoped the good would win out. Everything he asked and needed from you, you gave him, along with your hope. You kept him sane enough to live over thirty years of life, doing some really great things, while he wrestled with the demon side of himself. Think about it. He never killed anyone. Never hit anyone. If not for Miriam's frail bones, we might not have known, even now, about the double life he'd led."

"It was getting to be too much for him," Mason said. "When you left, and then with Gram growing older...his family on the law-abiding path was slipping away from him..."

She hadn't thought of it that way, but it made sense.

"I could've been the constant that kept him from—"

"From what?" she interrupted. "You were out of his life by *his* dictate," she reminded him. "And these past few months, you've been doing your best to be there for him. To protect him. Even getting the FBI to agree to bring him in with dignity."

Not that it had happened. He'd been found dead first.

"He didn't give you the chance to really help him, Mason. He never gave you the chance. Not in the past three months. Not in a lifetime of being a big brother," she added, fighting for the future. Hers. Mason's. Brianna's.

Fighting for her family.

"I'm scared to death that he's still in control, Mason. That we're going to let him choose our end, too."

He straightened at that, his gaze intent. Still, he said nothing.

"Five years ago, he sent you to me," Harper said, the words coming of their own accord from depths she'd been hiding for far too long. "Right here…he sent you here. Tonight, he sent me to you. Maybe he didn't mean to. I'm fairly sure he didn't. But I'm here because of him. Because I know that we can be in control if we choose to be."

His lips tightened, but he still kept his hands to himself. Harper figured she could be making a huge mistake, thought about that for a second and knew she didn't care.

If he didn't want her, didn't feel the same way she did, then they'd share an embarrassing moment and move on. Move forward in a different direction. Because there was no doubt they had some kind of future together.

Bruce was gone, but Brianna would always be there between them. With them. Connecting them.

Something much stronger than words had brought them together. They needed it now. Something much stronger than words.

Moving slowly, she slid over, then up onto her hands briefly as she settled herself on his lap. "I've only ever seduced a guy once in my life," she whispered, her hands on either side of his face. "I can't guarantee I'm good at it, but I can promise you it works." Her voice faded as, with each word, her lips moved closer to his, and she kissed him. Softly at first.

And then, his arms came around her, crushing her to him with such force that she thought she might have tasted blood. Hers. His. Both of them mingling their lives together in every possible way.

She hadn't intended to have sex on a cold beach that night.

Hadn't intended to do more than talk to him.

But when, an hour later, with the sand in her clothes scratching at her skin as she walked arm in arm with him up the beach back toward their cars, she wasn't the least bit sorry.

Or ashamed of what she'd done.

CHAPTER TWENTY-EIGHT

HE'D BEEN IN the darkest night his soul had ever known and she'd come to him. Not used to fanciful thinking, or at least to allowing it to enter his conscious thought, Mason walked up the beach feeling like he'd just been given new life. He'd been living in an emotional cocoon all his life, keeping his own feelings contained in order to make room for his brother's.

It was what Bruce—and to an extent his parents and grandparents—had expected of him. It was what he'd expected of himself once he became an adult.

He didn't regret the choice he'd made to protect his younger brother. He regretted the things he hadn't seen.

He hadn't been able to find a way to get past that. To live with it in any semblance of peace.

In one sentence, Harper had shown him the way.

They could choose. If they were to stop being victims of Bruce's manipulation, they had to choose.

He wasn't Mozart.

Neither was Bruce, but he'd been gifted. In a way, his brother had been the anti-Mozart.

"If I hadn't come here tonight, would you have called me? Ever?" She was looking up at him, but he didn't meet her gaze. Still trying to grasp the fact that Harper was there with him. Perhaps for more than a moment.

"I was going to come by tomorrow to see Brianna, you knew that."

"I know," she said, and let it drop.

But he couldn't. He hadn't called her five years ago, after the most incredible night of talk and sex, because of his brother.

And he'd been staying away for the same reason. Sort of. He'd just begun to understand how much that *sort of* mattered.

"I'm not going to pressure you, Harper," he told her. "Or try to convince you that we belong together. Nor am I going to suffocate you with what I need..."

She halted in the sand, her arm dropping away from behind him. "Would you stop?" she said, in the angriest tone she'd ever used with him. "You think I don't have the strength of mind to stand up to pressure? Because let me tell you—"

He stopped her with a finger to her lips and a smile on his face.

"Okay, tiger, I get it," he said. "And you're

right. That was insulting. You left Bruce. Do you realize you're the only one who was ever able to do that?"

"Not completely I didn't."

"Because you had Brianna. Without that, I'm sure you would have."

Her smile was sad, but her eyes glowed for him again. "Maybe. I hope so."

Suddenly he had a million things to say and had to get them lined up in his mind. "I think we should go on a date," he said. First things first. He'd been wanting to go out with her for six long years.

"We've had sex…twice. We have a daughter—and you're asking me out?"

"Yep." Pulling her up against him, he added, "I'm not saying that's all we'll do. We need to face facts, and a major fact is, we're combustible when we're together. But we're family. We share a daughter. It just seems like…if we're going to have it all, we should take a little time to date."

Harper's life was filled with beach, the air, the sea. "I love you, Mason Thomas," she said. And stopped, horror filling her eyes.

As though she felt guilty… As he should. No. Bruce had had his chance. He'd hurt everyone. Mason was going to spend the rest of his life doing what it took to make sure his brother never hurt anyone again.

"I love you, too, Harper Davidson, soon to be Thomas, I hope. And I'll stand on my brother's grave and tell you so. What Bruce brought into our lives wasn't a healthy love. This is, like a flower that blooms forever, *and* a burning fire, just like Gram said."

Harper pulled back. "Miriam... She's not going to like this. Bruce had her convinced that I was always after you, and that's why I took the first chance I had to get out of our marriage, because you never came around..."

He shook his head. Kissed her quiet. "Gram sees him for what he is now, Harper, or at least sees enough of what he was. Loving Elmer showed her the difference between dependence and love. And she sees you for what you've always been, too. She asked me this afternoon if I thought you'd ever forgive her."

"There's nothing to forgive," Harper said. "How do you blame a heart that was only doing its best to love?"

Her words hit him hard.

With her usual wisdom, Harper had just sent Bruce on a new journey away from them where, hopefully, his spirit would find, and be able to accept, real love.

Loving wasn't easy. It didn't guarantee there'd be no pain. But its promise, that it would be stronger than pain, stronger than evil, that it would be everlasting...was the ultimate truth. A truth that even Bruce couldn't reframe.

"YOU READY?" MORE nervous than she'd ever been, Harper looked down at her daughter a couple of months after her walk on the beach with Mason, loving the red velvet dress, the curly blond hair, the black patent shoes, but mostly, loving the open, engaging, trusting grin on Brianna's face.

"Yep!" Brianna said, "You ready?"

In a short black, figure-hugging dress with a big red satin bow on one hip, and wearing black two-inch heels, Harper squeezed Brianna's hand as they approached Mason's front door. "I'm ready," she said. There was no doubt in her mind about what they were about to do, about a choice she'd already made. But the emotion that accompanied everything these days was still a bit hard for her to get used to.

Why jittery knees and breathlessness, butterfly stomachs and rapid heartbeats had to go along with something so incredible, she had no idea.

"It's the best Christmas present ever, huh?" Brianna said, her voice almost a whisper. Harper just wanted to pick her up, hug her and never let go. The moment she'd given birth, she'd been introduced to Magic.

Mason deserved the same. "Yes, it is."

"Because you're the mom I always wanted," Brianna said, and Harper started to cry. She'd stop. She had to stop.

And had a smile plastered on her face as Mason opened the door. "I thought you'd never get here!" he said, swinging Brianna up and giving her a hug before putting her down, saying, "The tree's all bare and waiting for you." He motioned toward the other room, the family room where the three of them had spent a few evenings over the past couple of months. They'd decided to keep the place, so they could stay in a home of their own when they came to visit Gram and her parents in Albina. So they could entertain both sides of their family at the same time. As they were doing during this first Christmas together.

"I think we should do presents first." Brianna hadn't moved from the doorway. "Don't you, Mommy?" The look she gave Harper was clearly a hint.

"At least one," Harper agreed, standing back.

Brianna tugged Mason's hand. "Can you come down here?" she asked. Of course he bent immediately, putting himself on eye level with her.

Harper knew what was coming, what Brianna was going to tell him, but she didn't know exactly what the little girl would say. The idea had been Brianna's, so the gift was hers to give.

Brianna looked back at Harper as though for reassurance, and she smiled, nodded, in spite of the tears already in her eyes.

"I have a present that isn't like one you open," she told Mason, her tone steady and unmistakably serious.

"Okay." Mason smiled at her, waiting patiently.

"My present is you are the daddy I always wanted."

Love exploded around Harper, bathing her, healing her. Filling her.

Leave it to a four-year-old to know the perfect words.

Or…leave it to Brianna.

Harper started to sob. Bent over with the exquisite pain of loving—with the pain of letting go of the bad.

Mason hadn't moved. He had tears on his face, too. He was smiling at Brianna. And he hadn't moved.

"Mommy used to say that to me when I was a baby." Brianna just kept right on talking in her matter-of-fact way. "I don't 'member that part, but she says it to me when I'm sick or sad and it always makes me feel better, and I say it to her and she feels better, and now your present is to feel it, too."

Mason looked up at Harper. "You...when..."

"Mommy told me how you helped her one time, because my other...daddy asked you to when she was sad. She said how you helped her feel better and that made you my daddy. She said because we didn't want to hurt my other daddy's feelings, you were keeping that a secret. But now that he's in heaven he would want Mommy to tell."

It hadn't been quite like that, but close enough.

Mason lifted Brianna off the ground and into his arms. "You're most definitely the baby I always wanted," he said to her, then reached for Harper, pulling her into their hug. "And Mommy is the mommy I always wanted, too," he said. His voice was strong, sure, but his eyes were still glazed with tears. "I had a special present for tonight, too," he said, releasing Harper to reach into his pocket. He pulled out a black box and handed it to Brianna. "Open it."

And as she did, he said, "Harper and Brianna, will you marry me?"

Harper grinned, she cried, she opened her mouth, but before she could say a word, Brianna pulled the ring out of the box and said, "Oh, yes, we will! Won't we, Mommy?"

Without waiting for an answer, she grabbed

Harper's arm, pulling her hand up and putting the ring on the little finger of her left hand.

There were still some things to teach their daughter. And many things she was sure to teach them, but Harper knew all she had to know that night.

She loved. She was loved.

The rest would take care of itself.

* * * * *

*If you enjoyed this romance from
Tara Taylor Quinn,
you'll love other recent books from the*
WHERE SECRETS ARE SAFE *miniseries:*

*A FAMILY FOR CHRISTMAS
FOR JOY'S SAKE
THE FIREMAN'S SON*

*And don't miss
A DEFENDER'S HEART
available soon from
Harlequin Superromance!*

We hope you enjoyed this story from
Harlequin® Superromance.

Harlequin® Superromance is coming to an end soon,
but heartfelt tales of family, friendship, community
and love are around the corner with
Harlequin® Special Edition
and **Harlequin® Heartwarming**!

Romance is for life, and these stories show that
every chapter in a relationship has its challenges
and delights and that love can be
renewed with each turn of the page!

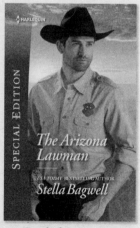

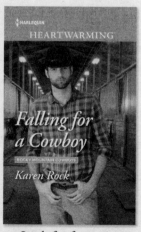

Look for six new
romances every month!

Look for four new
romances every month!

Get 2 Free Books,
<u>Plus</u> 2 Free Gifts –
just for trying the Reader Service!

Get 2 Free Books,
Plus 2 Free Gifts—
just for trying the Reader Service!